THE CYPHER

Matti McLean

Renaissance.
Diverse Canadian Voices

Cover and interior design by Matti McLean.

Edited by Joel Balkovec and Isabelle Shi.

Legal deposit, Library and Archives Canada, October 2020.

Paperback ISBN 978-1-987963-95-3
Ebook ISBN 978-1-987963-96-0

Renaissance Press
http://pressesrenaissancepress.ca
pressesrenaissancepress@gmail.com

Avaria

Thanks to all those who have helped to form this book into something worth reading:

Trevor, Robert, Rebecca and everyone else who has helped me out.

Big thanks to Nathan for taking such a risk on me.

Thanks to Stephen for pointing me in the right direction.

So many others: Cassandra, Nicole, Shawn, Owen and all of my audio book team- You've been wonderful.

And mostly thanks for Mo for inspiring my greatest adventure to date - not just in Avaria.

This is for you.

The night was still as death.

Penner slid his arm across the bed as a shiver shot through his body. He grasped the sheets. The bed was empty.

Fear gripped his chest and ripped him from his rest. It coursed through his veins as he prepared to erupt from his bed and storm the street.

But as soon as he opened his eyes, he saw Chess.

"Chess?" he began.

His lover was perched on the end of the bed, peering into the night like a vulture, his long, solid frame frozen against the night.

"Chess, what are you—"

Penner stretched out, but the second he touched Chess, it happened-

Like a spark bright enough to illuminate the entire room. A blast of heat that felt like they'd been dipped into a furnace, before being plunged into ice water. It was a thunderclap before deafening silence. It was only a moment, but it was enough.

Penner recoiled, thrown back onto the bed. Chess leapt through his skin and cleared the bed, landing in front of the open window with a grace that he'd never shown before. He whipped his attention back to Penner and blinked before recognising him. A wave of confusion washed over his face. His breath was rapid and shallow.

"Holy! I'm—Gods, I don't even—" Chess began, his speech rapid and incoherent, his eyes wide and wild.

"Chess? What was that?" Penner asked.

He looked down, realising that his hand was pulsing in pain. It felt like he'd slapped a fire. He looked from it to Chess and realised that he wasn't paying attention. Chess paced the room like a caged animal. His frame, though strong and tall, was shivering. His sharp, narrow features scanned the room, looking for distractions Penner couldn't see.

"Chess? Are YOU—"

"I have to leave!" Chess yelled. At first Penner was scared that Chess would wake the neighbours, but Chess didn't appear to care.

"Chess," he began. His throat was dry. "I know this place isn't—" He chose his words carefully. "Safe for us, but we can't just—" Chess held up his hand to silence Penner with a strange confusion, before bursting into laughter. He embraced Penner.

"We. We have to go. You need to come with me, I think. Or at least you should," Chess said, pushing Penner onto the bed and climbing on top of him. His face beamed with a smile that made him look drunk as coherence danced in and out of his face. His perfect teeth glistened, and for a moment Penner saw stars in his eyes.

2

They kissed before Chess winked at him and bounded to the closet.

"For a moment I thought you meant that you were—" Penner began, but stopped himself. He lay there for a moment, basking in the warmth that still radiated off their bed. It smelled like them. As he lay there, he ran through the words Chess had just said. He peeled his head off the bed and watched as Chess stuffed clothing into a satchel.

"Did you have a bad dream, or something?"

"No. Not a bad dream. A good dream. The best dream," he said as he clung to a ragged shirt with one hand, and a torn pair of pants with the other.

"Those are my pants."

"I need them. We need them," Chess said as he threw them into the bag that was almost bursting. "We need to pack light, though. Here." He threw Penner a small bag, which he caught before it slammed into his face. "Grab only what you need—we need. The toothbrushes, your pen. Oh! Bring your journal. You'll want it."

"Chess, what's going on?" Penner said, peeling himself off the bed and wrestling the bag out of Chess's hands. Chess looked at him, confused.

"I told you."

"No. You didn't."

"I didn't? I swear I—"

Penner gripped Chess's face, squishing his cheeks into his lips with his palms.

"Words. Use your words." Chess shook his head free and grabbed Penner's hands in his.

"Penner, I need you to listen to me. We don't have much time and I can't spend it talking to you about what needs to be done. Pack light and trust me."

Penner felt the bag grow heavy in his hands as the knot in his stomach grew. Chess had already returned to running around the room, throwing clothes and tools into the bag or discarding them on the floor.

"You wanna take a trip?"

"No. Not a trip."

"You're talking in fragments. I don't understand. Where are we going?" Penner frowned.

"Away," Chess said, a tinge of excitement in his voice. "Far away."

"We can't just leave."

"We must. I don't have a choice right now."

"When WILL we be back?" Penner asked.

"We won't," Chess said. "I mean, I won't. This is it."

Penner's mouth was dry. He tried to swallow but could barely breathe.

"You're asking me to leave with you without even knowing where we're going?"

"I'm asking you to come with me. But with or without you, I'm leaving. Don't make me leave alone."

Chess slid into a shirt and vest before packing a few more items in the bag. Penner wanted to argue, but there didn't appear to be any point. Chess looked serious, in fact he looked more serious than Penner had ever seen him. If Chess really was leaving, there didn't appear to be any choice. Anywhere Chess went, he'd follow. Gripping the small canvas bag, he ran into their washroom and began to pack.

"We need to leave in five. Be quick," Chess said as he rushed to the door.

"Chess!" Penner called out.

What?" Chess asked.

"Wear pants." Chess held his gaze for a moment before looking down.

"Right."

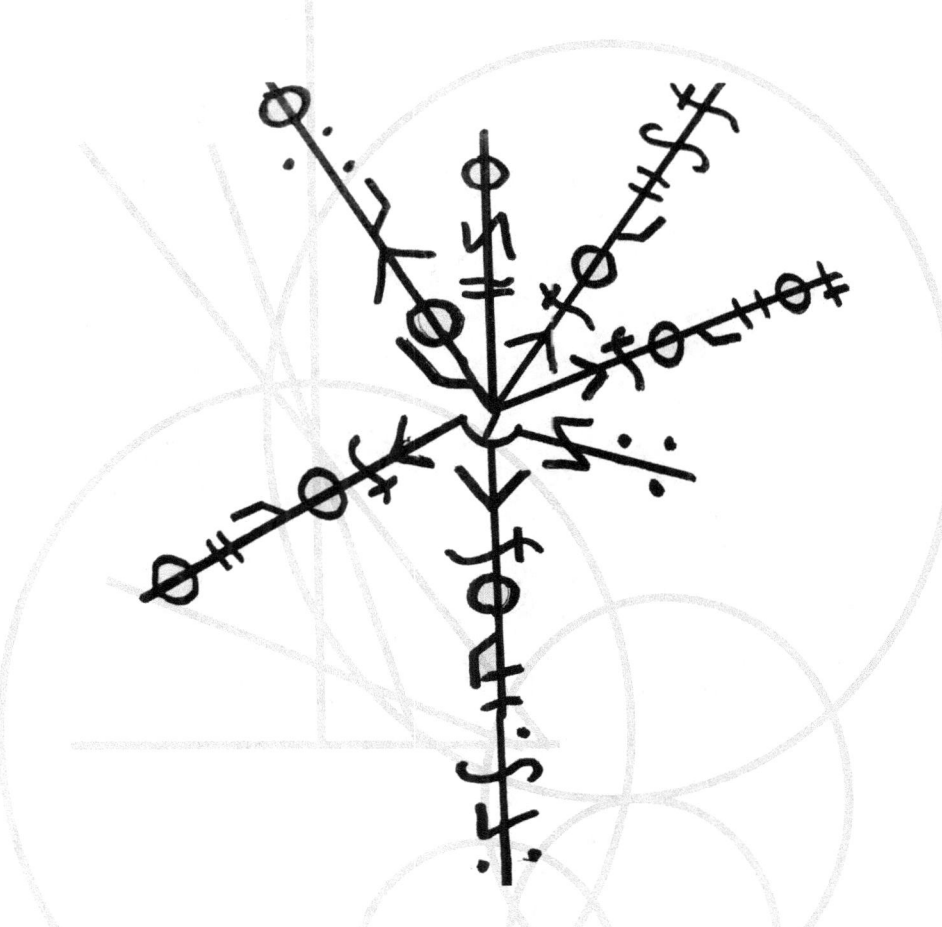

Arasia

N

Penner knew about being secretive. Years of living in a small town had taught him well. The town had barely ten thousand people, and was little more than a temple surrounded by a market, shops, and farms.

Though he'd always lived here, it had never felt like home.

As others were married in the temple, he poured himself into his books. Where others went out and drank, he avoided gatherings and festivities.

Most found him pleasant enough. Working as a clerk and upholding the peace was a good way to be seen and not heard. No one paid attention to the bookkeepers. He had never felt the persecution that so many others had. But he must have known his days here were numbered. Hiding had become more difficult upon discovering Chess, but his life had never been better.

Like most cities in the province, Arasia was dominated by a Temple in the middle, dedicated to the One Soul. Normally he could pass it without noticing, but tonight it stood like a watchtower: stony, unavoidable, and eerie. He felt like it was following them. At least they were wearing pants now.

They crossed the barren town square. Their footsteps echoed off the vacant buildings as he struggled to keep pace with Chess. Despite not knowing where they were headed, he still felt like they were going the wrong way.

Fear flooded his mind. He kept thinking that at any moment they'd be caught. He wasn't sure what would happen if they were, but he didn't want to FIND out. Technically, being out after dark wasn't a crime, but being with Chess would raise unwanted questions. Then Chess froze, gripped Penner by the lapels, and pulled him into an alley. Chess held him against the wall and hushed him. At first, Penner thought it was a romantic gesture and felt a flush of excitement. Then a black cape whipped by them and Penner breathed a sigh of relief. Luckily they hadn't been seen, but it had been close.

"You're doing great. Come on," Chess said as he slipped out of the dark alley and back into the street.

Penner barely recognised him. He would catch glimpses of his face in the moonlight, but it was determined and serious. Chess was never serious. He was the one who would chuckle for hours when someone stepped in dung. He was the one who would titter when someone said a dirty-sounding word. This new determination was strange and unfamiliar, and it made Penner feel like he'd never seen Chess before.

It took less than an hour to cross the city, and somehow they avoided detection the whole way. There were a few close calls, especially once the monks began to make their prayer rounds, but soon they were at the train station.

Compared to the rest of the village, the station was old and decrepit. Where other important buildings were covered in layers of opulence, the station was run down and dilapidated. Beams hung from the roof haphazardly and gave the impression you could bring the entire structure down with an unfortunately timed sneeze. To Penner's knowledge, the station had been built when the city had been founded, but had fallen out of fashion as fewer people opted to leave. It was a dark and dirty place, but at least it was open.

In contrast to the station was the train itself, a luxury steam vehicle with golden features and windows so clear they glistened. The steam spilled out from the engine like a waterfall that bathed the entire station. The vessel felt rich, and for the first time, Penner would get to board it, which delighted him.

As the skyline burned pink, they crossed the platform to the doors. They opened, exhaling a rich scent of pine needles and spice. Penner could feel himself shaking as the man in a velvet red garment approached him. Luckily, Chess intervened and presented the man with two shining, golden tickets.

Penner's eyes went wide as he looked at them. Where had Chess gotten those?

The man didn't appear to care. He took the tickets, punched them with his small silver trinket, and whisked them onboard. Behind them, a few small crates of wood and ore were being loaded into the back of the train, filling the station with the thick dusty smell of his hometown. Penner tried to get a better look at the mechanics of it, but before he could, the man closed the door behind them. The man nodded and retreated behind a small golden door which led to the front of the train, leaving the two of them in solitude.

"To our seats?" Chess asked, but Penner grabbed him by the shoulder and pulled him close. His voice was hushed but anxious.

"Where did you get those tickets?"

"Don't worry. They won't be missed," Chess said, his seriousness dissolving into his mysterious and enigmatic smile. "Let's grab a seat. They'll be leaving soon."

"Did you steal them?" Penner tried to whisper.

"Don't ask questions. Just have a seat," Chess said as he led the way through the iron door. After a moment, Penner followed and was shocked by what he found.

If he had thought the exterior of the train was luxurious, it was nothing compared to the inside. Golden walls, fur rugs, and crystals that hung from the ceilings cast rainbows on all surfaces. On one side, there was a space where moving picture shows were playing, showing exotic places and glamorous people. On another, there was a fountain of sparkling water cascading down a smooth stack of rocks. The chairs were oversized and looked more like golden beds than single seats. Sitting gave him a feeling of tremendous relaxation. Penner could feel his body melting into the soft cushions as Chess sat beside him. He felt Chess's rough fingers dance across his own. Shocked, Penner tried to retreat his hand, but Chess grabbed it in his.

"What are you doing?" Penner hissed.

"It's fine. This is our car. No one is going to see. We can do anything we want. Anything." The emphasis was clear. Penner's face was aflame. "Try to enjoy it." Penner glanced towards the door and pointed to it.

"But if they see—"

"This is our car, Father," Chess said with a laugh. Penner blinked at him before Chess pulled out the tickets and gave one to Penner. Penner's mouth went wide. It was papacy—they were impersonating the leaders of the Temple. No wonder the space was so expensive.

"How did you steal this?" Penner gasped. He leapt out of his seat and was about to bolt for the door when Chess grabbed him.

"Where are you going?"

"This is truly insane. I don't know what you're doing with these, or how you got your hands on them, but I need to get off of this train. If we're caught, we'll be charged. We'll be investigated."

"You're overreacting." Chess smirked.

"And you're posing as a Temple official! You're pretending to be a Father!"

"If we're being technical here, you're posing as the Father and I'd be your Assign. But I don't mind if you want to switch roles."

"They'll kill us!" Penner was yelling now, but his voice was drowned out by the train's whistle.

There was a lurch, and Penner could feel the train pulling away from the station. The power of the machine was stronger than anything he'd experienced before, and he was thrown into his chair. He clenched the armrests tight as the train began to race away from their hometown. There was nowhere he could go. He was stuck playing a role in a charade he didn't understand, and Chess was laughing at him. He wasn't sure what was going on, but he didn't like it.

Soon, they were out of the poor excuse for a station and racing away from everywhere they had ever known. The temple glowed a brilliant gold as they passed by it. Despite having no affection for the structure itself, he could feel a hot tear burn down his cheek as he realised this could be the last time he'd ever see it. His brain reeled. He was leaving behind everything he knew and posing as a temple official. He held his breath.

Pulling him out of his thoughts was Chess, whose hand felt hot and rough in his. Chess had made his living in the mines. His hands were calloused, but softened when Penner held them. Neither said anything, and before long they were through the city gates and traveling towards whatever it was that lay on the other side of the train.

After an hour, Penner looked out the window as the train snaked through the mountains. He could see the city in the distance, but it was little more than a dot now. The light reflected off the golden spire before it vanished into the distance. He felt Chess tighten his grip before placing his head on Penner's shoulder. He was grateful for the privacy as he began to play with Chess's ruffled hair. It smelled like dust and cinnamon.

"It's a beautiful view," Penner said as he replayed the memory in his head. If they were not going to return, he wanted to preserve this moment.

"It's nothing compared to what's next. Trust me," Chess said as he closed his eyes and began to snore.

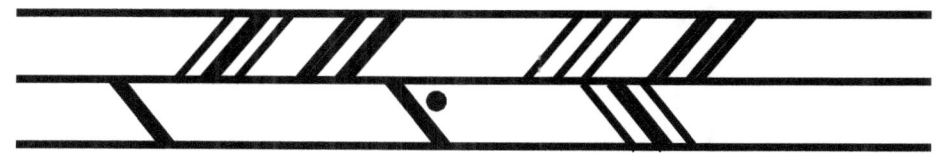

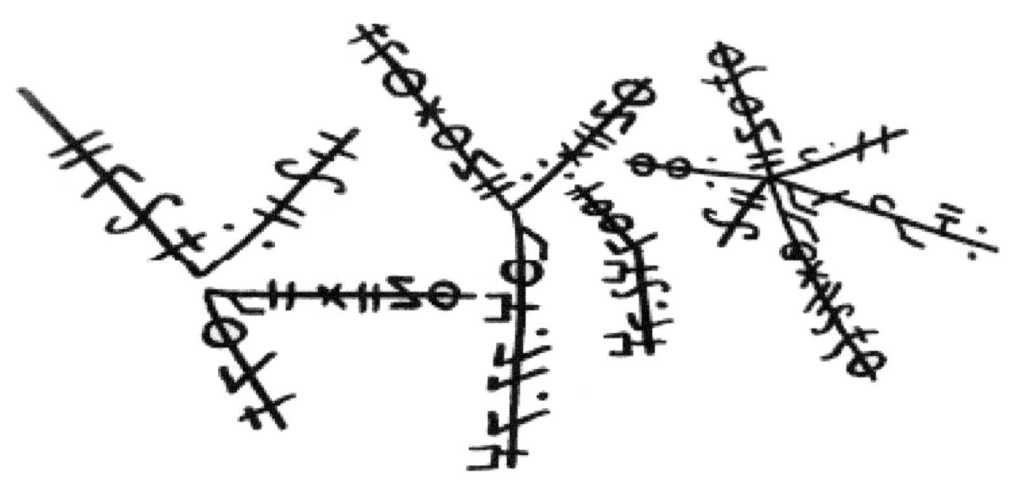

12

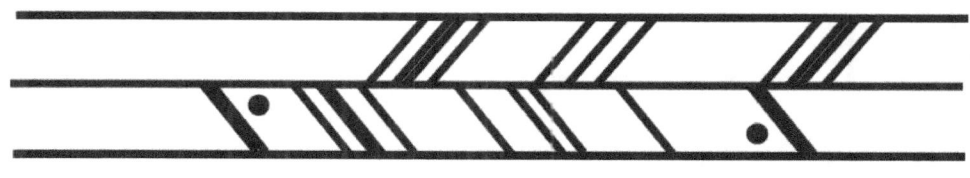

7/14/23

It's been less than a day, and already I miss home. I fear I will never go back, but at the same time I have never felt closer to Chess, or more terrified of what is happening.

He won't talk about last night. He's hardly spoken today. He's watched hours of the pictures but doesn't seem to see what's going on in them. He hasn't eaten. Granted, the food leaves much to be desired, which is strange for such an illustrious transport. Must be a penance thing. I wish I still had my stove. Funny how something so simple can leave such an impact.

He looks different. I've never seen him like this. The colour hasn't fully returned to his face. He looks tired. He keeps examining things that don't exist and he mutters under his breath. As we slept, he woke me up twice with screams. Thankfully there's no one else here to hear them. In the morning he claimed to have no memory of them, but I feel like he's lying to me. He looks worried, and I can't help but think it has to do with where we're going.

I don't know what is going on, but I hope that we find the answers in Sol. Apparently, that's where all the trains go. I never thought I'd ever be able to make it there, but here we are. Well, at least we will be there soon. Maybe we can start a new life in the bigger city. I hear there are entire blocks where we could be allowed to live together without judgement, — away from the clutches of the Temples.

I doubt that such a borough exists, but if it is out there, I hope we find it.

After two days on the train, Penner wasn't sure if he was more excited to see the city, or to eat real food again. The packaged meals had been service-able, but nothing compared to what Penner was used to creating.

Even with what he knew about the capital, nothing could prepare him for the sheer immensity of it. As they approached the massive walls, the city stood like a behemoth dominating the sky. Everything looked alien. Roads and wires hung like spiderwebs, covering buildings of countless shapes and sizes. Even the air was crowded, as airships of all shapes and sizes flew over-head as they wove their way through the metropolis.

They passed through the gate and Chess pulled away. Penner tried to grip him, but Chess shook his head. As the train began to slow down, it shook violently, as if it was trying to throw them off the rails. Penner gripped onto the sides of his chair as he closed his eyes. He breathed in and out, trying to calm his stomach as it lurched into his throat. Soon the shaking slowed, then stopped, and the door to the station swung open.

Grabbing their belongings, Chess guided Penner off the train.

"Exit through the back. We don't want them to know we were here."

Penner didn't argue and followed Chess through the back exit before the train stopped. A giant bloom of steam filled the room, and Chess and Penner leapt from the train, landing with a gentle thud on the galley. Chess landed with ease. Penner, on his face, but he was quickly on his feet and following Chess through the steam-filled area, just as some men in white garments swooped into the train.

As they rushed through the space, Penner immediately felt out of place. The station was abundance personified. He wasn't sure what he'd expected, but this was beyond it exponentially. The floor was fine, polished wood. Traces of gold ran along the walls, which stretched to an incredible height. Above them were large stained-glass windows depicting a Raven wearing a crown and clutching a pearl. Others depicted the Great Racoon, the Snake, and the Creator, each incredibly detailed. Penner's steps slowed down, but Chess grabbed him by the arm and guided him.

"Come on," Chess said as they raced out of the station.

Penner was overwhelmed. If he'd thought the station was incredible, the city centre was extreme. The buildings were so large that trying to look up made him dizzy. The air was strange and stank of copper and oil as the hustle of the city assaulted his ears. He gazed back at the station with its beautiful emerald and golden arches that were large and imposing. The entire city was bustling with excitement as trains, carriages, and people wove their way through the chaos. Penner was frozen in awe.

"You were perfect. No one saw us," Chess said, as he noticed Penner lost in the landscape. "We should get out of here before they start asking questions."

"It's incredible."

"You'll get used to it. Maybe." Chess slung his bag over his shoulder and turned to Penner with a smile. "You ready?"

"For what?" Penner asked.

Chess winked at him and took off into the crowd. Penner struggled to keep up and kept getting distracted by details. Which was unlike him, as Chess had the shorter attention span. This courtyard was twice as massive as the town square of Arasia. In the middle of the pale blue area was a golden pearl, which hung suspended in midair above the Snake, Raccoon, and Raven. The statue was bigger than any Penner had ever seen. He looked up at it, awestruck at the detail and execution of such a unique piece. He could see the individual feathers of the bird and the drips of venom from the snake's teeth. It looked to be made of gold, but there was so much of it he could hardly comprehend how they could get gold to float like that.

On the other side of the statue stood a building that looked to be a courthouse or a temple, or perhaps some perverse blend of the two. Its structure was heavily burnt and when he gazed into it, he could see strange black shadows moving around inside of it- though when he blinked, the shadows disappeared. Chess, however, didn't break his attention from the statue. His stare was so intense he looked to be burning a hole into it with his mind.

"It's amazing!" Penner broke the silence. He looked over to Chess, but his face was stone. His face frowned as his eyes danced around the monument, scouring its surface for something Penner couldn't see. "I've never seen such details before, and how did they get the wings to stay up like—"

"We have to go," Chess said, his voice cold as he turned away and jogged to the streets shooting off from the square. With little choice, Penner followed, taking one last look back at the globe before chasing after Chess.

"Where are we going?"

"Don't worry. I know where we need to go. Just follow me," Chess said. "Stay close."

Chess turned Penner around and raised his hand at him. For a second Penner flinched, but Chess's hand connected with another hand that had been attempting to reach into their bag. Penner saw the cloaked man for only a second before he was swallowed back into the crowds. Chess took the bag from Penner's hip and made Penner wrap his hands around it.

"Hold your bag in front of you. We can't afford to lose anything."

Penner was still trying to wrap his mind around what had happened.

"What was—"

"Just keep moving. Follow me," Chess said. Penner exhaled, unsure how long he'd been holding his breath. He trusted Chess and followed him. Gripping his bag tightly in his hands, he followed Chess through the crowds, and before long they arrived at an inn and went inside.

The Courtyard of Sol was a space where people used to gather to hear the wise words of the king before the maestro banished him and his family to the Under realm. All that remains is Royal Library- but none are allowed in there.

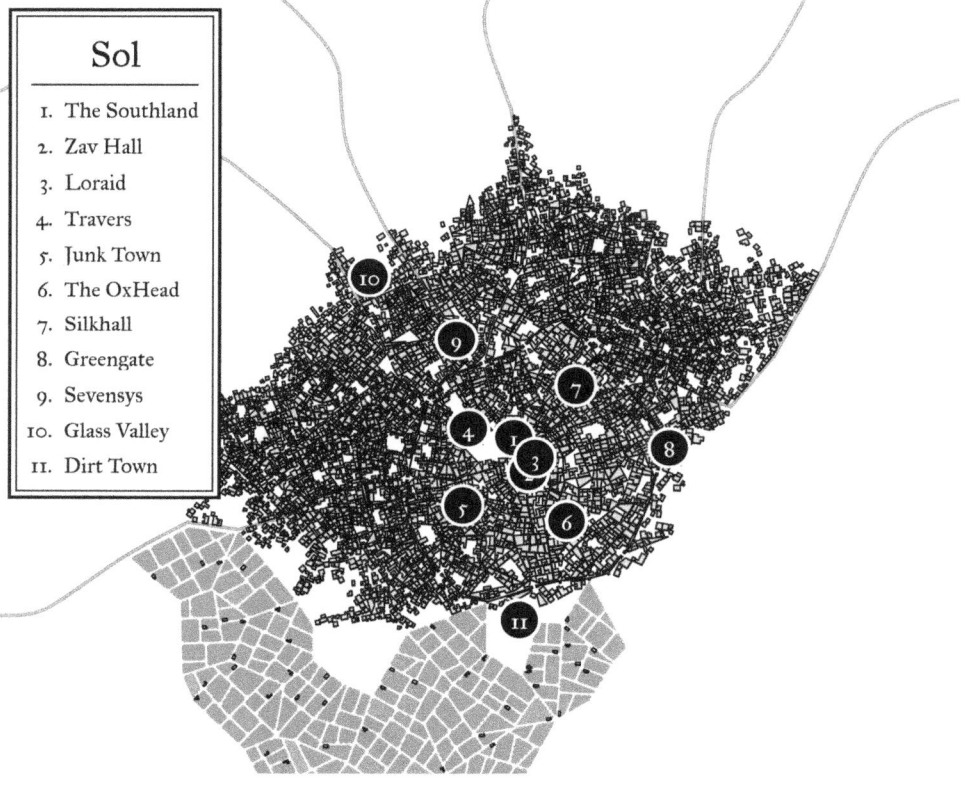

Sol

1. The Southland
2. Zav Hall
3. Loraid
4. Travers
5. Junk Town
6. The OxHead
7. Silkhall
8. Greengate
9. Sevensys
10. Glass Valley
11. Dirt Town

9/14/23

I don't know how Chess knows the city so well. To my knowledge he has never been here, but he moves through the streets like a native. I suppose I had always assumed he had lived his entire life in Arasi like I had, but here he was leading me through streets upon streets before stumbling upon an inn that was not only accepting of us, but seemed to know who we were when we entered. The owner said we had a look about us, but I can't shake an uneasy feeling about it. I feel like I've walked into a trap, but Chess just accepts it.

I am thankful to be here now, but Chess still won't talk to me about what happened. He keeps smiling and telling me to relax, but how can I when he's acting so strange? I just want him to sit back and stop, but he says there is more to do. He talked to the innkeeper for a solid hour as I arranged the room, and now we're to meet with someone tomorrow. He won't talk about it and he still hasn't eaten anything.

At least the food is edible now.

7ΛUVΠ⟨UV7 7ΛUVΠ⟨⟨LU)7 ⟨L7⟨UL⟨)⟨7⟩⟨Π
)7)L)7Π⟨ΛL Λⵉ) ΛΛⵉ)))L ⟨Uⵋ)7Π
ΠⵑV ΛΛⵉⵋ) ⟨L) U⟨JJ⟨ΛL Λ)ⵑ7
Πⵑ)Π 7)LΠ ΛV 7ⵑL Λ⟨Πⵑ ΠⵑV
VⵑV7 ΛΧΠ 7)L ΛV JVJΠ Λⵑ ΠⵑV 7ΛΧⵋ⁙

To Penner, the exterior of the building could be generously described as a bit much. If the station had been elaborate, this venue was extraordinary. The hallway was long and radiant, polished enough to glow. Above them hung opulent gold chandeliers, each more impressive than the last. Gemstones and crystals shattered the lights into a million fractals that made the room glimmer with life. Marble statues stood at every corner of the labyrinthian halls, each fierce and dominating and completely unfamiliar to Penner. Portraits of people in royal outfits sat upon the, all of them looking very important and supremely bored. The floors alternated between plush red carpets and complicated tile designs etched from gold and onyx. He had no business here and he knew it.

He followed Chess, who seemed like he had been here before. They followed two men dressed in black, with severe expressions and little sense of humour. They were silent and had remained so since they collected them in the atrium. He tried to ask what was going on, but they didn't acknowledge him. Though Penner wasn't sure what was going on, he felt it was important.

Penner walked with confusion, but Chess was walking with confidence. The entire time Penner was internally panicking, Chess was calm, collected and charming. His chin held high despite the scars he'd earned in the mines. Penner paused, and for a moment, he barely recognised him.

There had been something different about Chess since the dream. Penner had always been the one Chess had leaned upon, but now their situation was reversed. For the first time, Penner felt inadequate and uncomfortable. He didn't like not being the one in control.

After the strenuous stroll through the maze, they arrived at a large set of doors that were shiny and black as night. They approached and one of the guards held up a fist. Chess folded his hands behind his back and stood up straight. After Chess cleared his throat, Penner followed suit. The guard nodded, and the doors swung open and the scent of books and history washed over them. Penner gasped. In front of them was a huge library, with more books and artwork than he had ever seen before. His heart fluttered.

"She will be with you shortly," one of the guards said, while the other nodded and wandered off. With one ham-like arm, he ushered them inside.

"This is bigger than my house!" Penner exclaimed, unable to contain his excitement as he stepped into the centre of the room.

He felt himself being drawn to the wall when he was interrupted.

"Don't touch anything!" the soldier snapped as he left.

Penner froze as the doors closed, locking them in. For a moment, he realised they were trapped, but with the amount of knowledge around them, he didn't mind. He marvelled at the room: the oversized luxurious furniture, the larger than life portraits that adorned every wall, the hundreds — if not thousands — of books that smelled like history. It took all of his strength to not grab them and cuddle into them.

"There's enough books here for a lifetime."

"I wish we had the time to let you read them all." Penner looked at Chess as he paced the room.

"Who lives here?" Penner asked.

"She does."

"Who is she?"

"You'll see," Chess said, smiling at him. He looked amused and walked over to a globe. Chess peered into it and spun it. His long slender fingers slowly manoeuvred across it.

"You shouldn't touch that. The big guy looked serious," Chess chuckled.

Penner walked over to him and could see a strange sadness in his eyes. There was something bothering him, and Penner placed his hands on Chess's shoulders.

"Hey, you okay?" Penner asked with a squeeze.

"I'm fine," Chess said, shrugging Penner off. He turned to Penner with a sad smile. "Really, I am. It's just, this is something else entirely." Chess looked back at the globe as he gave it a spin. "There are so many mysteries in the world, but once you uncover them, that's it. The mystery is gone."

"That's a good thing. That's how progress is made."

"But maybe there are some things that are better left unknown."

"Like what?"

"SECRETS. I know some. But maybe there's some secrets that I shouldn't."

Penner frowned. He was trying to process what Chess was saying, but he wasn't following. He grabbed Chess's hand and smiled at him.

"You don't need to keep secrets from me," Penner said.

"But I do. At least these ones. It's not that I don't want to tell you. I just don't think you'll understand what I'm trying to say," Chess said.

Penner was about to respond when the doors clicked open.

Looking up, they both saw her at the same time. A beautiful woman in an elaborate red dress floated into the room. Her dress was massive, taking up the doorway. Her golden hair was long and beautiful, and draped elegantly around her slender shoulders. Her face was painted in majestic colours that Penner had never seen in person. Her hands were covered in black gloves that were adorned with jewels that matched her diamond necklace and earrings. The lights that dazzled from the jewels were almost blinding, and Penner had to squint to properly recognise her. When he did, his eyes went wide.

"Chess!" Penner whispered. "That's Raina Guilden!"

She smiled. Her face lit up as she clasped her hands together. "Welcome, Gentlemen," she said. Her voice was rich and smooth as honey, and though her accent was thick Penner had no issues comprehending her. He had seen her before, displayed dozens of feet tall on the sides of the temple in Arasi. They only got pictures a few times a year, and she'd been in dozens of them. She was just as stunning in person.

"Lady Raina. It's a pleasure to meet you," Chess said as he bowed to her. Raina nodded her approval at him and turned to Penner. Instantly, he forgot how to breathe.

"In the city, it's customary to bow to a lady," she said. Penner flushed. He followed Chess's lead. Pleased, she raised her hand, and Penner stood. He was surprised to see that she was almost as tall as he was, but he suspected that had more to do with her elegant shoes than her stature. He was a tall man, after all.

"I've been expecting you," she said. With the grace of a flower in a breeze, Raina cut between them before floating to one of her elaborate, oversized chairs. The wide, circular top made it look like she was being enveloped in a cocoon.

"You and your," She fished for the word. "—associate." She eyed Penner like a steak, and he had never felt so exposed. He was sure that she knew EVERYthing about them.

"I thank you for your time. I know you don't accept an audience with everyone," Chess said.

"Well, you're not just anyone, are you?" she chimed. "I can see it all over you. Modesty does you no favours. Barely in the aether for a week and standing before me. You and your—" She paused. "—associate—" She emphasized the ass, and Penner suddenly felt like a piece of meat. "—must be very special indeed."

"I'm sorry, do you know us?" Penner asked.

"Forgive me for blathering on. Can I offer you tea?"

Penner suddenly felt hot. The most famous face in the land was offering him tea.

"I would be honoured," Penner said. Chess nodded.

"Delightful. Chess, won't you assist me?" she cooed. Chess nodded and walked over to her to offer his assistance. He made a poor butler, but if he didn't have to pour the tea, maybe she wouldn't notice.

"Does he know?" Raina asked, quirking an eyebrow up at him.

Chess looked down and shook his head. Penner could clearly hear them, but didn't let on.

"Not yet."

"Good. Ignorance can be a gift. Don't ruin it for him until you have to. You don't want him to worry." She looked over at Penner. "He's a very pretty one."

Penner felt himself blush and tried to appear fascinated by the intricate weave of the carpet. He had never been called pretty before. At least not by someone famous. Grabbing two small teacups, Chess walked back to Penner and gave him the fuller one.

"You wanted sugar, right?" Raina said.

"It's how he likes it." Chess said and they each took a sip of the tea. It was very bitter. The sugar was appreciated.

Raina didn't work pouring the tea but she did appear to supervise. She winked at him and returned her attention to Chess. "What do you require from me?"

"I've seen the Mountain," Chess said.

"What mountain?" Penner asked. He hadn't heard anything about a mountain before now.

Raina, however, appeared to have heard of the mountain.

"Oh." She looked as if she'd been hurt. "You require transport?"

"We do."

"We do?" Penner asked.

"There's a pilot. They're the best I can offer. That particular journey is perilous. I hope you'll be—" She eyed Penner for a moment. "—careful."

"Why does he need to be careful? It's just a mountain. It can't be—" Penner asked.

"I'm sure it will be fine," Chess said. "We don't have much in the way of supplies."

"Is that going to be a problem? Do we need more supplies? Should I get more supplies?" Penner asked. Raina giggled and touched Penner's cheek. Penner felt himself flush.

"He's awful caring, isn't he?" Penner's voice suddenly failed him. She was touching him. He wasn't sure if he should touch her back, but he became acutely aware that he had forgotten how to breathe.

"This adventure. It's nothing too dangerous," Chess said. Penner wasn't convinced.

Raina walked over to Chess, put her hands on his shoulders and whispered in his ear. Penner bit his tongue, unsure whether he was jealous or annoyed. After a moment, she pulled away and he nodded. She turned to Penner and smiled.

"I'm afraid it won't be an easy ride for you. Your travel quarters will be tight. I'll arrange for the vessel to be waiting for you at precisely eight tomorrow." Penner frowned. "Is everything alright?"

"Are we leaving already? We've barely arrived and this place—" He paused and looked at Chess. "I had hoped we could spend some time in a place that was accepting. Of people like us."

"I understand. But I'm sorry. Time is of the essence. This captain is only in town for the day. I believe they'd make a perfect companion for you, and they will be gone with the morning wind," she said.

"Well... Perhaps we can come back here after?"

Chess and Raina looked at each other with a smile.

"Yes. I think we should," Chess said with a smile.

Penner felt his face light up again. He had never been good at hiding his emotions, but here he felt so at ease he wasn't trying to pretend he wasn't excited. It felt good not to hide.

"There will be a small ship awaiting you in the Northern Bay. It is being held under Cassius and will be departing at eight. Do not be late, or you will be stuck here. The captain, Fred, is a friend of mine. Short temper but incredibly resourceful. Should prove indispensable to you." She fixed her blue eyes on Penner and smiled. "Did you get all that?" He nodded. "Good boy."

"Two things that need to be resolved before we leave," Chess said.

"Have faith, my dear. Fred is unlikely to be bothered by your relationship."

"I require a Tome. Specifically, a Red Tome."

"A Red Tome." Raina looked at Chess with a frown. "Is that necessary? There are powerful binds in here. Deadly secrets that will put a target on your back. There are many who would kill for it, if it doesn't kill you first."

"We will guard it. I will ensure its safety."

Raina looked at him, before turning on her heels and grabbing a red book from the wall. It was small and thin, with a brilliant leather cover. Golden lines and complex patterns played across its cover. Raina held it for a second and breathed in the scent of the book. It appeared intoxicating. She took out a small square of red silk, wrapped the book in it and presented it to them like a gift.

"This goes against my better judgement. You must keep it safe."

"No. Not me. Him." Chess motioned to Penner.

"You're entrusting this power to him?"

"I trust him with my life. With him carrying it, we stand a chance." Raina turned to Penner, and offered him the book.

"Come and get it, Sugar. It's surprisingly heavy," she whispered.

Penner walked over, but before he could grab it, Raina snatched it out of reach. She shook her head. "You shouldn't touch such power with your hands. There are spirits who would use it against you. Place it in your satchel and only take it in case of emergency." She pulled him closer to her with a fierce expression. "You will know when. And do not let him read it."

"Why not?"

"It will kill him, of course." Penner looked at her, horrified, and she laughed. "No, sorry. Old prank. We have so few opportunities to use it."

Penner took the bag and closed it around the Tome. It was surprisingly light. It hardly felt like a book at all.

"You said you had two things you wished to ask me about?"

"Right, WHERE is your restroom?"

27

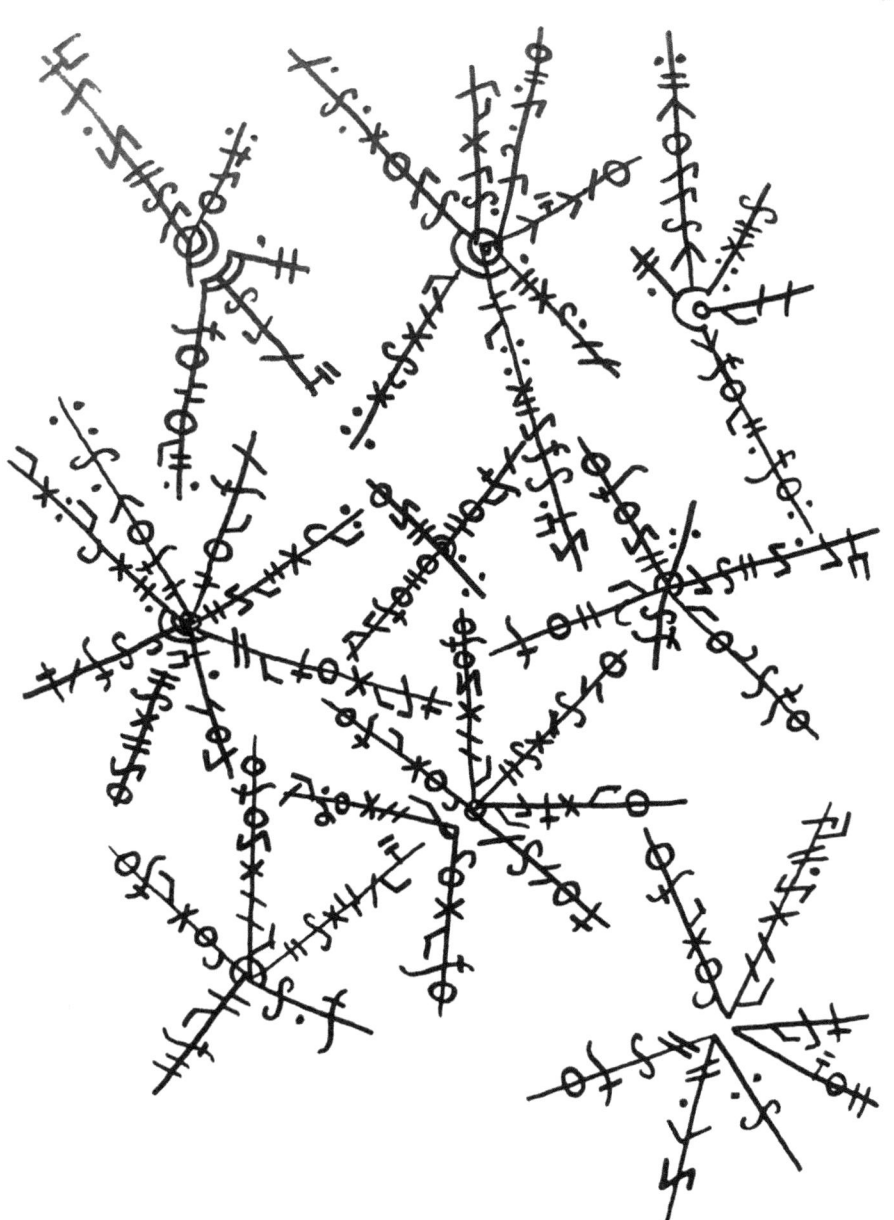

Having shared the room with Raina for THE past five minutes, Penner felt inadequate. He couldn't help it. Everything was so elaborate and beautiful. He kept scanning the room and marvelling at the books. He knew she was watching him, which was the reason he didn't grab them. There was so much knowledge here. Hundreds of stories just begging to be read.

"They're beautiful."

"You can touch them, IF you'd like."

Penner looked at her and then gazed back at the wall.

"Is this a trap? It feels like this is a trap."

Raina smiled at him. She hadn't taken her eyes off him since Chess had left. The attention was flattering but unnerving. After a minute, she chuckled to herself and smiled.

"This must be so awkward for YOU."

"There are worse things than being admired by royalty." Penner's cheeks burned. He felt emboldened.

"Do pardon my gaze. There is just something extraordinary about you," Raina said as she took a step towards him. Her eye contact was so intense it burnt. "You are a rare one."

Penner gulped.

"What makes you think that?"

"I can sense people. I can see them, who they are behind the pretence and customs of the world. It's a gift I've had since I was a girl. Comes in handy in the Southern cities. And I can see you, Penner. I can see right through you."

"I hope the view is enjoyable." He felt proud of himself for being able to flirt with her. He could've made toast on his cheeks. She took a second and nodded at him.

"Back there, where you came from. You were a clerk?"

"Of sorts. I was a negotiator. I worked in the courts, but kept many positions around the city. I went where I was needed and kept the peace when I had to," Penner said. His hands spasmed. She was making him nervous.

"A man of the law. Curious, considering your unconventional relationship."

"Knowing the law is the first step to knowing how to get around it." He smiled.

She laughed.

"A rebel as well. Very good, Penner! A man of many talents. Shame you couldn't stay. You'd be a most excellent addition to my affairs."

Penner couldn't help but notice her emphasis on affairs. With confidence, she walked to a large picture on the wall, of a raven with a crown. It was painted extraordinarily well. The details were so vivid, Penner was certain it would leap off the canvas.

"I was a painter, once," Raina said.

"Is this yours?" Penner asked eyeing the extraordinary canvas.

"This was a commission," she said. "I could never get the details. I just like to lay it all out there in broad, expressive strokes. Do you like it?"

"It is nice. It's a little…"

"A little what?"

Penner frowned as he chose his words carefully.

"Cleric-like? Especially with the Raven."

"I suppose. I guess I shouldn't have figured you as a man of faith."

"It's just a silly fable to keep children in line," Penner said.

"Every fable had to come from somewhere. Sometimes it's not the origin of the story that matters, but what the story means to you. It is possible to not believe in something and still recognise the importance of the story itself."

"I will think on it then," he said, turning back to the books. "How many stories are in here?"

She laughed. "Countless, I'd imagine. Some of them are even written in the books."

"I wish I could read them all."

"You just might. If we cross paths again, I will give you one."

"If?" She walked over to him, her perfume wafting towards him, leaving him breathless.

"You are a man of many questions. And so many of them are consuming

31

you. I can see that you are full of them," she said. "But you never ask Chess questions, do you?"

"It's more accurate to say he never answers them. Especially now."

She laughed.

"Do you trust him?"

"Unconditionally," Penner said.

"Even now? Through all this?"

"Through all this and more."

"And why do you think that is?" she asked.

"Sometimes when you know something, you just know."

Raina smiled at him.

"So you are a man of faith, after all," she quipped. "Your bond will help protect you, but what you are embarking on is a dangerous journey. To make it out alive, you must trust him."

"He's never given me a reason not to."

"Never?" Raina asked. "You know that he's different now. This is not the man you knew."

"I know, but he's still the man I love." He paused. "I can't explain it, I just—the past few days, I hardly recognise him. I know he still cares, but it's like he's somewhere else sometimes."

Penner wrung his hands. Raina put her hand on his shoulder and gave it an affectionate rub. He looked into her glassy eyes and could feel his emotion reflected in them. He knew that she understood. Maybe she'd gone through the exact same thing.

"Is there anything that you can tell me about all this?"

"I could, but TIME will make it known. I don't want to interfere before the right time," she said. "What I can tell you is that he needs you as much as you need him. Maybe more. You need to protect each other from what comes next. When people go through what he is going through, it can be hard to keep your anchor in reality. You will be good for him. Maybe you'll be able to protect him from himself," she said with a kind smile. She walked over to the large door and rapped three times. The hinges flew open and one of the large men filled the doorway.

"You're leaving?"

"I won't judge you. Love takes many forms. But you must be careful, Penner. I hope to see you again. Maybe even under happier circumstances. Farewell." With that, she walked out, leaving him with the guard. Looking at the man's impressive size, Penner turned to him and shrugged.

"Are you here to make sure I don't steal anything?" Penner asked as the door slammed shut behind her.

It echoed around the room like a gunshot. For a moment, he feared the man would rush him, but he didn't. He found himself drawn back to the wall. Admiring the rows of books and the intricate paintings. He turned to the Raven that Raina had been examining.

As he admired it, he was drawn to a small poem, framed beside the bird, that he hadn't noticed before:

REAL TRUTH.

IT SITS LIKE A STONE IN THE GULLET OF A BIRD-

IT BEGS TO BE SEEN. BUT IS NEVER UNDERSTOOD-

A PUZZLE- NEVER NOTICED. UNTIL IT IS FINISHED. BUT NEVER COMPLETED.

He found a portrait of Raina hidden in the grandeur of the room.

Though the painting appeared to be tarnishing, she appeared identical in it. In one hand, she held a scepter with a pearl embedded in it. In the other, a crystal goblet filled with black wine. On her shoulder, above her golden dress, was a large raven the size of her head. On its feathery head, it wore a large golden crown that appeared to be made of bones.

The door beside him swung opened, and he jumped as Chess walked in.

"Where did she go?" Chess asked.

"She left," Penner said.

"Did you have a good conversation?"

"A much-needed one," Penner said. He locked eyes with Chess, who smirked. "I was just admiring the art."

"It's good to admire the finer things in life." Chess winked.

"Subtle," Penner chuckled. "I just can't figure out what it means."

"Which part?" Chess walked over and began to scan the portrait with him.

"Well, I get the symbols. The raven and the pearl are obviously an allegory for—"

"A what?" Penner quirked his eyebrow.

"An allegory?" For a moment, Penner debated on explaining, but shook his head. "Nothing. Never mind. It's just that the pearl and the raven reference the origin story of the Creator's pearl, and the crown on the raven indicates she believes it to be the rightful owner of the jewel." Chess nodded, and Penner pointed to the goblet. "But the drink is black, and I can't figure out why. It could be poison, or oil."

"It's ink." Chess moved close to the painting. So close he looked like he was about to taste it. He breathed it in, and soon his eyes darted around the room. Like a shot, he bolted to the other side of the room and found a small goblet that looked similar to the one in the painting.

"How can you be sure?" Penner followed.

"I just know these things," Chess said, grabbing the small goblet and taking it back to the painting. Again Penner followed. Holding the goblet up to the portrait, Chess began TO turn it over in his hands. His eyes flickering back and forth between the two items at a rapid pace.

"What are you looking for?" Penner asked as he squinted at the cup.

"Symbols."

"Well, yeah. The raven could be a symbol of wisdom and strength, and a goblet of ink—" Penner began, but Chess cut him off.

"No, not that, the symbols. They're a key. They might be the key to all of this. Do you see the dots?"

Chess put the goblet down and his eyes began scouring the walls. Penner followed, until Chess grabbed a small frame and tried to rip it off the wall. Penner went to stop him, but then a large hand reached in and pulled Chess back. Penner recoiled, but Chess didn't notice, despite the fact that the large bodyguard was now grabbing him by the back of the shirt and dragging him to the door.

"I don't think you can touch the paintings," Penner said. Chess blinked.

After a breath, he finally snapped out of his trance and looked at Penner.

"It's not the paintings. It's the symbols," he said. His eyes went wide and he looked excited. "This is all about them."

"Sorry," Penner finally said to the guard, who gave him a disapproving look. He placed himself in front of Chess with his arms crossed. Though Chess was not short, he still had to LOOK up to the man's face. When he did, Chess smiled.

"You remind me of my old dog. Do you bark?" he asked.

"You should go," the guard said.

"We should go." Chess said nodding to the guard. He took one final look at the wall before shaking his head and walking back into the hallway. The bodyguard looked at Penner and gripped him by the back of the jacket and escorted him out.

Upon exiting the room, the man let go and escorted Penner to the side. The guard turned back to the library and slammed the door shut. He then turned to Chess and placed a letter in his hand. Chess took it and slid it into his pocket, and while Penner tried to TAKE a peek, the man blocked his gaze.

"You two best follow me out," the guard said as he began to walk through the hall. He quickly realised that Chess wasn't paying attention to their path. Instead his eyes were whipping across the letter he'd just received.

"What is it?" Penner asked in a whisper.

"Instructions," Chess replied. After a moment, he handed the letter to Penner. Curious, Penner opened the letter.

"These are instructions?" Penner asked, but he got no answer.

Penner frowned. He looked at the paper, but it was blank.

37

I found it. At first I could hardly believe that the space existed, but here it was, tucked away just a few hundred feet from the main city buildings. I watched a man kiss another in the front window of a butcher shop. I nearly fell over backwards from shock, but it was exciting.

I can't begin to explain how incredible it feels to be here! I feel like I belong. I want to stay here, but we can't. This mission, or whatever it is, demands we continue on. Maybe we'll be able to come back here after we've done what we need to.

I'm still shocked that I was fortunate enough to meet Raina Guilden. I never imagined meeting such a person. Who am I? A clerk from Arasia has no business consorting with a picture star. She's every bit as beautiful in person as I imagined, but I just wish I knew how she knew about Chess.
He's grown attached to a paper. Raina gave it to him, but when I try to read it, I don't see anything. I know it's blank, but I can't help but feel like I'm missing something.

Chess seems fine. He's quiet but focused. Maybe tonight I'll be able to spend time with him. On our way back to the inn we held hands in public without fear of what would happen. It was. Such a thrill. It felt so liberating. My hand is still tingling. Maybe the people in the city don't care about the laws of the Temple, or maybe there are just too many people to fight it, but it felt good to be able to feel his love without fear in a public place.

Maybe tomorrow I will kiss him in the street.

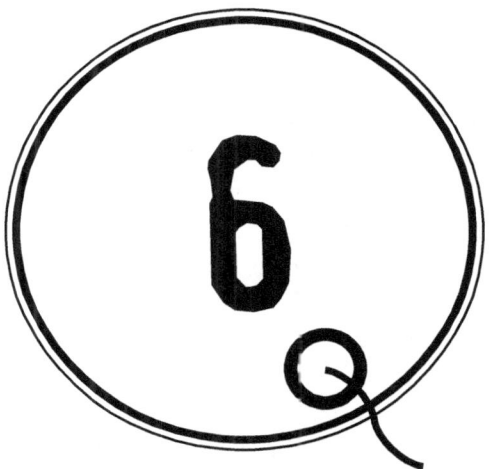

Even though it was getting dark, the city was alive. It was unlike anything Penner had ever seen before. All around him were impressive buildings of all shapes and sizes, slowly bursting into automated illumination. Every facade looked like a vertical star-scape. Technology integrated into the world seamlessly. The moon hung high in the sky, but seemed bigger surrounded by the buildings and airships. The stars were barely visible through the clouds, but the street lanterns made it look like they had fallen to the street.

The long cobblestone roads were buzzing as people and transportation zoomed along. Carriages, bicycles, and autos passed him, but the most popular mode of transportation was walking. He passed group after group of well-dressed folks in fancy clothes conversing on a wealth of topics he had no context for: discussions of the importance of their machines, and complaints about the municipal transport, and the mundanity of their jobs on the ships. A few times he slowed down to listen in.

"They expect top dollar for their cabins, but don't even offer access to their top decks. It's a scandal!" he overheard a man in a golden brocade jacket comment. The other people in his party shared his disgusted sentiments. Penner giggled to himself.

The complaints of the rich were so frivolous.

Despite the hour, many businesses were still open, their warm interiors beckoning all who passed by to come in and enjoy themselves. He walked by a tavern and marvelled at the large stills that held more types of spirits than he had ever seen before. He went into another and was shocked to find twelve different beers. He didn't have much coin on him, but the barkeep filled him a bag full of local breads and cheeses, and a container of fragrant stew. He'd never met anyone so friendly, and only realised after leaving that the barkeep had had a tail. He had never seen someone with a tail before and wondered whether or not to comment, but realised it was probably more polite not to.

He passed by an officer and slowed his pace. For a moment, he was terrified the man would sense he did not belong and attack him. But then the man looked at him and nodded and tipped his hat with a smile. Penner nodded back in relief. Joy filled his steps. He thought about Chess and his pace quickened, feeling eager to return to their room.

The inn was charming. A quaint white house with ivy covering the walls, illuminated by a single street lamp. Their orange blooms made the space smell like spices. Stepping inside, the warmth of the fireplace enveloped him. The innkeeper smiled at him and ushered him to the counter.

The man grabbed one of the small bags and looked inside, helping himself to a small hunk of cheese. Penner shrugged it off, shuffled the bags up the stairs, and fumbled his way into his room.

The room was dark and the curtains were drawn. Penner blinked to adjust his eyes and placed the items on a table by the door. He grabbed a match and lit the lamp that hung above the door. Once the flame was sparked, the room came alive with a balmy warm glow. To his surprise, Chess was in the exact position he'd been in when he'd left. He was slumped at the desk, resting on top of a pile of books. The open window made the pages flutter. Penner couldn't make out what was on them, but the pen was still clutched in Chess' hand.

"Chess?" he called. Chess's mouth hung open with spittle dripping from his lips. Chess had slept so little since they had left, Penner wasn't about to interrupt now. But curiosity got the best of him. He eyed the papers and tried to make them out, but the dim light prevented his view.

Crouching beside him, Penner perched on his toes as he did his best to balance, but still couldn't get a clear look. From this angle Chess looked peaceful. The scent of his skin hit Penner like a blast. Even when Chess had worked in the mines, he had always had a faint scent of cinnamon. Chess would chew on cinnamon stalks when he was anxious, which Penner commented would destroy his teeth, but Chess never cared. It took all Penner's strength to not kiss him. He had to let him sleep.

Still perched on his toes, Penner noticed a few papers had fallen off the desk. He picked them up and squinted at them, attempting to make sense of them. As he marvelled at them, the papers came alive with symbols, numbers, and strange writing written all over them. Their detail was amazing but confusing, and Penner could hardly make sense of which way they were supposed to be read.

Eventually, his legs cramped and he stood up. Curious to see more, he looked over at the papers that were trapped underneath Chess. As he looked at them, he could make out patterns similar to the ones that covered the pages in his hands. It began to look like they went together. He held one paper up and closed one eye, and observed how the lines that came off the page looked like they matched the lines on the paper Chess was on. He laid them beside each other to compare, but as he did so his hand grazed the other paper and he felt a shock.

His hand felt like it was on fire. A burning sensation that pierced his hand and made him flinch. There was a bright light, and though it was brief, it was blinding. He blinked as bright lights danced around him, and Chess bolted upright in his chair. His eyes were wide, and he sat up so fast the chair teetered backwards. Penner grabbed the chair and placed him back on the ground. Chess looked terrified and was breathing quickly as his eyes darted around the pages he had just created. After he realised where he was, Chess relaxed and looked up at Penner. He exhaled in what seemed like the first time in weeks.

"Hey, you," Penner said with a smile.

Chess, still breathing erratically, looked up at him. He didn't acknowledge him until Penner reached out and grabbed his shoulder, shocking him into consciousness.

"Penner?" he asked. "What are you—" Chess looked away and rifled through the pages. He turned them over and began to stack them on top of each other haphazardly. Penner wondered if he was looking for a pattern as Chess ran his eyes around them.

"What are you looking for?" Penner asked.

Chess looked at him, and Penner laughed. When he'd fallen asleep, the ink had transferred onto his face, making him look heavily tattooed. Black symbols stood out against his light skin.

"Ghosts," Chess said.

"What?" Penner asked.

"Do you believe in ghosts?" Chess asked as he picked up his pen. He began to scribble more symbols on the papers. He began to put different symbols on different pages, as if putting together a puzzle. There didn't appear to be any order to it.

"As much as anything else," Penner began. Chess looked at him, and then scanned the papers. "Are you okay?"

"It's not here!" Chess gritted his teeth in frustration. He threw the pen down so hard it snapped. The ink splattered, sending small blots of black ink over the papers and him. Chess hung his head. "And now I've made a mess." Chess tried to wipe himself off, but the small stains soon became massive stains of black that smeared all over his body. He began to rub it off more intensely and reached down to pick up the pieces of the pen. His hands flung themselves down, and as he did, Penner watched as he absentmindedly stabbed himself on a shard. Chess didn't seem to notice.

"Chess! Stop! What are you doing?" Penner exclaimed. Chess paused and Penner pointed at the blood pooling in his hand.

"Oh," he said. Penner gripped the hand and lifted it to stop the bleeding.

"You need to be more careful," Penner said.

"I'm fine," Chess said. Penner brought his hand over to the light and looked at the wound. "Really. Can I have my hand back?"

"Doesn't it hurt?" Penner said and let go.

"Doesn't what hurt?" Chess pulled his hand away and began to crawl on the floor, gathering the papers together.

Blood spilled onto the floor, causing Penner to follow him with a rag in an attempt to clean it up. Then, as it looked like he was calming down, he shot up, his head colliding with the underside of the desk. He managed to get to his feet, but barely.

"You okay?" Penner asked.

"I feel—a bit like myself." Chess threw the papers on the desk and turned to the bed. With a shaky step, his knees buckled and he collapsed. Penner had less than a second to react, but managed to catch Chess before he crashed onto the ground.

"Hey, hey. It's okay. You're okay," Penner purred as he helped Chess to the bed.

He was heavier than Penner had expected him to be, but he managed to drape Chess on the edge of the bed. Racing to his bag, he grabbed a shirt and tore off a strip to use as a sling . He had never liked this shirt anyway. Penner wrapped it around Chess's hand and wondered if he'd cracked his head open as well. Chess said nothing. He stared at the papers on the desk—crumpled and wrinkled from his sudden outburst.

"I'm not, you know."

"What?" Penner asked.

"I'm not okay, Penner," Chess said after a long silence. His voice was urgent but fragile.

After a moment he tried to push Penner away, but Penner wasn't going to let him escape his affection. He held his grip and pulled Chess in tighter giving him a kiss on the forehead, which seemed to calm Chess, albeit slightly.

"You are," Penner began. "You will be. Whatever this is, it'll pass."

"It won't."

"It will." Chess began to squirm and tried to push Penner away, but Penner simply held him tighter. "I'm not letting go."

"I'll tickle you," Chess threatened.

"You wouldn't dare."

"You should go," Chess peeped. "I'm only going to hurt you. You should leave. For your own good."

"You can't get rid of me that easily. I'll follow you," Penner said.

"You can't. That's the problem. I wish you could, but you can't," Chess said.

Penner said nothing. Outside, someone had started playing piano. It bathed the room in a calm, gentle melody. Chess began to shiver. A few loud sobs came out and Penner felt his shirt moisten from tears, but he continued to stroke Chess's back.

"It's okay," he kept repeating.

"It's not okay."

"Just shut up and take it," Penner said.

Chess chuckled through his tears.

"You sound like me."

"Someone has to."

Slowly, Chess began to calm down, and Penner laid him down on the bed. He placed him under the covers as his breathing became more calm and controlled. After a few minutes, the smell of the food became too much, and Penner was about to indulge when Chess reached out and gripped his hand so tight that it hurt. Penner froze and then turned back to Chess.

"Stay. Please," he begged, and Penner complied, settling back down on the bed and stroking Chess's legs through the warm blanket.

"Whatever you need, I'm here."

"I know," Chess said. "I'm scared. I keep seeing things, but I don't know. It's like a puzzle. Some pictures are so clear, but I don't know how they fit together, but I know they do. But when I connect them, I don't know what will happen."

"We'll worry about that when it comes."

"If anything happens to you, I—" Chess went silent and Penner gripped his hand.

"Don't worry about me," Penner said, trying to sound as calm as he could. He was trying to be reassuring and although he knew he was failing, Chess smiled at him anyway.

"Worry about this." Penner poked the center of Chess's forehead and, for a second, felt a gentle spark between them. He shook his hand, cursing the dryness of the room.

"I can't help it," Chess said. After a moment he closed his eyes, and the clutch on Penner's hand finally loosened. After he was sure Chess was sleeping, Penner took his hand back and blew out the lamp. In the dark of the room, he went back to the bed and crawled under the covers with Chess. Penner felt Chess's hand fold into his own.

"Hold onto that," Chess mumbled. Penner smiled, and held him tight as Chess began to snore. For the next few hours, all was still, but Penner couldn't sleep.

12/16/23

I don't want to leave.

Strange how a place we've barely arrived in already feels so comfortable. I think we could be happy here. I'd love to stay. Where there's a city, there's always a need for a clerk. I'd fit in here, maybe even better than in Brattan.

But Chess...

Truthfully, I never thought he'd ever wanted to leave the mines. He always spoke so highly of them and his experiences under the earth. I always found them claustrophobic, but him? He called them divine.

I can't explain what I saw tonight. Yes, it was him doing everything. I saw him. But it was something else as well. A madness I never thought he'd possessed, on display in terrifying glory.

He still won't tell me about his dreams, but they seem to be getting worse. He talks in his sleep. Sometimes I feel like he's just talking to me even when he's asleep. I just wish I knew what to do. I feel so powerless, being able to do nothing but dress his wounds. He needs to be more careful, but seems to just be getting more reckless.

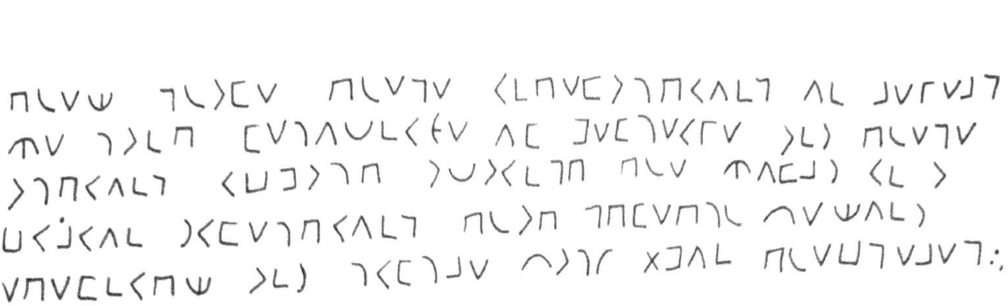

The journey to the airpad was short. The sun had risen, casting the world in a beautiful glow as it hung hot and heavy in the sky. All around them, traffic bustled along the path. The city never slowed down, even in the morning.

The boundary of the airpad was little more than a wall that separated the city from a long, flat tarmac with giant numbers painted all over. Above them hung dozens, MAYBE hundreds, of ships of varying sizes, each docked to the platforms that crossed the skies. Some were there for maintenance, while others looked ready for battle. Penner had never seen so many in one place and couldn't help but stare at them. The thought of idling in one of those magnificent machines began to excite him. He'd never been on one before. He was getting nervous.

All around them, the pavement radiated with heat so intense that it was hard to breathe. Penner cursed his clothing choice, wishing that he'd packed something lighter instead of the heavy pants and buttoned shirt.

Chess had prepared better, wearing a loose-fitting shirt and pants torn above the knee that allowed his legs to move freely. He fit right in as he strutted confidently across the tarmac. Penner looked like a tourist.

In fact, Chess seemed like he had walked these paths many times. The place seemed designed to disorient, with signs stacked on top of each other at every intersection. Around them, sky ships and buggies passed by as pillars of steam poured into the sky. Golden spherical cameras zipped around snapping photos, hovering in the air on rotating blades. Gigantic pneumatic arms clamped tightly to aircrafts to prevent them from floating away. Hundreds, if not thousands, of people were bustling at a rapid pace. Penner had never seen anything so chaotic yet still somehow organised. It made him jealous.

They approached a gate with several men in formal uniforms blocking the entrance. Chess walked towards them, but Penner hesitated. They didn't seem friendly.

"Is there another way around?" Penner asked.

Chess shook his head.

"You'll be fine. Trust me."

Penner looked at Chess. Hours before, he had been rocking him to sleep. Now, Chess was marching across the tarmac like he owned it. Penner bit his cheek and nodded. He followed as they approached one of the larger gaurds at the gate.

"Must we approach THE largest one?" Penner whispered.

"How can I assist?" the large guard asked. Their shirt struggled to contain their ample frame, but their voice was inviting and warm. Penner couldn't see their face through the screen on his helmet, but the uniform was bulky and shiny.

"We have a shuttle and need to enter this section," Chess spoke with authority and with an accent Penner had never heard before. The guard either was used to the accent, or didn't care.

"What name is the reservation under?"

"We should be under Cassius," Chess said. The guard nodded as lights and numbers began to flash across their helmet. Soon, one of the luminescent lines began to blink and the guard went silent, turning their attention back to Chess.

"It's a dragonfly-class. A little small for two, no?"

"A matter of necessity, I assure you," Chess said. "We were hired by Lady Raina to find locations for her next mover. She's looking for an exotic locale in the Water Tribes."

"Very well. Proceed down the tarmac. Safe travels. Blessings of the One Soul."

"Blessings of the One Soul," Penner and Chess replied in unison as they passed by the guard and entered onto a long flat blue tarmac. When they were a few steps past them, Penner turned to Chess, beaming.

"That went well," Penner said as he smiled at Chess, but Chess either didn't hear him, or was too focused on finding the ship to answer. Penner could feel eyes on him as the small golden cameras flew around. After a short walk, they found the ship, and Chess quickened his pace.

"Fifteen minutes early," Chess said.

"There's a first TIME for everything."

"Shut up."

Chess smiled and smacked him. For a moment Chess was himself again. No accent or pretense. But as soon as he'd smiled, he was drawn back to the ship.

The ship was small but impressive. It was called a dragonfly ship because of the bulbous shape of its hull, which looked like a metallic bug. Hardly bigger than their room at the inn, with a bottom deck that doubled as the living quarters, and a deck on top that could be covered by cloths in case of rain. A single mast rose from the middle of the deck where the silver sails attached to guide the vessel. The entire ship was painted a brilliant gold that reflected the sun . The side door was open and inviting, and Penner could see some of the brilliant mechanical engines chugging away inside. Things would certainly be tight, but he could feel himself becoming excited as he approached. He had always been fascinated by these types of ship, and was now going to live inside one.

As they approached, a tall, thin woman appeared on top of the vessel. She had a thick rope slung around her shoulder and wore clothes that seemed designed for the sky. A beige jacket hugged her torso, and the tapered pants seemed designed to showcase just how long her legs were. Her hair was short and dark and hung around her ears, billowing as if it were made of wind. With a wave of her hand, she took the rope, slung it around a post, and leapt off the vessel. Using the rope, she twisted to land beside them with a gentle thud.

"Good morning, Gents," she said, standing to her full height. To Penner's surprise, she was as tall as he was.

"Very impressive," Penner said with a few gentle claps.

She nodded.

"Are you here to examine my ship?"

"No. Actually, we are here to procure it." Penner smiled.

"I'm sorry?" She crossed her arms. Her eyebrow lifted as she smirked.

"We were told that this would be our ship?" Penner asked.

The woman smiled and shook her head.

"You must be mistaken. This ship belongs to no one. Cassandra is a maiden of the skies and flies where she will. I keep her safe and she protects me."

"Right. Of course." Penner chuckled to himself.

"Why are you gentlemen here?"

Penner stopped laughing.

"There must be some miscommunication. We were told this vessel would be waiting for us. Lady Raina sent us here and—"

"Right," the woman said as she shook her head.

"We had a reservation under Cassius?" Penner asked.

She shook her head and pressed her fingers to her forehead.

"Right. Of course. Lady Raina demanded that I get involved in—You know what? I'm not interested. Whatever this is about, I am not your captain and this—"

"You've been through this before," Chess said as he looked at her face. She looked at him and took a moment to examine his eyes. "I know you weren't expecting us, but I think that she sent us to you for a reason."

She smirked.

"You think so?"

"It's Fred, right?"

She nodded. "That's me."

"I'm Chess," he said as he shook her hand.

Fred motioned to Penner.

"Who IS he?"

"He's Penner."

"And is he here for something?"

Penner crossed his arms. "I can hear you."

"He's mine."

"He's your what?"

"He's my Cassius," Chess said with a smile.

Fred looked at him in shock.

"How do you—" She stopped herself. "That's why Raina sent you to me." She walked over to Penner and shook his hand. Her grip was strong. Penner had to force himself not to wince. "Very well. Let's do this."

"I'm Penner," he said.

"I got that part," Fred responded, looking deep into his eyes. "You've got nice eyes. Very brown. Brown eyes are the most honest. They don't hide anything."

"Thank you," Penner said, massaging out his hand as he slipped away from her vice-like grip. Chess walked over to the ship and pressed his face against it. For a moment it looked like they were cuddling. "Your ship is beautiful."

"Flattery will get you nowhere," she said. "You are free to come aboard but I warn you, Cassandra is a mighty ship, and it takes a savage determination to ride her. But treat her right and she'll take care of you. Come on, Boys, we've got to cast off," Fred said as she slung a thick, heavy rope over her shoulder.

Penner hesitated.

"Wait! You're not coming with us, are you?" he asked.

Fred sauntered to him.

"Of course I am. This is my ship. She goes nowhere without me," she said with a smile.

"Didn't you just say that she belongs to no one?"

"Who else would you say that I am?" Fred grinned.

"There must be some sort of mistake. I thought that this was a private—" Penner paused. He had no idea what he thought this trip was.

He turned to Chess, looking for support, but found none. Chess was running his hands over the ship with a big smile on his face.

"This ain't no honeymoon, boyo," she said. "Come on, NOW. Grab a rope and start coiling." She extended her hand and grabbed a rope and, with incredible grace, began TO hoist herself to the top of her ship. Looking over at Chess, Penner watched as he traced invisible lines around the hull.

"There are symbols all over this vessel," Chess said as he stared at the ship.

Penner frowned.

"I don't see anything."

"Just trust me," Chess said. "It looks like an alphabet."

"If only you could read."

"We didn't have books in the mines, but that doesn't mean I can't read," Chess said, still peering deeply into the ship. He looked so enamored with it that Penner couldn't help but feel excited as well.

"She seems like a stern woman," Penner whispered.

"She is," Fred called out from above them. He looked up. Fred was smiling at them from the top of the ship.

"It's rude to eavesdrop," Penner said.

"'Tis more rude to speak ill of someone who's letting you aboard their ship."

Penner grunted. She had him there.

She grabbed hold of a rope and rappelled down so that she was hovering just above them, like a spider dangling over its prey. "These ships are notoriously difficult to fly. And based on my experiences with these journeys, the road can be treacherous and unpredictable."

"I'm a fast learner. Flying this can't be that different," Penner said.

Fred laughed and landed uncomfortably close to him. Her pale eyes pierced his.

"Have you adjusted a ship before? Leveled the ballast or hoisted the sails? Airships require a delicate touch and considering you and your—friend." She punched the word hard. "You will require unique assistance. I'm likely the only one who can offer you two the proper amount of discretion and take you where you need to go without judgement."

Penner bit his lip as he looked back to Chess, who had begun to gently pet the ship's hull like it was a dog. He appeared to be cooing to it.

"Don't worry, Penner," she continued. "I'll take care of you. Just follow my instructions and you won't find any trouble aboard Cassandra. I can teach you the basics of flying, if you'd like. If you're lucky, you might even survive long enough to enjoy it."

She winked at him before giving him a smack on his behind. Penner was shocked, but before he could protest, she was already climbing back up to the top of the ship.

"Survive what?" Penner asked, but Fred had already gone. With a sigh, he gripped at his bag, adjusted it over his shoulder, and walked over to Chess. He placed his hand on his shoulder and Chess blinked out of his trance.

"She's perfect," Chess said with a smile.

"I find her abrasive."

"Not her," Chess said as he took Penner's hand and placed it on the ship.

"What are—"

"Shh." Chess put his finger to Penner's lips to silence him and motioned for him to close his eyes. "Feel it."

54

Penner rolled his eyes and followed instructions.

"It's very smooth."

"Not that. You can feel the fire inside of it. You can feel the steam rushing through the pipes. You can feel the wood just itching to float away. It's perfect. This is what I need."

Penner couldn't feel any of this and opened his eyes. His eyes pierced the ship, scanning every inch of the hull. He didn't get it. Chess, however, with his eyes closed and his hand pressed firmly into the wood, looked so peaceful. He looked like himself.

"I don't feel anything."

"You will. Soon enough," Chess said. Then, he yelped and ripped his hand away from the vessel. He clutched at his hand as if it had just been bitten by a snake. Penner looked at his palm and thought he saw blood, but Chess hid it from him.

"Come on, we should get aboard," Penner said as Chess turned back to him and nodded. "Onwards to the mountain."

"Right. Aye-aye, Captain." Chess followed him aboard.

Penner suddenly felt like he had said something wrong, but Chess no longer seemed to care.

ᚠᚢ ᚦᚲᚢ ᚦᛚ ᚨᚾᚢᚦᛚ ᚨᛃ ᚾᛚᚨᚷᚢᛚᚾ ᚦᛏᚥᚢᚾᚲᚢ ᚨᛃ
ᚾᚲᚢᚦᚾᚲᚨᛚ ᚦᛚᛃ ᛃ ᛏᛃᛃ ᛃᚦᚾᛚᚢᚾᚲᛏ ᚨᛚᛃᛃᚨᚠ ᚨᛃ ᚾᛚᚢ
ᛃᚦᛏᚾ ᚦᛚᛃ ᚾᛚᚢ ᛃᚷᚾᚷᚲᚢ᛬

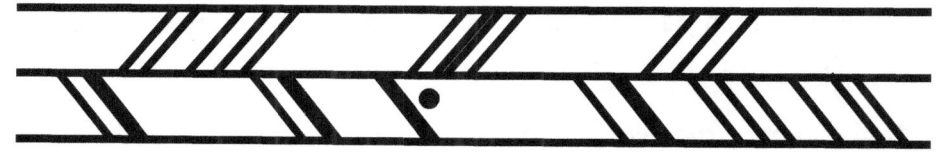

55

The ship was compact. The cabin was small and dark, with only a couple of circular windows to let some light in. It did little to brighten up the space. The interior was crowded with machines, gears, and tanks that stuck out from the walls at odd angles and made it difficult to get around. The space could adequately fit one person, but three would be challenging. There was a corner for sleeping, and one for the toilet sectioned off with a curtain. The lack of privacy was unnerving. It had not been designed for comfort and would take some getting used to before Penner could enjoy it. As a man accustomed to a bed with sheets, sleeping on a wooden floor or in a hammock left much to be desired.

"Sails up!" Fred yelled as Penner and Chess emerged onto the top deck of the ship.

Still compact, the deck was more spacious than below, but it was also covered in ropes and machinery to keep the ship afloat. Fred stood at the front and pulled a lever, causing the sails to unfold and snap into place. They caught the wind, sending silver ripples over the translucent fabric. The image was hypnotic, and Penner was mesmerized by their waving.

"Let's cast off, Boys! We've got a long way to go!" Fred hollered.

She began to untie the ropes that connected them to the tarmac and cast them over the side. Chess joined her, untying ropes as if he had been doing it for years. Penner stood back and tried to stay out of the way, having no idea where to begin. He marvelled at the way Fred seemed to dance across the deck of her ship. She moved with such precision and grace that it looked like she was dancing. With each untied rope the ship rose with a jolt, until there was nothing left holding them back.

Then the ship was floating. Rising above the chaos of the tarmac and rocking as the wind battered the vessel. Penner clutched a railing in an attempt to keep his equilibrium, but it was difficult. As soon as he'd found his balance, another burst would make him stumble. When he looked over the edge, he saw the streets shrink below him, and the image made his vision spin.

"You'll get used to the height. Just keep breathing," Fred called out to him.

Penner nodded, unsure what would happen if he tried to speak. Despite his earlier protestations, he was now acutely aware of how needed Fred was.

He heard the sounds of carriages and autos zooming around below as the ship made its way past the tarmac and towards the edge of the city. Buildings that had seemed so large from the ground were becoming smaller as they rode away from them. Before long, they were in the sky, easily fifty feet off the ground, and Penner felt a combination of exhilaration and terror. He'd never dreamed of getting to ride in a ship like this before, and now the experience was overwhelming. He could feel a tear floating in his eye, but he was unsure which emotion had triggered it.

"Keep your wits about you. These ships can take a while to get used to. The rocking will stop, but if you're not used to the sky, it'll mess with your head," Fred said.

Her enthusiasm for the sky was admirable, but Penner wasn't comforted. As they began moving towards the city walls, he peeled his eyes away from the town below and focused on the horizon. She was right, this was different from gliding. Gliding had been gentle and safe. This felt like riding a bull through a storm. It was more nerve-wracking than he had expected. His insides were twisted into leaden knots, and he wondered whether it was because of the ship or what was coming next.

He looked to the mountains he'd grown up in, now bumps barely visible over the horizon. Somewhere over there was Arasia. The place where he was born, had grown up. The place where he had met Chess. He had never been sentimental, but floating above the city brought it out of him. He realised they were moving further away from home, and he wondered if he would ever get to see it again. Then he had an even more alarming thought: what if he didn't want to?

"Portside, Boys!" Fred called out swiftly as she gripped onto a rope and climbed up the mast.

She hung on it and Penner was too focused on this to realise what was happening. With a sharp turn, the ship heaved to one side and Penner, not expecting the maneuver, toppled along with it. With a gasp, he attempted to grab back onto the railing, but missed. His hands clutched air as he could feel the world open up below him and the weight of gravity begin to pull him down. Luckily, Chess was prepared and caught Penner. Pulling him back onto the deck, he tied a small rope to the mast that he slid into Penner's hand.

"Best be careful," Chess said. "Almost lost you there."

Once his heartbeat returned, Penner smiled back. He felt foolish, but Chess kissed him on the cheek as if to tell him it was okay. He wrapped his arm around Penner and held him up as Penner regained his footing, and held him there for a moment longer than necessary.

"Thanks for saving me."

Chess winked at him. "Just returning the favour."

After he'd regained his balance, Penner gripped onto the rope and relaxed. Chess let go and galloped to the bow of the ship and balanced on the railing. Fred dropped down from above and stood beside him. Penner wondered how he could be so confident in his balance. If he was at the front, he'd either tumble over the edge or have a heart attack.

"It's beautiful!" Chess exclaimed. His voice exploded with excitement as they passed between the tall buildings that surrounded the city gate.

"You haven't seen anything yet," Fred said as she secured a rope to a wheel, allowing it to creak back and forth. "This should hold us until we pass through the city limits. After that I'll take us higher and we can go further."

"How high will we go?" Penner asked, clenching the rope so tight he could feel blisters forming.

"High enough," Fred said. "Depends on the heat and the air currents, but I reckon we can add a hundred feet or so."

"A hundred feet?" Penner exclaimed.

"This is amazing!" Chess said as he closed his eyes and took a deep breath.

"It's definitely something," Penner said. "Be careful up there!"

"Don't worry. I'm not going to fall," Chess said. He looked up and smiled as a sail swung past him, nearly knocking him over. After that he decided to step off the railing. "Sorry." He shrugged.

There was a massive clang as the ship approached the portal on the wall. Fred cranked a few levers, which slowed down their approach as steam poured into the sky.

"What do we do?" Penner asked.

"Just be calm. Soon we'll be through the gate, and then it's smooth sailing into the unknown." Fred walked to the front of the ship and waited.

Penner watched as three small golden balls approached the ship. Much like the cameras on the tarmac, each hung from a propeller, with small sparks flying from their shiny shells. They approached Fred, who held up a sheet of paper and allowed them to scan it. They beeped and bobbed as Penner studied them. They were cute in their own way, and he was trying to figure out how they worked. Their workings looked so intricate.

He watched as they came to the bow of the ship and hovered in front of Fred. She didn't move as they ran up and down her body like dogs looking for a treat. Once they hit the letter, they paused and turned to each other before nodding. One whistled at Fred, who gave them a thumbs up, and with that they departed to the next ship coming up behind them.

When Penner looked back, he could see a procession of ships looking to leave the city. One was massive and covered in illustrious white sails, with the insignia of the One Soul all over it. Even the Temple's transport vessels were more decadent than anything he could ever dream of affording. It had to be as tall as the temple back home. Perhaps they were transporting a maestro to one of the havens, or sending another gathering of monks on a Mission. Whatever the case, he just hoped they wouldn't pay much attention to their small vessel as they skipped through the gates. As Cassandra turned to the front, the massive gates opened, revealing a marvelous vision of the world around them. Through the portal he could see blue skies, violet mountains, and fields and forests spreading out before them.

The view was amazing, but his stomach hated it.

"Where are we going?" Penner asked once his vision stopped spinning.

"West. I reckon Cassandra can take us to the mountains if the weather is warm. If not, there's a couple villages closer that we can stay at."

"Right. But where are we going?" Penner said, watching as the gates below them opened for a swarm of people pushing carts.

Hundreds of farmers flocked into the city to sell their goods, which were so fresh Penner could smell them from the ship. The busy city landscape had been replaced with miles of farmland. The dark and grimy smell of the city was replaced with a fresh scent of fields in bloom. It still wasn't pleasant, but at least it reminded him of home. He looked below at the small farmhouses that were nestled amongst crops and animals that seemed to roam free in the fields. As he listened, he could hear the bleats and calls of livestock. Or was that just his stomach?

"It's beautiful, isn't it? Have you ever seen anything so amazing?" Chess exclaimed as he sidled up beside Penner.

"Just once," Penner said, smiling at Chess.

Chess rolled his eyes but blushed. For the first time, Penner got a good look and realised that Chess still had several markings on his face from his furious scribblings on the desk. After he passed out, the ink must've transferred to his face. Penner wondered why it had taken him so long to notice it. The patterns etched a perfect design around his eyes that made it look like they had been deliberately placed there.

"You've got something on your face," Penner said as he licked his fingers and gently placed his hand on Chess's cheek. As soon as his hand made contact, there was a flash of light and a piercing scream.

Terrified, they both stumbled backwards, and Chess knocked his head against the mast. Penner felt like the air had been kicked out of him. He tried to crawl to his feet, but couldn't as he felt a convulsion shoot up from his stomach. He threw his head over the railing as he vomited onto some poor sheep far below them. His throat was burning as he wiped his face with his sleeve. He could feel the foul smell burning his nose as his shaky hands pulled him back around. He saw Chess kneeling beside the mast, with his hands on the back of his head.

"Oh my—Chess, are you okay?" he said as he crawled beside him.

"Fine! I-I'm fine," Chess stuttered, avoiding Penner's eyes. He was shaking. Penner went to comfort him, but Chess pushed him away.

"I'm fine. I'm okay. Just—don't come any closer," Chess said, backing away from Penner and racing down into the cabin. Penner went to pursue him, but Fred stepped in between and stopped him.

"Stop. You're not going below deck yet. Give him a moment."

"I need to help him," he insisted.

Fred shook her head.

"He'll be okay," she said.

"Will he?" Penner asked.

Fred opened her mouth as if to respond, but hesitated. Penner looked out over the horizon and exhaled. Coming beside him, Fred put her hand on his shoulder and gave it a squeeze.

"Just give him time."

"I appreciate your concern, but he needs me," Penner said, trying once again to enter the galley, but he found his path blocked once more by Fred. She was quicker than he'd expected.

"He needs space."

"He needs me!" he snapped. For a moment neither moved. He gritted his teeth and he swore he could see her resolve weaken.

"Just be careful." She stepped aside, allowing Penner enough space to squeeze past and go down the slippery steps. Underneath, he found Chess in the corner, vigorously rubbing his face with a wet rag. Penner approached with his hands raised as he tried to sound as comforting as possible.

"Chess?" Penner asked.

"It's not coming off," Chess said as he scratched at his skin with a rag.

"Just be careful. There's no need to—"

"I can't get it off," Chess spat. "Why isn't it coming off?"

"It will. Just relax. Just let it wash off. Calm down. Breathe," Penner said as he crept over to Chess. His hands outstretched as if he was trying to disarm him.

The way Chess was furiously rubbing at his face made his skin crawl. He didn't touch him, but as Penner got closer Chess began to scrape slower. With a few deep breaths, Chess put the washcloth down, and Penner saw that his cheek was bright red, with smears of blood glistening on his cheeks.

"Put the cloth down, Chess."

"It's not going away," Chess said. Penner looked at the cheek, and sure enough, despite his furious rubbing, he was right. The black marks were still there, albeit faint beneath the bright red of his skin.

"They will. It's just pen marks."

"Pen comes off."

"It will. Trust me," Penner said.

He felt silly having to explain to Chess that pen will rub off. He grabbed Chess's hand and smiled. Chess flinched, as if he was expecting another scream to erupt from their contact, but there was no scream and they both relaxed. Penner took the cloth and pulled it away from Chess.

For a moment Chess tightened his grip, but Penner hushed him, "Put the cloth down. Relax."

Chess hesitated, but exhaled and put the cloth in the sink. A few small drops of blood stained the white basin before falling down the drain.

"I trust you," Chess said, as he turned to look at himself in the mirror. "I just don't trust him."

VⲢVL ⟨J ⋔V ⟩ΛLⲘ ⲄLΛ⋔ ⋔L⟩ⲛ J⟩ᴜⲚ ᴧVᴡᴧL⟩
XⲚ LΛ⋔ ⋔V ⟩Λ ⲄLΛ⋔ ⲛL⟩ⲛ ⟩ⲛ JV⟩Ⲛⲛ ⋔V ⟩ᴄV
LVᴄV LΛ⋔

63

I heard something. The way Chess reacted. I know he heard it too. Is this what he's hearing all the time? What he's seeing? I want to know what's going on in his head, but he's shutting down. He's pulling away and I don't know what to do.

We've only been flying for a few hours and I'm exhausted. This ship is comfortable on the deck, but underneath it could use some work. Flying through the sky is incredible but gut-wrenching. The beauty is captivating. I haven't seen anything so gorgeous in my life. The air is so pure you can smell energy in the sky. There is magic here that I've never felt before.

Our captain, on the other hand, is strange. She clearly has no issue with me and Chess, but she speaks so brazenly that it's off-putting. I've met plenty of strong-willed women before, but it's like she lives on a completely different planet. Maybe she does. Maybe the sky transforms you into some bullheaded warrior. That being said, I feel like she's not telling us everything. She seems to know what is going on with Chess, but keeps preventing me from trying to help him. There's something about her I don't trust yet. What's to prevent her from turning us in to the authorities at her earliest convenience?

Despite my own opinions, her sailing skills are remarkable. Full credit to her there. She's at one with this ship and commands it with such ease that it's breathtaking. Maybe one day, I'll be able to move as fluidly as her across the deck without feeling like there's a cat trying to escape my throat.

Maybe this vessel is the answer to our problem and the sky is our escape. I don't know where his mind is right now, but if there's one place where he can return to me, this is it.

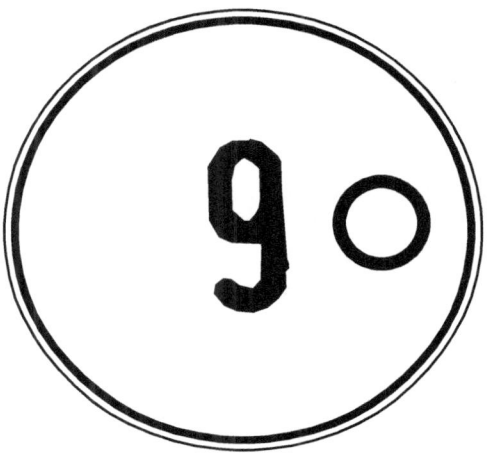

By midday, the fields and farmland had turned into a beautiful, rocky green forest. Thick, dense underbrush vegetation obscured the ground, and Penner wondered how anyone had been able to travel through the forest before roads. The ground was uneven and smothered in plants bigger than any Penner had seen, some green, some brown, some red. Even from their height, he could make out the trees that seemed to be clawing at the sky. Their long branches would look terrifying from below, but even from above they had a creepy quality that made him uneasy.

Fred said they were sailing at around eighty feet. From the glimpses Penner could manage over the side of the ship, he had no doubt. He couldn't comprehend being so high up, and when he caught a glimpse of the ground, it made him feel dizzy. That with the near-constant nausea he'd felt since the ship had begun its ascent was enough to incapacitate him.

Currently he was slumped in a chair beside Fred. She told him that it was only a temporary feeling and that within a day or two he'd be fine, but that was little consolation right now. He felt like death. He looked like it too. Fred seemed satisfied with the course of the vessel. She had pulled out a small easel and canvas and was currently painting the landscape.

"When you spend as much time in the sky as me, you really learn to appreciate the view."

"I'll have to take your word on it," he croaked. "How long have you been flying?"

"As long as I care to remember," she said, smearing some green over the canvas.

"And how long has that been?"

"Long enough. I rescued Cassandra from the scrap heap, but I like to think she rescued me. She was set to be torn up, few people know how to steer a dragonfly vessel anymore, much less one of this size. Once I saw her, I knew that I couldn't just let her fall away and be used for scrap. I left my old life and traded it in for the sky. Haven't looked back since." She pulled her eyes away from the painting and smirked at Penner. "You really shouldn't stay in one spot like that. Only way to get your body accustomed to the feeling is to move around. Come over here."

"I'm fine over here."

"Consider it an order from the Captain."

He looked up at her, intrigued, and was struck by how attractive and powerful she looked. Her smile was warm and inviting, and her eyes had a glamorous twinkle. He wanted to resist, but with a grunt, he pulled himself up from the chair and dragged himself across the deck. He felt his insides wobble like they were unattached. His legs were shaky, but he managed to slither over to her and took a glimpse of what she had been working on.

"You're quite good!" he exclaimed—a little louder than he intended.

"You sound shocked."

"Just seems an odd hobby for an aviatrix."

"It's one of the more honest ways to earn a living in the sky. I always keep supplies around in case inspiration hits. Some villages pay handsomely for fine art."

"I trust it's not the only way to make a living in the sky."

Fred turned to him.

"Is that an accusation?" she asked.

"It's—nothing. Never mind."

"I have a wide variety of jobs I do to keep my ship in the air. It's important to diversify. Keeps the brain fresh. Always thinking. Always making new avenues for financial success. Ain't nothing wrong with doing many things to get back." She picked up her brush once again and smiled at her creation. "Some options require a bit more finesse than painting, but all require great skill. With enough time and practice, they all can be mastered."

"Are they all legal?" Penner asked.

"Legality is a formality for those tied to the earth. Morality, doubly so. The sky has a looser law system. You're not chained to the rule of one country, so it's important to follow your own moral compass." Penner grunted, and she turned to him. "Not that you and Chess have ever done anything outside legality before."

"Well—" Penner felt himself flush and had to turn his gaze towards the sky.

"I see through you, Penner. More than you realise. But at least the view is decent."

He coughed and fiddled with his pocket watch. He pulled it from his vest pocket, trying to see what time it was. He was so flustered he didn't even realise it wasn't working.

"Your watch won't work. You're in a different place now. The magnetism in the air is too strong."

Penner frowned and shut the watch, then took a couple steps back towards the cabin.

"I'm going to see how he's doing," Penner said.

"You should give him some space," Fred said. "He'll need that right now."

"Your concern is noted but—"

"He's sorting through his brain. He requires time and space. Give it to him."

"My—whatever is happening to Chess is—" he stuttered.

"It's not madness."

Penner paused and looked at her.

"It's not normal."

"Who are you to say anything is normal?" Fred laughed. "Something very unexplainable has happened and he's just trying to sort it all out. Let him do that."

"You act like you know him."

"I've seen it before."

Penner hesitated.

"And?"

"Quiet. I need silence to capture this," she said as she held her brush up to the sky. She smeared more paint onto the canvas and Penner sat back down.

For a few minutes neither said anything, but Penner found his eyes growing heavy. Before they could continue their conversation, he drifted off to sleep.

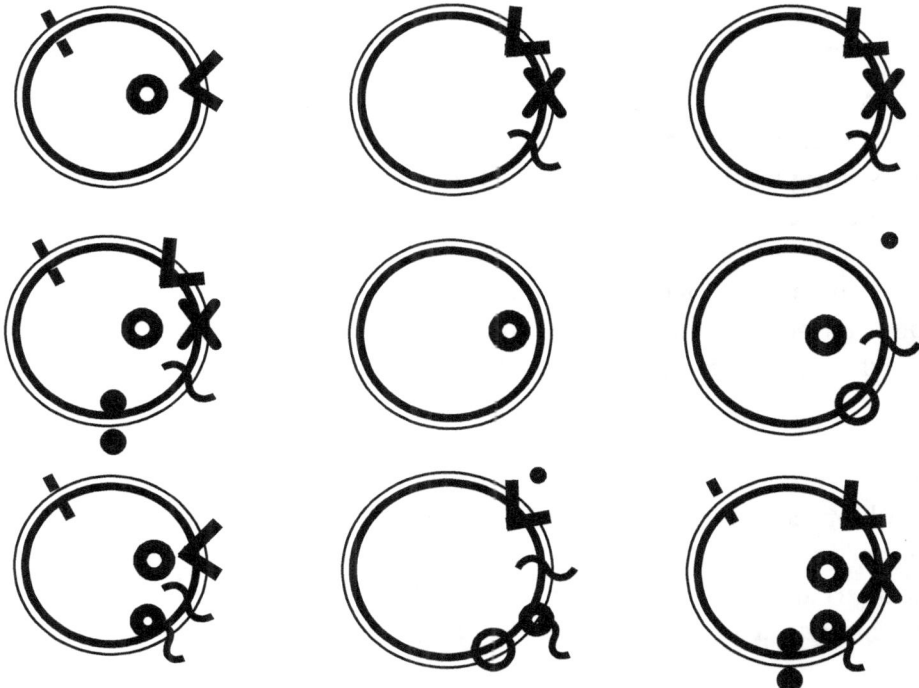

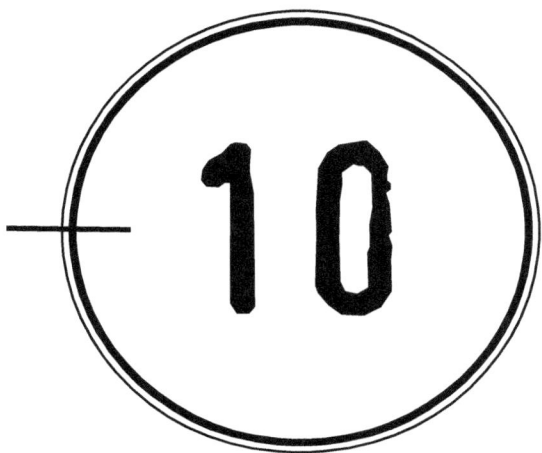

Approaching nightfall, the land below became rocky and strange. Villages were few and far between, and only distinguished by small flecks of light that sprung up through the forest. The sky was a fiery orange with pink and red smeared through as the sun began to sink low on the horizon.

Penner could feel the beginning of cool night touch his skin and was about to mention this to Fred, but she was one step ahead of him. Fred had launched into action and was bringing the ship down to the ground.

Giant plumes of steam burst from exhausts around the deck. In minutes, they were nestled into an alcove surrounded by trees that reached so high they blocked out what was left of the indigo sky. The sounds of the forest were strange and unfamiliar, which made Penner anxious. He wasn't sure what the plan was at this point. He had prepared for adventure, but he had neglected the thought that he may not be sleeping in a bed.

"We can make camp here," Fred said.

"Can we?" Penner asked as she anchored them into the alcove with a series of ropes.

"You'll be fine. I have some hammocks down in the cabin." Fred said. "And don't worry, I won't peek. I like to sleep on the deck and keep watch."

She was quick and moved rope-to-rope throwing them over the side and connecting them to the tree trunks. Penner yawned. Despite his nap, or more likely naps, he was exhausted. He'd seen little of Chess today, and just as he was about to go below to see him, Chess stumbled onto the deck like a new-born deer with a big yawn.

"There's a village a few paces east of here. We could get there in twenty minutes if we wanted," Penner replied.

Chess staggered towards them and hiccupped.

"How did you see that?" Penner asked.

"I don't think we want to go there," Fred responded. "It's a temple village. They'd be pretty devout." Fred walked over to him and smirked. "Besides, you don't look like you should be going anywhere right now."

"What? I'm fine. I'm great. I'm gr-great," Chess slurred. And Penner paused.

"Are you drunk?" Penner walked over to him and smelled wine all over him.

"I'm not drunk. You're—what?" Chess leant against the railing. Penner rushed to his side to ensure he didn't fall overboard.

"Come on you, let's go to bed. In our hammock." Penner turned to Fred. "Will we both fit in there?"

"You'll be fine. Let me go anchor it for you." As she left, Chess took his hand and clumsily smushed it into Penner's face.

"Your face is all smushy," he chuckled.

"You were supposed to be resting."

"You rest. You need it."

"Have you slept at all?" Penner exhaled. "What have you been drinking?"

"No." Chess's breath smelled like wine and Penner quirked his eyebrow.

"You got no sleep?"

"No. Yes. Maybe."

Penner grit his teeth.

"How did you—"

"I'm not drunk, you're drunk."

Penner frowned. Questions abounded, like why had he been drinking? Where did he find the wine? Most importantly, why hadn't he shared it?

"Are you mad?"

"A little, yeah."

"Don't be mad. Be happy." Chess pushed his fingers into Penner's mouth and made him smile. Penner was not amused.

"About what?"

"You got to fly today."

Penner paused. He did have that.

"I guess."

"Hold that thought. I feel sick."

"Right. Come with me." Penner put his head in the crook of Chess's arm and carefully guided him to the deck. He sat cross-legged and placed Chess's head in his lap. Chess looked up at the stars and Penner began to play with his hair.

"There they are," Chess said as his eyes began to flutter close he marveled at the sky. "I almost missed them."

"The stars?"

"Them. All of them," Chess said as his breath slowed. "And now, here they are." He smiled. Despite his annoyance that Chess would drink without him, Penner smiled as well. He stroked Chess's head and watched his eyes flutter and eventually close. "You're the only one who—" Chess's voice disappeared into a sleepy haze and he began to snore. Penner continued to play with his hair, and sat with Chess in his lap despite the fact that their hammock was ready below deck.

After a few minutes, Fred walked back up and the two nodded to each other. She sat opposite them, opting to sit on the deck instead of a chair so that she and Penner could be on the same level. After a moment she tapped a baseboard which opened, revealing a small bar. She took out a small flask and handed it over to Penner, who graciously accepted. There wasn't much inside, but she seemed insistent he have it.

"No fair for him to have all the fun."

"I appreciate it. Thanks," Penner said as he lifted the flask up in a toast. He tried the drink, which was sweet and stung his throat. Now that they were anchored to the ground, he hoped he would be able to keep it down. "It's good."

"It's from the tribes to the south. They make fantastic blends."

"I'll have to try them," he said as he felt Chess turn in his lap. He snored again and Penner hushed him, as he handed the now empty flask back to Fred.

"I think he's out," she said with a smile.

"Do you have more wine below deck?" Penner asked.

"I always keep a stash around. He didn't drink it, though. Must've got wine from somewhere else."

"Do you have any more?" Penner asked.

"I'll pick up a few bottles when we hit Nicholls. In the meantime, enjoy the view," she said as she looked up. For a moment Penner was struck by her figure. The graceful way her body was assembled as a fierce blend of strength and length. She was beautiful, and every time Penner looked at her, he found himself less inclined to look away. He wondered if she was aware of his gaze, but if she was, she didn't mind.

"They're amazing! I've never seen them so bright," Penner said as he began to shift his body back so he was leaning against the railing. He could smell Chess's hair and it filled his spirit. After what felt like forever yet no time at all, he and Fred helped to maneuver Chess back down into the hammock. He crawled in beside him and felt Chess latch onto him like a sloth. Though he was uncomfortable, the sound of Chess's heartbeat was enough to relax him, and soon he was asleep.

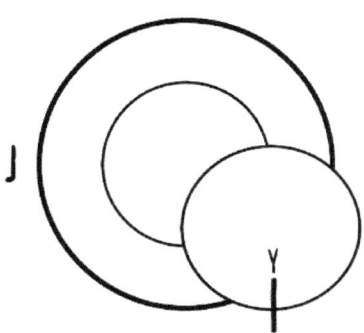

The sound was terrifying. Penner awoke to the sounds of grunting coming from outside and the chattering of a woodland creature. A wave of confusion overcame him. At first he thought it was a dream, but it was too cold. He knew something was wrong, but couldn't figure it out. Soon the pieces started coming together:

One, he was in a strange box-like room.

Two, he was sleeping in a net.

Three, Chess was gone.

He shot up as the memories flooded back to him. Yes, they were in a ship and he was sleeping in a hammock. But the sounds were not that. He saw that the door on the side was open. He shivered as the cold air poured in. He grabbed his shirt and threw it on as he raced into the night.

The chill hit him like a brick. The cold was so intense that his eyes stung and his nose ran. He wished there was something heavier to throw around him. As his eyes adjusted, he saw the black outline of a figure grunting and groaning as he lugged around a massive plank. Watching him was painful, and Penner couldn't figure out what he was doing. Then he realised it was Chess, and the plank was a tree trunk that looked like it had been ripped from the ground.

"Chess?" Penner asked, unsure of whether or not that was him. He had always been strong, but this strength was impossible. He sounded like he was in pain, but continued to drag the trunk along the ground. "What are you doing?" Penner called. There was no answer.

Chess turned, sending small pieces of bark and tinder flying around as he furiously carved into the ground like a man possessed. The trenches he left in the ground were massive and deep. His groans were guttural and pained.

"Chess! Stop!" Penner yelled.

For a moment, the world froze, and Chess stopped in his tracks as he turned to Penner.

"What are you—" He sounded exhausted.

Penner ran to him and threw his shirt over Chess. He had no idea how long he had been out here, but he was freezing. As soon as Penner made contact with him, Chess let go of the trunk. It landed with a thud so heavy that the ground underneath them shook. It had to be hundreds of pounds, and Penner was stunned. How had Chess even lifted it, much less used it to carve so deep into the ground? The lines were at least two feet deep and a foot across. Penner had to be careful not to step into one, or he could twist his ankle.

"The symbols," Chess breathed.

He held Chess both in awe and fear of what he'd done. While he tried to be comforting, he was terrified. He had no idea how Chess had managed to move the trunk, much less rip it from the ground. Chess felt cold and clammy and began to convulse.

"Penner? Is that you?" Fred called out from the ship.

"We're over here!" Penner replied as Chess began to feel more fragile in his hands.

He began to shake slightly, and though his skin was ice, Penner could feel a warmth radiating off of him. He smelled terrible, and when Penner pulled away he could feel a stickiness cling onto his skin. As he tried to wipe off the feeling, Fred emerged from the ship and shone a torch on them. Penner felt sick to his stomach as he looked at Chess, who shone a bright red. Penner looked down at his hands and the thick smell of blood filled his nose.

Chess was hardly recognisable under the shiny red flood that covered him. All over his body were thick dark lines carved into his skin. Blood poured from them and his skin was a mess of sickly white and crimson.

Penner felt sick as he realised what he had seen earlier. It hadn't been pieces of the tree that had splattered off of Chess. It had been skin and blood.

He soon realised that all around them, puddles of blood covered the ground with footprints smeared all over. He was standing in one right now. Then Chess collapsed. Penner felt so horrified, he almost didn't catch him. The force of his fall almost knocked Penner off his feet.

"Chess—Chess!"

He was horrified. The smell of blood was so thick it made his stomach turn, and he had to stop himself from vomiting. He had served time as a nurse, but he had never seen so much blood come out of someone before. It looked like someone had slaughtered an entire army. Penner could feel the puddle seeping up his knees as he knelt beside Chess and sought a pulse.

"What happened here?" Fred asked as she rushed over to them. Penner used the light to examine Chess. The lines were cut into his skin, but not deep.

"He's hurt," Penner said.

"I figured that much. Did he do this to himself?" she asked.

"He must've. Where were you?" Penner spat. His nursing training flooded back to him. He grabbed onto his wrist and felt a pulse, albeit faint. "He's lost a lot of blood. I can patch up someone in a crunch, but he needs help beyond what I can give."

"He's still breathing, but it's faint," Fred said reassuringly, placing her hand by his mouth. Penner nodded and looked at her.

"We need to get him somewhere."

"We could take Cassandra, but without the wind it would be dangerous. Wouldn't want to career back down into the forest. Plus, with no wind we'd be traveling slow."

"Any other options?"

"The temple," she said.

Penner felt his stomach drop.

"They'll kill us. We're heretics."

"They won't turn away someone in need. Just don't say you love him and I think you'll be okay. I doubt they have a doctor, but they'd have healers and—"

"As long as they have equipment to keep him breathing, I can do the rest," Penner said. "How can we get him there?"

"We need to carry him. The torch should keep the wolves at bay."

"Fine. I'll carry him." Penner could feel adrenaline pumping through him. Chess needed him, and he felt stronger than ever. "Help me get him on," Penner said.

Fred nodded and helped Penner position Chess on his back. Grabbing some bandages and ropes from the ship, they patched up the deeper wounds and hoped the pressure would keep him together until they got to the temple. With time running out, they tied the ropes to carry Chess on his back and began to run.

He'd never been as strong as Chess, but right now, he felt like a beast. Despite the choking darkness, he sprinted like a wolf. His body felt sticky and hot. Sweat and blood coated him. He hardly noticed. He had to get there. Every drop fueled him. He had to get there.

His mind flooded with questions. What was going on? How had he even moved the trunk, much less lifted it from the ground? What had possessed him to cut into himself? But mostly one word kept repeating as it bounced around his skull. Why? There were no answers, but the questions continued to multiply. Would they make it? Was it too late? The questions were choking him. They overwhelmed his mind and he was drowning.

After what felt like an eternity, they arrived at the temple. The large stone walls were carved into the mountain, and a sweet-smelling smoke poured out of windows. The doors were marble slabs, each a brilliant white with a glistening shine. A set of stone steps led up to the temple doors, each carved into the mountain over the course of decades, maybe even centuries. The sight would fill him with contempt, but Penner didn't care right now. He had to get Chess help.

Like an arrow, he shot to the top of the stairs and pounded on the doors. Fred moved quickly and untied the knots that held Chess to Penner, and the two of them delicately laid Chess on the stairs. Feeling the weight of Chess slide off of him made him weak. The adrenaline that had fueled him evaporated. Vomit pooled in his throat. He couldn't breathe.

"He'll be okay," she whispered.

"He better be," Penner said.

"Remember where we are," Fred insisted.

Penner looked from her to the doors and after a moment, he nodded. His stomach was knots and his mouth was dry. His hands shook and his vision blurred. His heart was beating so loud he could feel it in his head. Each beat pounding on his skull like a drum. He was drenched with blood, sweat, and fears as he found himself praying that someone would answer the door. He felt like a hypocrite, but just as he was chastising himself, the door creaked open and a man in a red robe appeared.

"Glory to the One Soul, travellers."

"Glory to the One Soul," Penner cried. "Chess—he needs help. He—he—" Penner found his voice failing him as a violent sob burst from his throat. All the fear and anger that had been simmering inside of him exploded. His hands shook violently, and he began to shiver uncontrollably as he gripped the monk by the robe. "Please. Help."

The monk looked at him, and then down to the body of Chess at his feet. The monk bent down to Chess and felt his forehead.

"Give me space," the monk said, looking shaken for a moment before gathering his composure and running inside. He pulled a long golden rope, and a bell sounded so loudly that the mountain shook. Penner watched as a flickering of candles began to illuminate the sides of the temple. The temple looked like it was on fire.

"Help me get him inside," the monk said. Penner nodded and grabbed Chess by the arms as Fred gripped his feet. Lifting him up, the two of them maneuvered Chess inside as a series of robed monks rushed in.

"Brother Jacob, what is it?" the new monk said, her face tired from sleep as she scanned Penner and Fred. She didn't look impressed to have visitors.

"Brother Charlotte, this traveller is hurt. We must help him."

Her eyes went wide after seeing Chess.

"My—" She motioned for several of the other monks to help. They swooped in like a well-coordinated machine and whisked Chess away from Penner and Fred before they could protest. "Take him to the tabernacle."

"As you wish," Brother Jacob said as he bowed away. Penner instinctively took a step to follow them, but Brother Jacob stopped him before he could.

"Let me go with him. I can help," Penner insisted. "I was a nurse once and—"

"Leave him to our care." Brother Jacob gripped him by the arm and held him back.

"I was trained. I can help."

"You've done more than enough by bringing him here. We will do all we can to help your friend."

"He's not just my friend!" Penner shouted. "Let me through."

"Brother, you are in a holy place. Remember yourself," he said.

"I can patch him up. I know how to help him," Penner insisted, but the monk shook his head.

"I am sorry, Ivalice. But we are in a holy place. Only those who have taken the oath can continue into the tabernacle. Your concern is appreciated, but at this point there is nothing more you can do for him. Let the healers work. They are the best in the Valley."

"They'll do all they can to help him," she said.

"Is that enough?" he asked.

"Do you feel well?" Brother Jacob asked.

Penner nodded, but as soon as the monk said it, he realised how exhausted he felt. He'd just ran miles through a forest with Chess tied to his back.

"I'm fine," he said, but he sounded exhausted.

"Come, brother. Clean yourself off. All will be well." He gripped Penner's shoulder and guided him into the space. Penner nodded and looked up, to try to see where they'd taken him, but couldn't see anything. "You're welcome to stay as well, brother."

"I have a ship waiting for me," Fred answered. "But I'll be back for these two."

"We shall keep them safe. Thank you for your help in getting them to us. Blessing go with you."

"And with you," Fred said as she turned, giving Penner one last affirmative nod before walking out through the front gates.

The monk wrapped Penner's arm around himself as they left the massive atrium. He hadn't realised how weak he was until he tried to move. His legs buckled every few steps. The monk escorted him up into the back halls of the temple, and Penner hoped that Chess would be alright. He could hear echoes through the halls and just hoped Chess was still breathing. He had never felt further from Chess, and he just hoped to see him again in the morning.

The sponge was rough and cold. Penner pressed it to his skin and felt layers of dirt and blood fall off him. As the water trickled down, it stung every new scrape and scratch he'd acquired in his race here. Running shirtless through the underbrush had left him worse for wear. As the adrenaline in his system wore off, each one of the scrapes stung him like a dagger. He watched red water circle down the drain and couldn't tell what blood was his and what was Chess's. The thought made him sick. He tried to find comfort in the lavender scent of the room, but he felt dead. He wondered how Fred was doing back at the ship. Would she even wait for them?

He didn't want to stay here longer than he had to, but the thought made him worry he'd have no escape. How was Chess? Where was he?

How could he be so close but so powerless to help him?

Stepping out of the basin, he walked to a set of robes that the monk had left him. His legs were shaking, but the shower made him feel strong enough to get to his bed. At least the robes were comfortable. Tying a knot around his waist kept the billowing fabric together as he exited the room and followed the path back to the entrance. However, walking was cumbersome, and he struggled to not trip as he shuffled in the oversized apparel.

In the chaos, he hardly noticed his surroundings. The walls were stone, seemingly carved into the mountain, with beams of beautifully varnished wood that held the ceiling. Every inch of the hallway was bare but beautiful. It looked as if they polished the place every day. It shone so beautifully that even in the minimal candlelight, it glistened with an incredible brilliance.

He entered the main atrium and was awestruck. Everything was carved from the mountain: the rows of pews, the stone altar, the brilliant chandeliers that hung down from the domed ceiling. Above the altar was a statue of the Great Raven and Snake with a white Pearl being held between them. Everything was precise and flawless. It wasn't overly large, but it was big enough to seat a congregation of thirty devout followers. He wondered to himself how many monks were tending to Chess right now. Was he still breathing? Was he looking better? Penner's mind was lost in thought. He focused his attention on the altar. It was beautiful, with carvings of a white sphere adorning its front.

He wasn't sure what he was feeling. Was it guilt? Fear? Resentment? The last time he had been in a holy place, things had not gone well for him. He had seen the one he loved sentenced to death for being a corrupted soul. He wrung his hands, unsure of whether he was angry, sad, or terrified. His head spun as he tried to relax into the seat. It wasn't easy with the solid rock jutting into his back, but he tried. He bit his lip as he scoured the altar. He had sworn to never come back to these places, but in this world they were unavoidable.

Finally, he exhaled. He was desperate for help and they were the only ones who could save Chess. He knew that there was a chance that if they knew the full truth of their situation, he and Chess could be executed. Last time he had been protected, now he had to protect Chess. The thought made him sick as he stared up at the Raven. He wondered if it would spring to life and slice him in half just for being here.

He wasn't sure if he'd fallen asleep, but after what felt like a lifetime, a solitary monk wandered into the room and looked at Penner. He felt himself start to shake as the man sat next to him and grabbed his shoulder. His eyes were pale blue and lined with life. His wrinkled hand pulled the red hood back, revealing a full head of white hair and a kind smile.

"Glory to the One Soul," the man greeted him kindly. "Your friend is stable."

Penner exhaled.

"Where is he?"

"He is breathing and a few of the monks are tending to his wounds. We removed him from the tabernacle and into a space where he can rest."

"May I go help them?" Penner asked.

"You should rest. It's almost dawn," he said.

"I don't care what time it is, I just want to help. I have to make sure he's okay," Penner replied. "I've seen wounds before. I've treated the sick. I know how to take care of patients."

"Are you a medic?"

"I enlisted when I was young. I was terrible with a rifle, so they gave me a medical kit."

The man looked at Penner.

"Were you a good medic?"

Penner hesitated and the man smiled as he turned to the altar. "He means a great deal to you, doesn't he?" he asked.

"He does."

"Then I'll help however I can," he said, brushing the wrinkles out of his robe. "I'll bring you to him, but you shouldn't stay long. You both need rest. Follow me."

"Thank you."

The man nodded and slowly got off the pew. With no real other option, Penner followed.

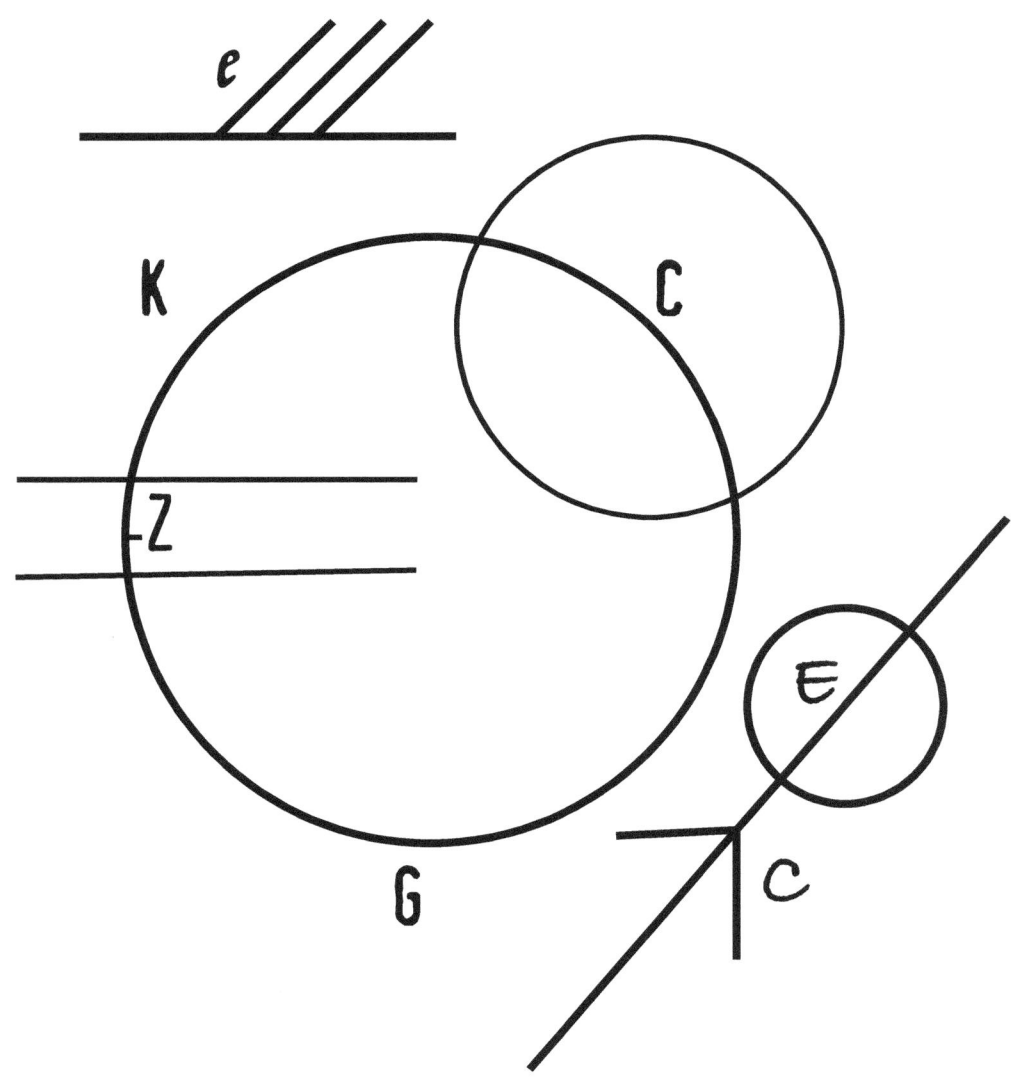

13/14/23

He is stable. For now, that is enough.

I can't begin to explain last night's events. They baffle me. I have never seen anything like it, but every detail is scarred into my mind. The smell of blood. The feeling of his cold body weighing heavy on my back. The thought that I'd lost him.

He'll never look the same again. To think otherwise would be foolish. Seeing him there half-stitched is something I won't forget.

I have always been good with a needle, but these monks are incredible. The speed at which they patched him up was remarkable. They don't talk much, but then again, what is there to say? How does one explain this? The wounds are far too calculated to be accidental and I suspect more than a few of them think I did this to him. One man couldn't do this to himself.

He hasn't woken up yet, but I hope he does soon. I need to hear his voice. I need him to tell me he's okay.

This place may be a sanctuary, but it is far from safe. I want to get out of here.

I need him to wake up.

The warm sun on his face woke Penner. A few birds chirped through the open window as he pushed a rough, threadbare blanket off of him. The air was fresh, and for a second he thought he was back home. He looked at his hands to see them stained with blood, and everything flooded back at once. Even though he'd showered, he still felt dirty. The smell of blood was still thick in the air.

He wasn't sure how long ago he'd stitched up Chess with the monks, but the sun had been out by the time they had finished. The entire experience had been traumatic, but comforting. On the one hand, he had made sure that Chess was okay. On the other, the pain made it hard to look at him.

Whatever Chess had used, it had been precise. The cuts started at his chest and criss-crossed down his arms and legs. Some less than inch long, others extending almost the full length of his body. Stitch by stitch, they had closed every wound and applied a strange green salve on top.
They had assured him that Chess would be okay and helped him back to his

chambers. He hadn't wanted to leave but he'd had to. They had both needed to rest, and as soon as his head had hit the bed, he had been out.

How long had he been asleep? Judging by the height of the sun, he guessed it was close to noon. He quickly got out of the bed and threw on his clothes, which had been tended to by the monks. They hadn't been successful at removing the stains, and what remained of his shirt had been sewn together after they'd cut it off of Chess. The bloodstains rendered it now a copper brown, and it made him sick to look at. But he had to wear something. Every muscle ached as he put it on. Moving his legs was agony, but he willed himself into the hall. He raced to the main cathedral's chapel area where the monks were doing their prayers. Thick, fragrant smoke poured out of their hands as herbs burned, making them look like ghosts.

"Brother, welcome." One of the monks came up to him and took his hand in a comforting fashion. "I hope your sleep was untroubled."

"Thank you," Penner said, feeling uncomfortable. He realised this was one of the gentlemen who had helped them out last night. "Brother Jacob, right?"

"You remember. Welcome," he said with a warm smile on his handsome face. "Your friend is doing well. He's still asleep, but seems to be feeling much better."

"Good. I'm glad. Can I see him?"

"You'd best let him rest. I imagine he'll be in quite a bit of pain when he comes to. We have our best healers praying for him, but it's unlikely that they'll let him wake up today."

Penner bit his lip.

"Your help was appreciated last night, but sometimes the best cure is time," the monk continued.

"Right. Well, thank you for being so warm," Penner said as he looked around the sanctum. "Has my companion come by? The female I was here with?"

"Not yet. If you wish to go find her, your friend will remain in good company."

"Okay. Yes. Thank you. Thank you for everything."

Brother Jacob nodded and motioned towards the door. With a nod, Penner walked through the exit and into the daylight. The contrast blinded him as he made his way back to the ship. Broken branches and blood splatters made the trail easy to follow. It took him longer to walk back than he thought it would. How fast had he been running last night? After stumbling and dragging his heavy body for what felt like hours, he managed to tumble back into the clearing where Cassandra was moored, but found no sign of Fred.

Scouring the sides of the forest, he took a few steps into the field and looked to see if Fred was on deck. He walked to the ship and felt a hand clap down on his shoulder so fast he jumped out of his skin. Fred appeared behind him with a rabbit slung across her back.

"Hungry?" she asked. Despite the smell of the rabbit, he felt his stomach rumble.

"I guess so," he said. In all the chaos, he hadn't eaten. Fred flung the rabbit into his hands and ascended to the top of Cassandra's deck. A small metal item shot into the air and landed in front of him. He looked down to see the handle of a knife, barely a foot away from where he was standing.

"That could've hit me!" he yelled. With a grunt, he sat on a rock and began to skin the carcass.

Dressing the rabbit was soothing. The menial activity took his mind off last night, and the knife was sharp enough to make it easy work. Within minutes he had skinned and gutted the beast, and he walked to where Fred had started a small fire. They attached the rabbit to a spit and began to cook. Fred had also gathered a few vegetables and fruits and offered him a small collection of green leaves.

"It's a herb. Should tide you over until the rabbit is done."

"Thanks. I won't be seeing anything strange, will I?" he asked.

"Only if you look in a mirror."

He took a bite of the strange herb and chewed. It was bitter, but serviceable.

After a few moments of turning the spit, she finally broke the silence.

"How is he?"

"Alive."

"I figured that much."

"He's stable. They say they've got their best healers working on him, but they're going to be keeping him for today. See how he's healing. They said he won't wake up until tomorrow or so."

"That's good. He'll heal faster if he sleeps," she said, taking a bite of her herbs. She chewed with her mouth open. "We did all we could. He's going to be okay."

"Is he?" Penner asked. "I mean, he's—He was hauling around a log and carving god knows what into the dirt. He cut into himself and—"

"I know," she said. "These things, all this divine stuff, it takes time to process and the human brain is only so big. He's just being overloaded with everything right now. He's coping, but he'll be fine."

"You speak like you know from experience," Penner said.

"His name was Cassius. And I was Jessica."

Penner looked at her, confused.

"So you went through this sort of thing?"

"Something like it."

"And—these things are normal? What was it—"

"Hard. These things—this thing—it changes a person."

"Have you seen many people like us out there?"

"I've heard stories. Lady Raina spoke about her disciples often enough."

"Did she know Cassius?"

"She did. Told us to go east. By then he was lost in his thoughts, so he did, but I'm not sure that she had anything to do with it." She paused. "He's already doing much better than Cassius."

"You're kidding, right? You saw what he did to himself."

"But he can still talk. He still knows who you are. He doesn't attack you when you try to do something for him. I've seen much, much worse."

"How many?"

"Enough." She stopped turning the spit and Penner used the moment to get a good look at her.

"Who were you before?" Fred laughed.

"Someone very different."

"Where were you from?"

"The Southern Kingdoms. The cities of Pearl."

"I hear they're beautiful."

"They're okay. I prefer the country to the seas myself," she said as she looked around the forest clearing. "Gives you more places to hide. I was the daughter of a judge, and fell in love with a merchant. I thought my life would be nothing but rearing children and growing old with him. Destiny had other plans."

"So what happened?" Penner asked.

"What do you think? I'm here and he's—well, he's not anymore." Fred paused and turned to the ship. She got up and pointed to the rabbit. "Keep turning the spit, you don't want it to burn."

"Are you—"

"I'm not hungry anymore," she said as she climbed back on top of the deck.

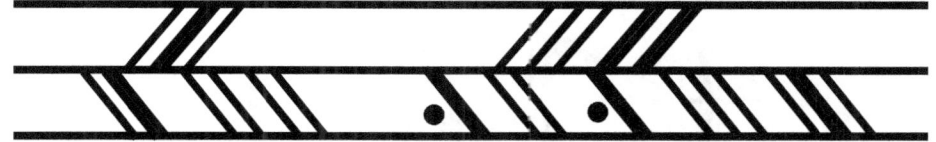

The creator was lonely, he sought to make creatures that would keep him company. His first companion was to be fair, virtuous and ordered. However, because the creator had never made anything before, he considered the creatures who did not serve a purpose a mistake.

This is why Tolin is a snake – lovely and beautiful, but they became the guardians of the seas. The need for legs was never given, and as a result, they were long and flat.

The next was Zav who the creator made great at swimming, and as a result he gave them arms and legs than any creature. The creator however made them joyful, but they were considered... for walking. Instead they were winged which allowed them to fly and be given dominion of the land.

Finally there was Mobo – the forgotten. When Mobo was created, they became selfish and used his aims to cause trickery and chaos through the land– but when he saw how selfish they were, he refused the creator when the creator wanted them to stop. However, when they were complete, he was supposed to be given dominion of the land– but he resented the other creatures and has ever since.

93

The next two days were uneventful. The camp was far enough away from the village to allow privacy. The people who did come by were either hunters or traders that Fred would do business with. During the day, Fred would HUNT and Penner would forage, gathering herbs, mushrooms, and vegetables. He hated to kill animals, but had no problem cleaning them once they were dead.

He chose to spend his time with Fred at the ship, but would return to the temple to check up on Chess and talk to the monks every morning and evening before dark. Despite himself, he enjoyed the monks' company and started joining them FOR meals. Brother Jacob was proving to be a good conversationalist, and the two would get into friendly debates about Classical writings.

Penner was shocked by how easily the old doctrines came back to him, but he enjoyed that they could discuss matters without either side taking offense. Brother Harper would trade them snacks in exchange for gardening.

Despite the hard work, it was appreciated. It took Penner's mind off of Chess. Only one man, the white-haired man who had comforted him, hadn't made any effort to talk to Penner since their arrival. When he had asked Brother Jacob about the man, he had been dismissive. The man was a hermit who rarely interacted with the rest of the congregation. But whenever that man was around, Penner knew he was being watched.

The healers had been working over Chess since his arrival, and by the third day, Penner was able to see him again. He was guided into the room where he had helped to stitch together Chess's wounds. His heart leapt. The wounds looked much better, still red and fresh, but in shockingly good shape, considering. Chess was able to move his body with relative ease, and they assured him that with the proper healing he would be able to move freely in less than a week.

"Hey you," Chess said.

Penner smiled as tears began to well in his eyes. He had to fight every urge to launch himself at Chess and smother him in kisses and choke him for putting him in this absurd situation. Anger gave way to relief, and despite his better judgement, he walked over and embraced him. Chess hugged him back. The monks smiled.

"You're awake. You're alive," Penner whispered.

"I'm still me. Still here," he squeaked. "Tight."

Penner released his grip and Chess coughed.

"Sorry," he said, somewhere between a laugh and a sob. "I just—"

"I know."

"He's doing fine. I thought you'd appreciate getting to see him before we continue our work," Brother Jacob said. "His recovery is remarkable. His spirit is very compatible with this treatment."

"Of course. Thank you. I-I'm glad you're doing better," Penner began, but Chess shushed him before pointing to a jagged line that criss-crossed his chest.

"Connect the dots," Chess said with a smile before laying back on the cot.

He closed his eyes as the healers began to work their hands over him, applying a shiny balm onto his skin. For a moment Penner wondered if they'd let him join THEM, but their techniques were far beyond what he'd learned. He would just have to let strangers rub their oily hands all over his partner, and he would go back to the ship and sleep in his hammock. He sighed.

"Connect the dots," he said to himself. It sounded important, but he couldn't figure out why.

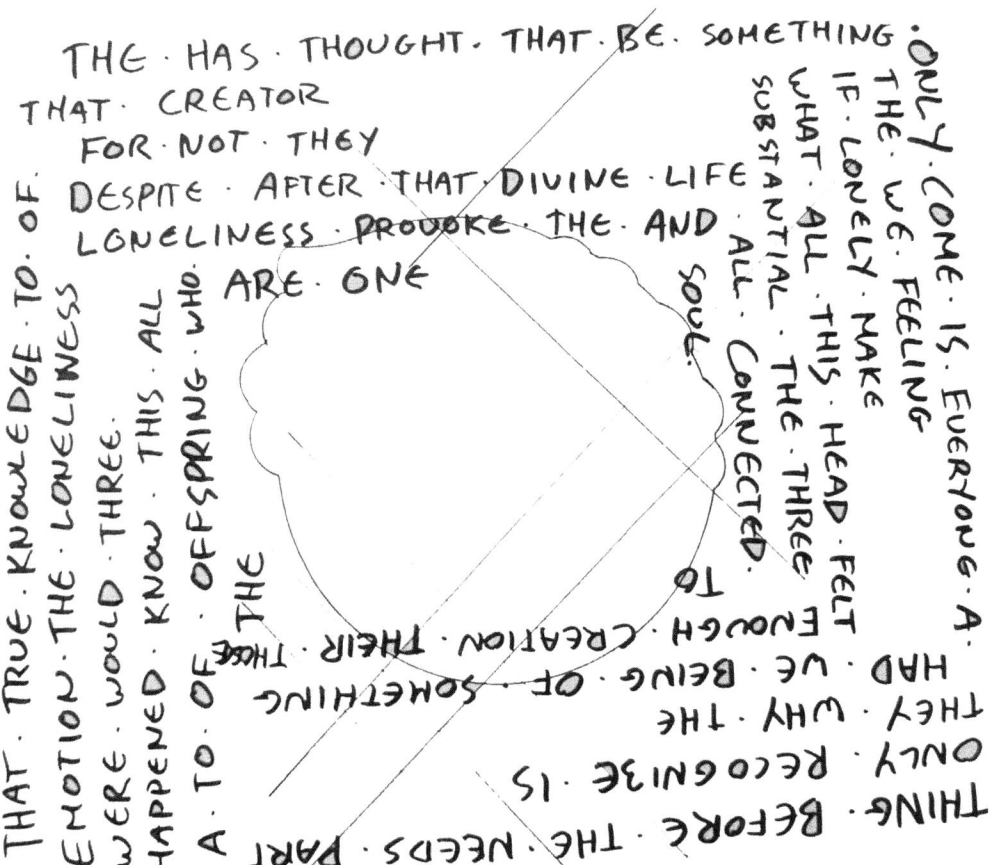

It was evening. The monks were out having their supper and Penner sat in the main hall, looking up at the Snake and Raven. Both were carved so intricately they looked like they could burst to life any moment. He sat with his journal in his hands and looked down at it. He hadn't been able to bring himself to write in it since the night of the incident. There was still some blood splattered on the cover, and he wondered if he'd ever get it out.

"Who was right?" a voice behind him asked. The shock made Penner jump, as he turned around to find the silver-haired monk looking at him. "Apologies. I didn't mean to frighten you."

"It's fine. I didn't hear you come in," Penner said.

"I will attempt to be louder next time. These old bones don't travel as loudly as they used to," he said with a warm smile on his wrinkled face. Penner nodded and returned his attention to the altar. He peered at it for a moment before the man spoke again. "You are not a believer, are you?"

"Not for a while, now," Penner said. "Feels like a lifetime ago."

"And yet fate brought you here," the monk replied.

"Desperation brought me here. I don't want to be here. I don't like being here. It brings back too many bad memories."

"Have you been here before?" Penner shook his head.

"Not here, no. I grew up a long way from here."

"And yet, you treat this place like it hurts you."

Penner bit his lip.

"Maybe not this place, but one like it. My hometown has a Temple."

"Every hometown has a Temple," the man said with a laugh.

"Well, let's just say it didn't paint the rest of them in a good light. They took something from me. Something very important."

"No one here means you any harm," the monk said.

"No one here knows who I am."

"I don't think that would change anything. Maybe you paint us all in a bad light."

"I'm only here because of him. I'm only here so he can get better. Where he goes, I go."

"Strange how your friend had this happen, to force you to come into such a place."

"What are you implying?"

"Maybe he's not the reason that you came here. Perhaps this destination was for you," the man said with a kind smile. "Maybe there's a part of you that needed this place."

"I doubt that," Penner said, stifling a laugh.

"Life is a mysterious force. The One Soul is even more so. The One Soul brought you here to sit with me. Here, now, in this place. There must be some significance in this. Of all the temples in this world, you walk into this one. He is not your brother, and you declared him to be more than a friend."

Penner felt his mouth go dry. He clenched his hands around his journal.

"I know him very well."

"He is all over your heart, my boy. Don't be afraid. I will not tell anyone. It is no secret here. There are no secrets. The One Soul sees all."

Penner looked at him. He looked earnest, but Penner knew better than to trust him.

"Why are you telling me this? Is this a threat?" he whispered.

"Not all who wear the cloth carry a whip. Not all who preach condemn. You will have friends in every corner of this earth, just as you will always have enemies who will masquerade as friends." He nodded to the altar and Penner followed his gaze. "You have a good heart. Its purity is probably what brought you to him in the first place. Just be careful. Even here. Even now. Not all who help seek what is best for you."

"And you?" Penner turned to the man as a tear ran down his cheek.

"I had a man once," he whispered. "We lived together in a village not far from here. For a time we lived in harmony with the world. It wasn't a long time, but it was an important time. But in an instant the world changed. The riots of the Southern Kingdom sent ripples throughout the world and when the revolts happened in our town, things got complicated. He went to fight and though I waited, I never heard from him again. I sought shelter and came here. One can only wait so long before the world conspires against you. I had to do what was best for me AND hid in the words of our forefathers," he said as they stared at the altar in front of them.

"Did you ever see him again?"

"Not in this life, I'm afraid. Perhaps in my next loop, I will SEE myself through his eyes and find out what happened. Until then, I will stay here." He looked at Penner and smiled. "Perhaps you're the reason I've stayed here as long as I have."

"Perhaps." Penner brushed away a tear he hadn't realised was there as the man stood. He reached into his pocket and pulled out a small piece of wood with a snake carved on one side, and a raven on the other. He offered it to Penner for a closer look. Penner took it and marvelled at the incredibly detailed carvings. It looked like this small piece of wood had taken days, if not weeks, to complete. For its size, it was incredibly dense and felt heavy in his hand.

"Is this Tardan wood? How did you get it here?"

"There are ways," he said as he began to walk to the altar. "I chose not to believe in accidents a long time ago. I think now you are proving me right." Penner held out his hand to return the plank to the monk, but he was already walking away.

"Sir, you left—"

"If you had known it was a gift, would you have taken it?" he asked with a smile as he threw the hood over his head and disappeared into the back hallways. Penner tried to follow but by the time he was on his feet, the man was gone. Penner looked back at the wood piece and placed it in the chest pocket of his vest. He wasn't sure what the monk had been thinking, but he was touched. Suddenly he felt a wave of sadness. He hadn't caught the man's name, and he had a feeling that he would never get another chance.

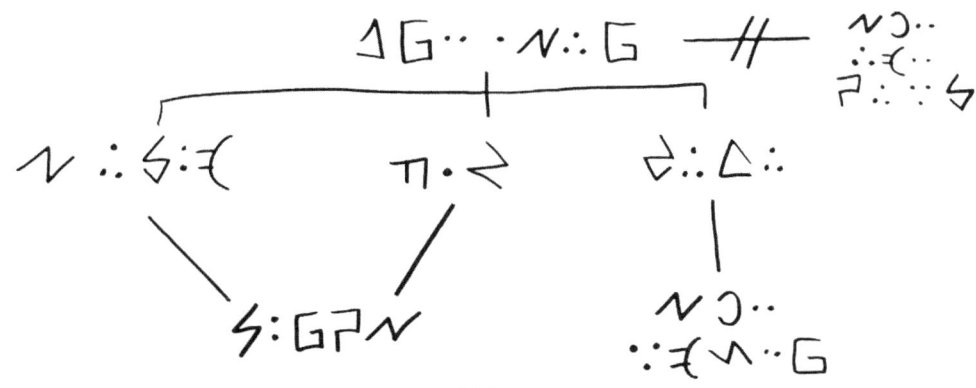

The word of the moment was discomfort.

Penner awoke to the feeling of stone jutting into his back. He wasn't sure how long he'd been asleep, but it had to be late because the room was still. He must have passed out in front of the altar. When he tried to get up, his back refused to cooperate. Then Chess stormed into the space and stood at the head of the cathedral. He was wearing a gown that covered his front half, leaving his backside exposed. Wires and cables stuck out of him at odd angles as he hovered at the front.

"Chess?" he asked, still half asleep, but Chess didn't answer.

Was this a dream?

Penner yawned as he gripped the back of the pew in front of him and pulled himself to his feet. His body felt heavy and weak, but Chess was bounding so fast it was hard to track him. Then he froze, standing in front of the giant statues behind the altar. A cold breeze erupted from the front and whipped him across the face, fully waking him up.

"What the hell was that?" Penner asked.

He looked to Chess, but he didn't respond. Penner paused. Why was he out of the recovery space? He didn't look well enough to be walking around yet. The bright pink lines still laced his skin. His hair was messy and standing on end, and drops of blood pooled underneath him.

"Chess, you shouldn't be up there." Penner frowned. He hated sounding like a parent.

"Can you see it? The window?" Chess asked.

"Why are you up? You need to get down from—"

Before Penner could finish, Chess leapt onto the altar, landing on top of it like a cat. The entire sanctum rumbled with fury. The cool breeze whipped around the space again. The candles that lined the walls of the atrium burned brighter. Penner hadn't even noticed that they'd been lit.

"It's closing," Chess said.

"Just let it," Penner urged. "It's not safe! If they catch you up there, they'll—"

Chess stood on the altar and reached over his head. As he did, something flickered above him. It was a translucent circle Penner hadn't seen before.

As Chess grabbed it, the candles blazed brighter. The breeze picked up speed and it felt more like it was sucking them into the circle.

"I can get it!" Chess exclaimed.

"Don't!"

It was fruitless.

With his arm stretched above him, Chess leapt high into the air. His hand gripped at the circle, and it began to flicker. Penner didn't notice. He was more concerned about catching Chess as he fell. He launched himself from his seat and rushed towards Chess as fast as he could. But he knew it was hopeless. There was no way he would be able to reach Chess in time to cushion his fall. Chess was about to fall back onto the altar and undo all of the good the monks had done. He would break every stitch and crack his head on the ground. If he was lucky, he would just break his back.

But then time seemed to slow, and everything froze.

The wind grew stronger. It beat against his shirt as the air in the room was sucked towards Chess. It was sudden but strong, and Penner could feel himself being pulled by it.

The candles exploded into torrents of fire.

One by one they danced as the wind pulled them into long spires of heat. They raced towards Chess and his outstretched arm that still clenched at the circle in the air above him. They looked like fiery tentacles trying to burn Chess's hand off. Before Penner could comprehend what was going on, the fire around Chess's hand had grown so fierce that Penner could feel the heat blasting against his face.

Then Penner realised he wasn't breathing.

The flames erupted into the shape of burning wings that stretched out to either side of the cathedral. Each wing a flurry of energy that blasted with a heat so intense, it radiated through Penner's body. A head emerged with a long, sharp beak that was made from a blue fire so intense, it looked black. The creature was massive. It was almost incomprehensible. It opened its beak to scream and the sound was a thunderclap, shaking the room with such ferocity that the mountain felt like it was exploding. The chandeliers collapsed and smashed into the pews, which crumbled all around him.

The altar burst into dust and scattered to the ends of the room. The world ceased to exist, and for a moment the beast was reality. It continued to grow until the flames seemed to envelop the world, and standing in the centre of its chest, bathed in lightning, was Chess. He hung suspended, as if the creature were cradling him within itself.

Penner couldn't breathe as his eyes stung from the heat and a voice smashed through his skull, "For the good of it all, you must—"

Then everything vanished.

In a blink, the world was black. In another, everything returned to how it was before. The chaos evaporated into a wisp of smoke, and the world reset with everything back and intact.

Still sitting in the pew, Penner shot to his feet. He wasn't sure how high Chess had jumped, but he was falling. He collapsed in a heap in front of the altar, missing it by inches. Scrambling over the pews, Penner rushed to Chess and laid him on his back, cradling his neck in his hands. He didn't feel broken and he appeared to be breathing, which was encouraging. Some stitches had come undone, but nothing as bad as he'd expected.

"Chess, are you okay?" he asked, grabbing his face. For a moment Chess was quiet, but soon his eyes fluttered open and he looked up at Penner.

"I almost had it. It was right there, and it slipped through my fingers." Chess looked at his hands, which were red and blistered.

"What was—What was that?" Penner asked.

Chess didn't seem to care and seemed lost in his own thoughts. He pulled himself up to his knees and looked around the room.

"You shouldn't move right now." Then, with a smile, Chess pointed at the Raven statue.

"Look!" Chess exclaimed.

Penner followed his gaze. He noticed a collection of dots that formed a strange pattern on the statue's chest. Chess pushed Penner off despite his protestations and raced over to it. The holes were dark and deep, and smoke poured out of them. They looked as if they had been blasted into the marble, but when Penner felt it, the statue was cold. He touched the circles and despite the smoke, they were just as cold.

"Connect the dots," Chess said as he burst into a smile and turned to

104

Penner. He held out his arm, which Penner accepted. Chess traced along one of the lines that had been carved into his arm and then traced along the dots on the raven statue.

Penner had to examine it a few times to make sure he was seeing what he was seeing. His mouth went wide.

"They match. They're a perfect match," Penner whispered. "How are they—"

Chess pulled down the remnants of his tattered sleeve and nodded at the doorways.

"Like the gullet of a bird." He said more to himself than to Penner. "We should probably get out of here. Fast," Chess said as the sounds of rustling echoed through the halls. Chess turned to go, but Penner held him still.

Surprising himself, Penner was hesitant to leave. Had Chess healed enough to leave now? What would they gain by leaving?

"We can't leave," Penner whispered.

"We must. It's time. I know where we're going next."

Penner looked at Chess and frowned. The monks had treated them decently. He'd grown comfortable here. But with one look back at the statue, he knew that Chess was right. The monks were strict about appearances, and dark burning holes on a marble statue would be impossible to explain.

"Trust me."

Before he could react, Chess gripped him by the wrist and made a dash for the door. He stumbled behind Chess. He feared for Chess's body as he ran, scared that at any moment the pain would be too much. Any second, the wounds could rip open. No one should be able to run with that many stitches, but Chess didn't slow down. He moved with such agility that within moments, they were at the door. With a kick, Chess flung open the doors to escape into the night.

Penner had assumed the doors were too heavy to do that, but in seconds they were outside. The cold night slapped him in the face as he realised how hot the air had become. He looked back and saw Brother Jacob running into the atrium. When they got to the bottom of the stairs, Chess held up his hand, and a small blast of wind to erupted from them as the doors in the cathedral slammed shut.

"Be quick. We don't have much time," Chess said.

"What was that?"

"I closed the doors." Chess began to walk towards the ship, but Penner stopped him.

"You shot a blast of wind from your hands!" he exclaimed.

"Technically not me, but there's no time to explain," Chess exclaimed.

"Try!"

"We have to go. We don't have much time."

"Until what?" Penner asked.

"Until they hunt us down like dogs. We need to run back to the ship and get out of here. I've bought us a minute. Maybe two."

"But it's night. Even if we get back to the ship, we can't—"

"Just follow me!" Chess bellowed as he ran into the forest.

Penner hesitated. His legs felt like marble. He was rooted to the ground as his knees shook. Then the sound of a bang as the doors reverberated. The monks were trying to get out. Within seconds they'd come after them.

With no choice, Penner began to run after Chess. In the darkness, he found it difficult to keep up, but did his best. Despite his injuries, Chess was moving quicker than Penner expected. Leaping onto rocks and bounding off trees. He looked more like an ape than a man. The pain Penner imagined him to be feeling was no hindrance as he moved better and faster than him. Guided only by moonlight, Penner kept tripping over roots and slamming into trees. He was moving slow, and the noises behind him were getting louder each minute.

In a particularly nasty moment, he tripped and slammed against a trunk so hard he froze. For a moment he was afraid that they'd be caught, then Chess reappeared and slung his arm around Penner and helped him up. Using Chess as leverage, Penner could follow along, and they began to move more quickly again. They weren't going to set any speed records, but they were outpacing the growing crowd that followed them.

By the time they arrived at Cassandra, Penner felt more battered and bruised than Chess. Taking his arm back, Chess sprinted across the meadow and leapt over the trenches he'd carved into the ground. Within moments he was back at the ship, untying knots like a captain. Penner had trouble keeping up. He was out of breath and limped as fast as he could in a futile attempt to keep up. By the time he got to the door, he could hear the engines warming up.

Then, looking angry, Fred appeared and gripped him by the shirt. "Penner! WHAT the hell is going on?" she yelled.

"I-I don't know. I was in the cathedral and woke up, and he was just standing there and acting like this."

Cassandra heaved forwards, her heavy bow knocking Penner off of his feet as he attempted to climb into the vessel. Fred tightened her grip and pulled him aboard, saving his legs from getting crushed by the ship.

"We shouldn't launch her at night. We need the sun to—"

The ship heaved again, this time slamming into the ground so hard the meadow shook.

Fred swore as she glared at Penner. "If anything happens to her, I'm holding you responsible," she threatened before launching into action.

She bounded up to the top deck, and Penner pushed himself to his feet and attempted to follow as the ship lurched to the side. He felt his head slam into the wall and he toppled to the ground. His head spun and he felt like he was going to throw up. He gripped onto the railing and clawed himself halfway up the stairwell, which provided him a glimpse above deck.

Though he wanted to get on deck, he knew he couldn't. But he could see what was happening.

Chess was moving with such ease, it left Penner speechless. He easily glided across the deck and quickly untied the remaining ropes.

"You can't launch her. We need the sun to open the sails and guide us!" she screamed.

"We don't need power. We just need to float. I'll take care of the rest!" Chess called out. "It needs to be tonight! It needs to be now!"

"What's that sound?" Fred asked. She looked over the side of the ship and cursed. Penner looked over and could see the torches of the mob growing closer by the second. Chess raced over to Penner on the stairs, and helped drag him up onto the deck as the ship lurched upwards. Penner turned to see Fred unlatching the final rope, and Cassandra began to rise.

"We're rising too slow. We won't be able to get out of here at this rate," Fred said.

"We're going to be fine. Trust me," Chess said as he stepped to the edge of the deck.

For a second, he looked like he would throw himself over and Penner raced to his feet.

He wasn't able to make it over to him, but he was relieved when Chess stopped at the edge and fished into his pocket. He pulled out a long, slender match and Penner paused.

"Is that from the temple?" Penner asked. After a moment, Chess took his hand and dragged the match against the rough grain of the ship. It flashed a brilliant pink spark, and he tossed it over the side of the ship.

For a moment it looked like nothing happened. Then the entire meadow lit up in brilliant hot flames. A flash of fire spread across the ground below them, filling the trenches that Chess had dug up. The sudden burst of heat seemed to make Cassandra buzz with energy. As the field burst into flames, they felt themselves rising fast enough to pin Penner to the ground.

"You should see this," Chess said.

Penner had to blink to clear his eyes, but soon noticed that the lines formed very distinct yet familiar patterns. He looked to Chess and gripped him by the arm as he traced several of the fire lines with his finger. Chess removed his shirt and began to trace the patterns. The lines dug into the ground matched the lines on Chess's body perfectly. Penner gazed at it and noticed that in the middle were the five dots that had also appeared on the chest of the raven.

"Connect the dots," Chess said.

"They match? How?"

"It's what it needs to be," Chess said as he pointed towards a very specific point on the horizon. As if on cue, a blast of light appeared in the sky, illuminating a far-off mountain that Penner could hardly see. Despite the distance, it was very clearly the same outline as the line pattern on Chess and the ground.

"That's where we are going next!" Chess exclaimed. "That is where we need to be."

Fred looked at him, dumbfounded, before turning to Penner.

"That's the mountain? What's so special about—" Penner yelled, but his voice was still raspy.

"We need to go to the mountain. That mountain!" Chess exclaimed at Fred, who looked back at Chess, then the ground, and then to the horizon.

"That mountain? Chess, you can't—"

"How long to get there?" Chess asked.

"A few days. Could be a week if the winds aren't with us. Hard to say. I mean, we shouldn't even be flying at night, and she's been grounded a few days. We will need to find someplace to charge in the next day or so."

"Let's go!" Chess exclaimed.

They heard a rumble from just out of range that caused the three of them to look down. A small burst of flame exploded against the side of the ship. The force rocked the ship, and Penner looked down to see the figures loading up a small catapult.

"Is that the monks?" Penner asked. "How'd they get that?"

"You don't want to find out," Chess replied as he whipped behind the wheel and turned to Fred. "We need to go there. Let's get moving."

"Fine. Let's leave."

With a gentle swivel of his wrist, the entire ship surged to the side as a cold wind slammed against them. In seconds they were moving. The heat had given them enough height that now all they had to do was try to glide the ship back to the ground. A few tree branches crunched and snapped under Cassandra's heavy bow, but they were moving. They wouldn't be able to get far, but they were in the sky, meaning they could outpace the mob below them.

"I know a place we can go," Fred said as Penner turned back to see a few people attempt to throw items after them.

They looked like the monks, but instead of dressing in robes, they were clad in armour. Some clenched ropes and bows in their hands. They looked more like an army.

"They actually had me thinking they were our friends."

"Maybe in another life," Fred said. "But for now, we just have to keep moving forwards," she said as they felt a crunch of branches beneath them.

His legs went weak, and Chess caught him and brought him below deck. He lifted Penner into the hammock and brushed the hair out of his face.

"Rest. I need you in the morning."

Penner didn't want to sleep, but felt his eyes close as he exhaled. The ship rocking back and forth was relaxing, but he still couldn't get the image of the raven out of his mind. He could still feel the wind erupting from Chess's hand and dreamt that the wind had blasted him to pieces.

Z	T	H	E	R	C	M	O	B	O	E
A	V	A	R	I	A	A	N	I	S	N
V	O	R	T	T	S	E	E	R	U	T
A	H	A	O	O	S	S	S	H	N	C
N	T	S	O	L	A	T	O	E	L	R
I	O	I	A	I	N	R	U	L	E	E
A	M	A	E	N	O	O	L	I	L	A
R	E	H	T	O	R	B	Y	O	P	T
P	E	R	H	H	A	V	E	N	M	O
C	E	P	E	T	I	M	L	A	E	R
O	N	B	R	A	T	T	A	N	T	S

17/16/23

I wish I could say I had been expecting this. I once again find my-self at a loss of words to explain how I feel. I hadn't been inside any kind of holy place in years. It feels like longer. But being in there and talking to the men—I began to hope that they were different.

What confuses me is they were adorned in their battle garments when they pursued us. The weapons they had far outmatched what a regu-lar monastery would have. There's no way they could have changed so fast. They followed us with such perfect targeting, it leads me to believe that they had planned to do something terrible to us whether we had burnt the statue or not.

I hardly slept and when I woke up, he was asleep. I know what I felt last night. The wind was pouring from his hands, and it was strong. The circle above his head was so strange, but I have no idea where it went. Ev-erything about this space is unfamiliar and now everything just feels more abnormal by the day.

On top of everything, he needs to go to the mountain. I didn't recog-nise it before, but now I do. Mount Spira. Not just any mountain, but the supposed birthplace of the entire religion. Of our entire world. It's bound to be swarming with monks or holy energy, or whatever fresh hell lives there. At this point I wouldn't be surprised if a dragon reared its head from the ground and severed our ship in two.

Actually, I probably shouldn't joke about that. At least he's alive. At least he's here with me.

At least we're together.

The gentle humming of the ship woke him. Penner wasn't sure how he'd slept through the night, but there was a strange feeling in the air. It almost felt like calm. He hadn't felt that in a while.

The weather was fair as Penner emerged onto the deck to feel the breeze kiss his face. He looked across the deck to see Fred hanging casually off the railing. One wrong move and she'd plummet to her death. Despite this, she dangled and drank tea. How she stayed up all night and still looked fresh and alert was a mystery. When she saw him, she motioned to the tea. Penner ambled over to her and looked at Chess, who was sleeping in a chair.

"What happened?"

"We got away," Fred said. "Then I made tea."

"And the monks?" Penner poured himself a cup of the earthy-smelling tea. It wasn't pleasant.

"Haven't seen any of your friends since we left the clearing."

"They're not friends. Certainly not mine. I don't know what they were."

"Well, they didn't look happy."

"Don't blame them. Especially considering we desecrated their Temple."

"You did what?" she exclaimed. Penner realised he'd never seen her look shocked before. He couldn't figure out whether she was angry or amused.

"It's fine. They're fine. They're intact," Penner said. Fred still looked perplexed. "Chess had a—I don't know. Something happened. It was big."

"Be specific." Fred smirked. "Was it bad?"

"I don't know. He was reaching for something, and then there was a flash, and fire filled the room. But the fire was alive. I know it sounds crazy, but I could feel it breathing. He was floating in the air. But then he fell and I ran to him." He paused. "I don't know what exactly it was, but it left a mark: five dots in a row, burnt straight into the marble, that matched the marks in his arm and the lines in the ground exactly. The exact same five dots. The same mountaintop shape in three separate places. It matches the mountain exactly, but I—" Penner could feel himself getting flustered.

"You what?" Fred stopped hanging and slid into a seat opposite Penner.

"This is all insane. I thought I was here to help him, but he keeps needing to rescue me. Why am I even here if I can't even help?"

"Well, you stopped him in the forest when he was—possessed. There's always that. Who knows what would have happened if you hadn't been there."

"That's another thing that scares me." Penner's fists clenched. "There's something going on here that I've never seen before. It's bigger and more intense and insane than I thought it could be. And it's all happening around him. The same symbol three times is impossible. It's physically impossible and yet —"

"Impossible is relative."

114

"Impossible is impossible. It shouldn't happen." He looked over at Chess, who kicked in his sleep. He looked like a puppy. "This is bigger than I thought it would be."

"That depends. How big does your mind go?"

Penner twiddled his thumbs.

"I've always just assumed that everything was the way it was. I mean, I used to believe in bigger things, but now I feel like I've seen things that I can't explain. I've seen Chess become a weapon. I saw a giant flaming bird burst into existence and disappear. I was content with my world the way it was. Now I realise that all along, I must've been wrong." He put the tea down. "And after seeing that, whatever it was, what do I even do with this knowledge? If these things are true, then what else is true? Are the teachings—is it all true?"

"I wish I could tell you," Fred said.

"What does that say about us? About what we are. What we do." His throat went dry.

"If that kind of love was so bad, I doubt they'd insist you were brought along for the trip. What I do know is he needs YOU now. Perhaps more than ever. If you're confused, just imagine how he feels."

"How can he be confused? He always looks so sure. It's like he's expecting all this madness."

"He might know what he needs to do, but he doesn't know why. I'm sure he's struggling with this just as much as you."

Penner looked over at Chess. He snored.

"Do you know what's going on? Was it the same for you? With the whole Cassius thing?"

Fred shook her head. "It was similar. I don't think it's ever the same."

"How'd you handle it?" Fred took a long sip of tea before putting the cup beside her.

"I suppose in many ways I didn't." She peered to the horizon and pointed. "It's about two days away if the wind is with us. We've put a bit of distance between us and the temple, but I'm not sure it's enough. I'm not crazy about touching down again so soon, but I think it's wise. We need to resupply, and you should probably get some of your bruises checked out."

"I'm fine," he lied. His head felt like it was split open. His legs burned. His stomach felt like he'd been stabbed. He knew that he should have someone check him. He wasn't made of steel.

"Let's get started, then," she said as she grabbed a thick rope and slung it over her shoulder.

"Shouldn't we—"

"You're of more use to me right now than him. Let's open the sails so we can get the engines heated. The night launch should have destroyed us, and it's about time we gave Cassandra some love," she said.

"Won't we wake him?"

"The way he's sleeping? Right now, I'm not sure the Three could wake him. Come on. I'll teach you how to steer."

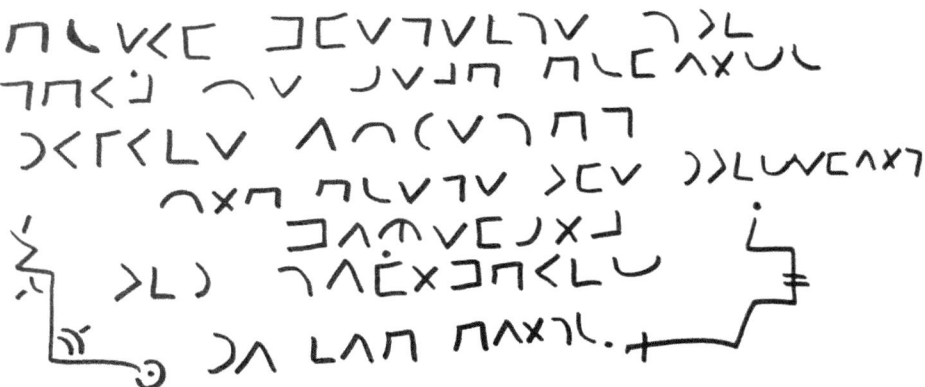

Resting in the hammock, Chess looked peaceful. While it was hard to see him in his current state, the wounds were healing. It was clear the scars would never go away, but that didn't matter. As long as Chess was alive.

"Don't look at me," Chess cooed.

"Can't help it," Penner said.

"Not you," Chess said. Without moving his head, he pointed at the window. There Penner saw a beautiful emerald spider the size of a coin, sitting in its web. It reflected a bright green light and Penner wasn't sure how he'd missed it before.

"It's not poisonous, is it?"

"Not overly. It's fine. She's just a little cranky," Chess said as he craned his head to Penner. "Are you going to join me?"

117

"In the hammock? You want me to—with your everything?"

"Just get in here." Chess motioned to him and Penner smiled. He stepped up into the hammock and cuddled against Chess. He could feel the heat from the wounds radiate off of him. He tried to ignore it, but the position he had to lie in was very uncomfortable. He shifted until eventually he could cradle him without feeling like he was ripping Chess apart. Penner closed his eyes and brushed his hands through Chess's hair.

"I'm sorry," Chess exhaled.

Penner froze.

"Did I pull something?" he asked.

"No. I'm fine. I said I'm sorry. Me. Not you." Chess sounded like he was falling asleep.

"For what?" Penner asked.

"Everything. This. Nothing. I know that this is weird but, it's strange and I'm—"

"You're fine. You're okay," Penner said. "You're going to be okay."

"I'm still sorry."

"There's nothing to apologise for. I'm with you. That's the important thing."

"Is it?"

"I'm here now."

"Are you?" Chess shivered. Penner held him tighter. "I feel like I'm losing myself."

"Then we will find you together. You've got to still be in there some-where. I won't let anything happen to you until then."

"You won't be able to stop anything. You won't be able to protect me. There might be a time when you need to let me go."

"I won't do that," Penner whispered. He squeezed Chess tight. "Good luck getting out of this hammock because I'm not letting you leave." Chess wriggled, but relaxed into Penner with a smile on his face. He pressed his body into Penner's and brushed his hand through his hair.

"You win this round," Chess said before closing his eyes and falling asleep.

Once he was sure Chess was asleep, Penner tried to get out of the hammock. When he moved his arm, Chess gripped it tighter, locking him in the cuddle. Penner sighed, resigning himself to the fact that his arm would be trapped until Chess woke up. With a smirk, Penner relaxed into the netting and slowly let the feeling of warmth and comfort ease him into a nap.

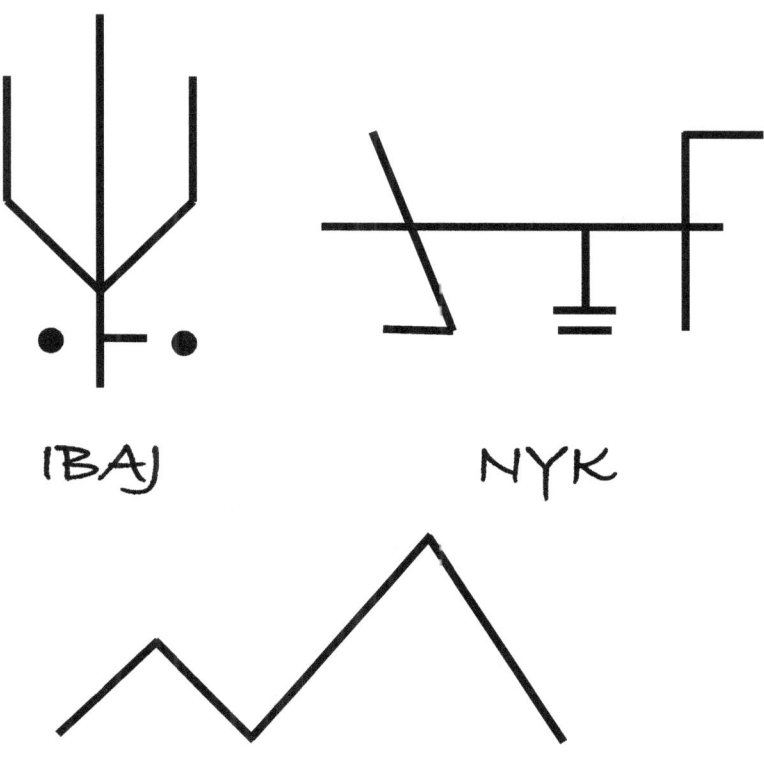

Thunder ripped Penner from his slumber.

The ship rocked back and forth. The movements were aggressive and disorienting. Chess was still curled up next to him, comfortably wrapped in his dreams. For a moment, Penner contemplated waking him, but if Chess was finally resting, he wasn't about to keep him from that.

Penner threw his legs out of the hammock and wrenched his arm out from under Chess. He didn't even notice, and Penner bounded up the stairs to see Fred lassoing lines along the edge of the ship. Her expression was severe, and Penner wasn't sure if he should be more afraid of the storm or her.

"Sleep well?" she asked, throwing him a rope as soon as he emerged. He almost didn't catch it, but ran it to the edge and tied it off.

Above them, the skies were thick and heavy, churning as Penner felt a tremendous heat rip through the air.

"What's going on?"

"We're above a Helion forest. Storms like these CAN whip out of no-where above these damn trees. We need to tie everything down and find a place to settle down until it's done."

Penner didn't know much about these types of forests, but what he had heard was not good. These forests were built around volcanic outposts, and were made of large but light trees. The trees were so light that if they were not rooted into the ground, they would float away. Practically every airship was made out of these trees, but their lightness made the forests unpredictable.

"What do we need?" Penner asked. "What can I do?"

"Tie everything down!" Fred exclaimed as Penner grabbed another rope and began to tie it around the edge of the ship. She cursed as she wiped a torrent of water out of her eyes. "Just look for a clearing, or a field, or some-thing—anything to get away from these damn trees!"

There was a pop, and the ship was thrown to the right. Penner was knocked down and skidded across the deck as a torrent of water was dumped on them. He couldn't breathe. The world around them was black. The down-pour pelted rain like bullets. He tried to stand, but the wind pinned him. There was another burst and he was thrown back. Before he cracked his head open, a hand caught him. He looked up at Chess gripping his shoulders and walking him to the mast.

"Grab it," Chess ordered.

Penner was barely able to see, but gripped it tight. He feared the mast would evaporate in his grip or snap in half and crush him. Cassandra surged forwards, and the torrential downpour paused. He gasped.

His heart raced as the sound of pops grew stronger and the world around him became hot. Pockets of gas ignited as several trees burst into flames be-low them. The rain pelted them again, but this time it was hotter. The air around them began to heat up. Penner was afraid he'd be broiled. The steam began to sting, but in a moment everything began to soften. A red light il-luminated them from below as Cassandra rapidly rose higher. Soon the ship was still, and Penner let go of the mast. The mist was thick and sticky and burned as he breathed. Then, Fred appeared before him, drifting into view like a ghost as the rain dissipated.

"You okay?" she asked.

"Fine." Penner rolled up his sleeves. The heat was becoming unbearable. Sweat soaked his shirt. "What happened?"

"Chess happened. Steered us into the eye of the storm," she said.

Penner coughed. The air felt thinner. He turned to see Chess walk over to them as he surveyed the deck.

"Why is it so hot?" he asked.

"Because we're over the mouth of a volcano," Chess said. "Only safe space around here for the time being."

"Won't you damage the ship?" Penner asked.

"Cassandra is fine. We're well above the fires. The heat is keeping us above the storm. As long as we don't spend too long here, we'll be fine. That was some quick thinking, sailor." Fred sounded proud.

"How long do we have to wait?" Penner asked. He gasped for breath.

"Storm like this could last a few minutes or a few hours," Fred said as she whipped off her shirt.

Penner's mouth hung open as he turned away.

"You—your shirt—"

"This heat isn't going anywhere. Best get cozy," she said as she stretched up to the sky. Penner was flustered as Chess disappeared below deck.

"You sure you want to—" Penner held his tongue when Fred looked at him with a smirk.

"You don't mind, do you?" Penner stuttered, and Fred looked at him with an amused smile. Then she laughed. She covered her chest with her arm and walked towards the ship's bow. "I'm sorry, I just assumed that you—"

"It-it's complicated," Penner began, feeling his cheeks flush as he attempted to speak. "And you are a—fine—" His mouth went dry.

"It's too hot to wear much else," she said. "Best adapt, or you'll pass out."

"Right. Of course. Excuse me." Penner tried not to look. But he realised he was still looking. He pried himself away and made his way below deck. He regretted it, as it felt like an oven. The heat was so dense. He gasped as his body was drenched in sweat. Each breath burnt his throat. It felt like he was swallowing fire. He unbuttoned his collar, but it gave him no relief. He wiped his brow, but the sweat was too thick.

Then he saw Chess.

At first, he thought he was hallucinating due to the heat, but in front of him Chess stood naked. His body was covered in stitches and scars and nothing else. Staring at him was mesmerising, and Penner felt the urge to trace every inch of him. Chess looked graceful as he stood in front of the window. The entire room danced with embers that shimmered in the heat. Wisps of steam whipped past them. But all he could see was Chess. The lines on his body seemed to glow. He looked confident and powerful.

He turned his beautiful eyes and smiled at Penner. Even his eyes were glowing.

"Hey, you." Chess smirked.

Penner didn't hesitate. Within seconds he was standing with Chess. He held his body close and kissed him. The kiss was electric, and he could feel his entire body come alive at the contact. The heat pooled around them as their hands slid over each other. Chess pulled away and whipped the shirt off Penner. He kissed down his chest, which sent small waves of ecstasy over him. Standing back up, Penner felt everything spin. Whether that was from passion or the suffocating heat, he didn't care. Feeling Chess this way was amazing.

Every touch, every kiss, every second their skin touched, energy coursed through them both.

It had been ages since they had touched, and now here they were. Penner kissed Chess's body as he squirmed beneath his lips. Penner ran his hands over every inch he could reach. He wanted to remember how Chess felt in his embrace.

Feeling Chess's strong fingers interlock in his hair, Penner made his way down his lithe, bruised body. Hovering lower, he felt fingers run through his hair as the heat enveloped them. For a time, everything was heat and they were inseparable. He felt every inch of his body and plunged into him. The gasp of pleasure that erupted from them was explosive, and in that moment Penner felt complete. The entire adventure had been worth it. Everything they had gone through was over and whatever was to come didn't stand a chance.

For as long as he'd known how he was different, he had questioned himself. He Hs questioned what the Order of the One Soul would do to him. Despite turning from the Order long ago, some part of him had kept the shame. Though he knew it was false, a part of him had always worried about what the Temples and sanctums had taught. Now, lying naked and spent beside his lover, all those fears went away. Everything evaporated, and it was only them. He looked down at Chess and ran his hands along the scars on his body.

"I love you," he whispered. Chess looked up and smiled at him before closing his eyes and nestling into his side. "I get nothing?"

"If you don't know by now, you're a fool," Chess said. Penner kissed him on the forehead and, despite the sickening heat, they held each other.

"Would still be nice."

"I bet it would." Then Penner tickled him.

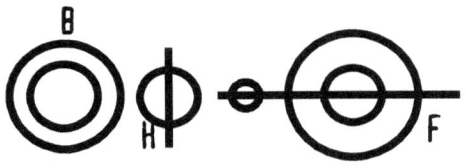

18/16/23

At least he feels the same. I know this body beside me. I know every inch of his skin. He smells the same. He tastes the same. His skin now has scars on it, but it's still the same skin. Every day I get to lie beside him feels amazing.

So much has happened in so little time. There are brief glances when I see him how he was. He'll smile or laugh and I'll be back to there—where we were before all this. But those times are getting fewer and farther between. He's unmistakably a new man now. I love him no less, but I just wish I knew how to get him back.

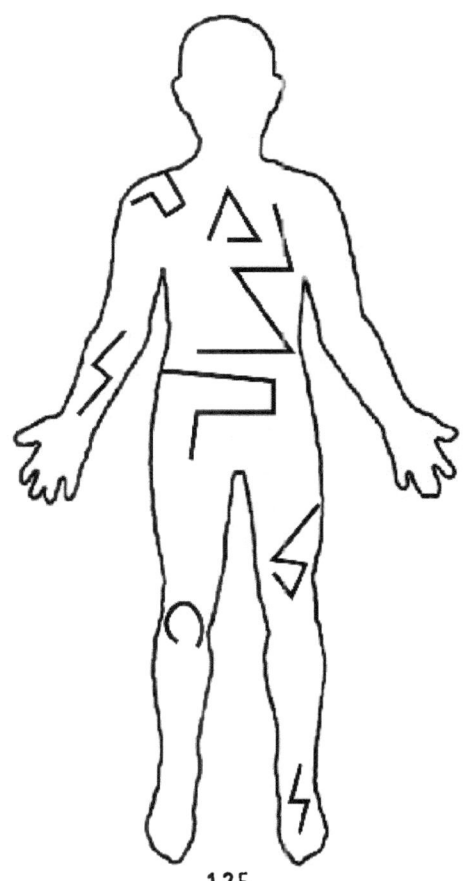

creation know because world understand creator all one speak love creations selfish time three broken pearl make creatures result only say

corrupted much spread instead severed company beautiful anything life therefore despite web substantial

follow given little keep other each made through brief self more nothing divine

Once the storm subsided, Fred wasted no time in clearing the volcano and getting out of the Helion forest. Penner and Chess had no choice but to leave the comfort of the hammock and make their way above deck. Penner felt invigorated. It was the first time in a long while that he felt like Chess belonged to him. But it didn't last. The day was smooth sailing as they floated their way to the ground without opening the sails. The power they'd stored was enough to make a smooth landing miles away from the troublesome trees. It was an easy journey, and with little to do, Chess went below deck to sleep.

Together with Fred, Penner gave Cassandra a thorough inspection. There were a few burns and scuff marks, but no lasting damage. Fred got Penner to rub off a few of the lighter singe marks with a rag, until the hull shone like gold. Satisfied with his work, she made a small cup of green tea that smelled like honey. Penner wondered how many teas she had tucked away.

"People often pay more for tea than ale. It's smart to have a good stock."

She took a sip.

"Should we be drinking it, then?"

"Tea is meant to be drunk. Plus, if you know what stock to get where, it can be cheap. Also, you can make your own when you're in the sky. I've pioneered two blends myself, so far." She looked over to him, but he avoided her gaze. There was something fiercely attractive about her eyes. He'd been having trouble looking at them without blushing.

"You look tired." She smirked. "It's late. You should get some shut-eye."

"Don't you need sleep too?"

"I didn't have the workout you did," she said with a smile, and Penner felt himself flush.

"Do you ever sleep?"

"There's too much to do," she said as her eyes danced over Cassandra's hull before returning to her tea. "I'm sorry if I made you uncomfortable earlier."

"I just never realised that you were so—bold."

"Bold is just another word for unconstrained," she said. "Life is different up here. You live by yourself on a ship for long enough and you tend to stop caring about customs and traditions. Why must a woman be modest? I hunt and forage for my food and make a fair wage. I do what I do to survive, and I don't feel the need to constrain myself to the expectations of others."

"You shouldn't have to," Penner said.

"And neither should you." She hesitated before putting down her tea and smiling at Penner. "You two sounded like you were having fun earlier."

"It was hot," Penner said, feeling a smile form. His face was so warm she could brew tea on it. "I mean the temperature was. It was very—"

Fred laughed. "Nothing to be ashamed of. It's natural." Penner smiled and paused. Fred looked concerned. "Did I say something?"

"You called it natural. I don't know if anyone—it's nothing. Well, I'm sorry if it bothered you," he stammered.

"I told you, I don't care. There's no law in the sky. We do what we want."

"Thank you." Penner smiled as he put down his tea and watched the sunset. "Not everyone is so kind."

"Just let me join next time." Penner froze as he was about to sip his tea.

"That's a joke, right?" Penner asked.

Fred shrugged, and then laughed to herself before going quiet.

"I know what you're going through right now. With Chess. How distant he seems and how different he is. Cassius—the same thing happened to him and I had to stand around and watch as he changed. The difference was he got in his head and he was stuck there. His thoughts became a cage and I wasn't able to get through anymore."

"I—" Penner couldn't find words.

"It's tough and it will change you. It will be brutal, and at the end of it, it killed me. To see him go through all that, and what it cost. I lost everything."

"Was it worth it?"

"In a way. But it's going to be different than you expect." She drew a sip. Penner reached across the fire pit and grabbed her hand. For a moment they smiled.

"Thanks. For everything," Penner said as she squeezed his hand. After a moment, they let go and watched the stars come out. In this moment the universe was still, and Penner reveled in it. He wondered how many others had gone through this before.

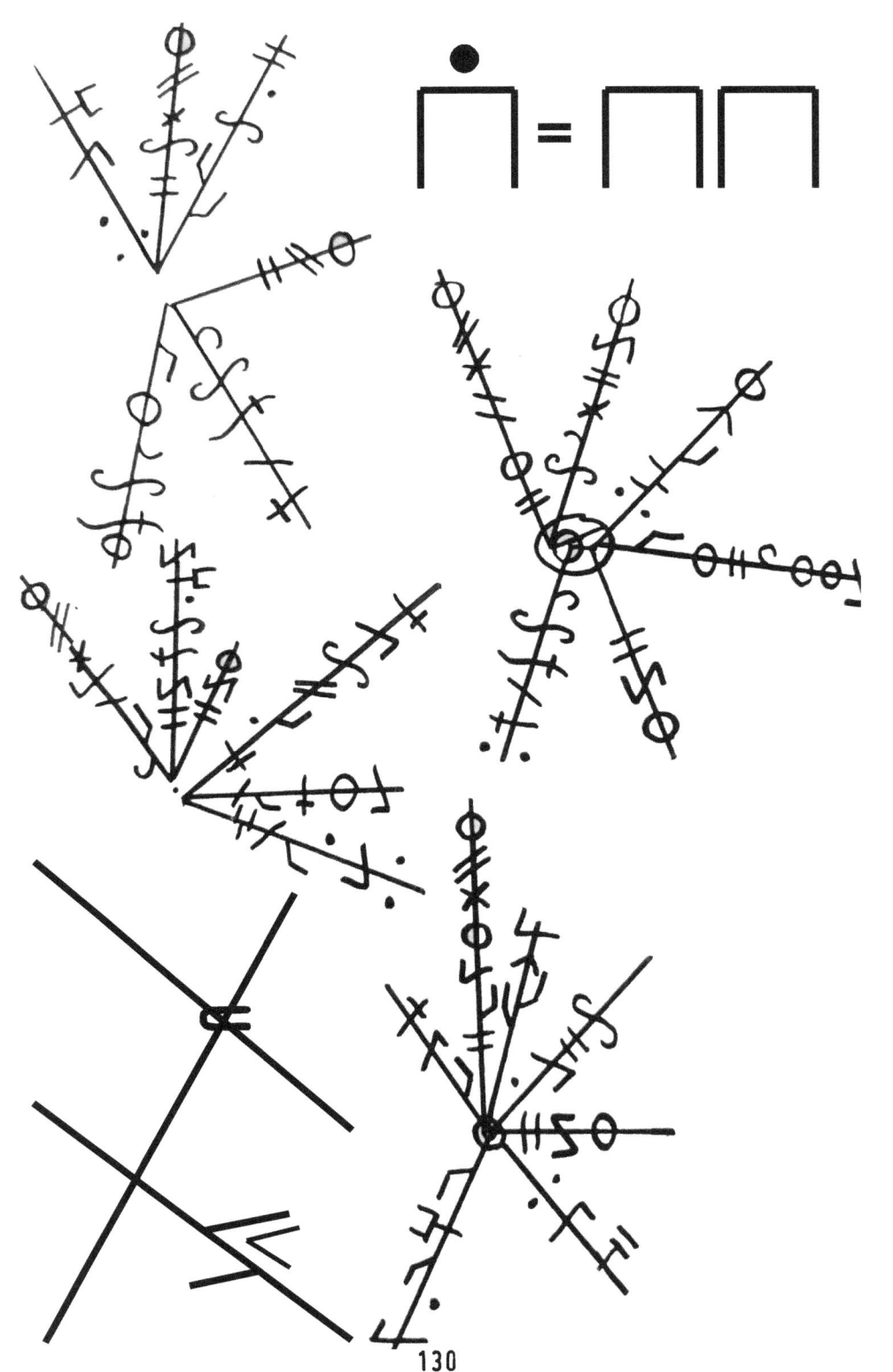

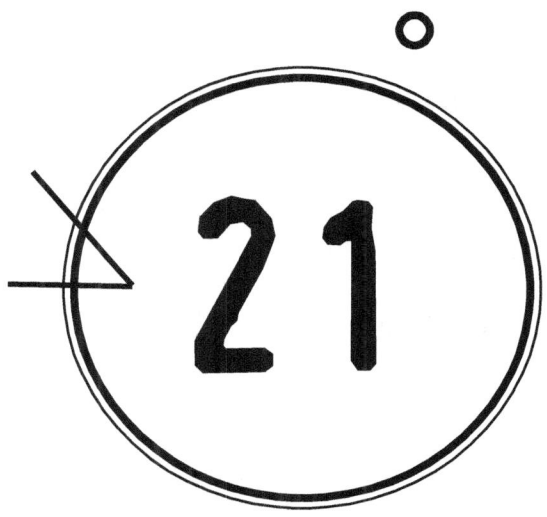

The air was still and silent as the sun beat down on them. The field was quiet. They were warm, and Chess laid his head on Penner's chest. Penner was twirling Chess's hair and swatting his hand away any time it would wander to the bandages that laced his arms.

"Stop scratching," Penner ordered. Chess frowned at him as a twelve-year-old would.

"It's itchy."

"It's itchy because you dug into your arms." Penner slapped his hands away again. He sounded like a caretaker, but judging by the way Chess nudged into him, he didn't mind. "It's amazing none of them became infected."

"It's fine. You've got some of me on you," he said, pointing to Penner's shirt. With a resigned sigh, Penner looked down at his formerly white, now dingy brown shirt. It had several fresh lines of red as the unbuttoned fabric flapped in the breeze.

"It's fine. I'm as resigned to this as I can get. I can't launder them anyway, so I might as well enjoy it," Penner said with a smile. "Just stop scratching and I won't have this problem."

"Scratching helps." Chess sounded like a child.

Penner shook his head. "Scratching will make it worse. Stop it."

"Fine. But I won't be happy about it."

"You'll thank me later." Penner said. "Smell the air."

"It smells like air."

"Clean air. It smells like pure, clean air. It's amazing, isn't it?"

"It smells more like gas." Chess smirked. Penner nudged him. He looked through the trees, and in the distance, he could see the mountain. It looked so much larger from this angle. Like it was inescapable. They were definitely getting closer to it. "You shouldn't worry about me so much."

"Hard not to," Penner said. Suddenly Chess lurched forwards, his nose shooting into the air.

"That's not gas," Chess said as his eyes went wide. He leapt to his feet and raced over to the ship. He looked like a man possessed, and when he turned around to Penner it sent a chill down his body. He ran back to Penner and grabbed him by the sides of his shirt.

"Get the Tome," Chess whispered. "It's under the deck with my bag. But whatever you do, don't touch it. Get it now."

"What's going on?" Penner asked, but Chess had already jumped off and was rushing towards the stern.

"No time!" he bellowed. "Fred!"

Penner saw Fred peek up from the deck. Since the volcano, she had taken to going topless as often as she could. It looked like she was enjoying their relaxation as much as they were. "What is—"

"We need to go! Now!" Chess exclaimed as he began unfurling the sails. Soon ropes began to snap around Penner as plumes of steam shot off the vessel. They weren't even bothering to fully untie the ship.

"You're still tied down—" Penner yelled up.

"What did I tell you?" Chess yelled as another blast of steam erupted from Cassandra. The ship was rising. Penner realised they would leave without him if he didn't react quickly. Before he could move, a flash of green shot before his eyes. An arrow landed with a thud behind him, missing him by inches. Someone was shooting at him. Today was about to become another interesting day.

Racing faster than he thought possible, Penner rushed towards the open door of the cabin. Another arrow flew by him, tearing his pant leg. He leapt into the ship and an arrow landed in the door, plunging deep into the wood.

He grunted and gripped tight onto the wall as Cassandra dragged the remaining ties out of the ground and began to rapidly ascend. The ship shifted forwards and Penner was flung to the bottom of the stairs. Chess appeared at the top of the stairs and raised his hand.

"Stay!" Chess commanded. Penner froze as Chess ducked. An arrow shot high above them. A flash of green struck inches from his face. He yelped and leapt backwards as Fred raced past him. She cranked levers and turned a wheel, and steam poured out of the ship.

"Cassandra doesn't handle quick takeoff well. She's not built for speed, she's built for endurance," Fred called out.

"Let's just hope she's fast enough to outrun them!" Chess exclaimed.

"What's happening? Who are they?" Penner pried himself off the wall.

"Got another incoming!" Chess yelled out, and Fred raced up the stairs. Penner was frozen. People were shooting at him. He had never been shot at before. Especially not with arrows. As he stood, Chess came to the top of the stairs and yelled down at him. "Aren't you forgetting something?"

He grit his teeth as another arrow flashed by them-his one flying close enough to catch the tip of Chess's shirt.

The Tome.

Penner had forgotten about the Tome. He rushed over to where he knew it was and pulled off the clothes that had fallen on it. He wasn't sure why Chess was so adamant about it, especially at a time like this.

He grabbed a shirt to wrap the book up with, but when he looked at the book, he felt something whisper in his head, "Open me."

The voice was eerie and gentle, like a long-tongued man licking his brain. He turned to see if there was someone behind him, but he was alone. He was unsure where the voice was coming from, but the more he stared at the book, the louder the voice became.

"Open me!" the voice insisted, but with a quick motion, he leapt at it, and wrapped it up in the shirt.

"Not happening," he said, more to himself than the book, but he hoped the book had heard.

He stood up and ran towards the deck when a large hook smashed through one of the windows. Glass and splinters showered the room.

Covering his eyes, he felt debris bounce off him. When he opened his eyes, he could see the harpoon digging into the wall. His stomach dropped as he crept over to it. He raced to the window, careful to avoid the detritus, and saw a massive man climbing up a rope that tailed off the hook's end.

The man was strong, launching himself up the rope several feet at a time. Penner grasped the hook and tried to dislodge it, but couldn't. He pulled and pushed against it, but whatever they had used to launch it had firmly lodged it in the side of the wall. The man was climbing fast; he knew that time was short. Thinking quickly, he looked at the rope. There was still about twenty feet of space between him and the man. Seeing no other option, he grabbed a large, jagged chunk of glass and began to saw the rope.

It was not as effective as a machete, it worked well enough. Though the jagged glass dug into his hand, he began slashing at the rope like a wild man. He sawed at it, and the man below struggled and nearly fell. Unfortunately, he caught himself and tightened his grip. He glared up at Penner. The beast of a man had blue eyes that looked afraid. Penner gulped. Could he really cut the rope? They were close to eighty feet above the trees, and the fall would likely kill the man. Penner felt his hands begin to tremble. The glass was cutting deeper into his palm. The blood began to run.

The man grunted and his fear dissipated. With newfound resolve, he leapt up the rope at a rapid pace. Penner's body reacted by itself. He quickly dug the shard into what was left of the rope and cut at it as fast as he could. He chopped at it, but the man was climbing faster. Inches from the ledge, Penner severed the rope and time stood still. The climber's eyes went wide as he reached up for the rope, only to have the final piece slip away from him. But the man managed to catch the side of the window. The wooden planks plunged into his hand as he threw his body up onto the anchor only a few feet from him. Penner looked up at the man and felt his stomach sink. He didn't know what he'd do, but he feared the worst.

The man was about to leap into the room when his arm slapped to his neck. He winced as a small emerald emerged from between his fingers—the small spider maneuvering expertly away from danger. The man staggered, and Penner took the moment to throw his shoulder into the man's chest. The man careened backwards. It was only a second, but it worked. The man slipped and staggered backwards through the window and began to plummet to the ground. Penner didn't want to look, but couldn't help it. As the man fell, he threw open the black robes that hugged his shoulders. His descent slowed, but whether it would be enough to save his life was unknown. A glint of green distracted him as the spider crawled back to its web.

Before he could relax, another harpoon was fired out of the forest. A barrage of arrows followed. One by one, he could hear them bounce off of the hull. Two of them burst through the hole in the wall, and Penner ran back above deck. He couldn't stay here. He did what he had come to do, clutching the Tome in his hands before stuffing it in his shirt.

With the book secure, he raced up to the deck, where three strange men were circling. They were tall and solid, clothed in black and golden symbols.

As he ran up, one man turned to him and raised a long sword over his head. As the man lifted his hand, a smaller hand reached up and grabbed his wrist. Chess appeared from behind the man and slammed their arms down with a sickening snap. The man's face contorted as he let out a scream that echoed across the ship.

The man spun around and lunged at Chess. He grabbed Chess by the shoulders and tried to push him back, but Chess ducked and the man toppled over. Straightening his legs, he launched the man over his back. His massive frame slammed into the mast with a crunch, and he slumped to the deck. Standing back up, another of the men appeared behind Chess and tried to choke him out. Penner stepped forward and flung his fist directly at them. Chess ducked at the perfect time and Penner felt a snap. The sharp stab of pain in his fist made him wonder whether he'd broken his fist or the man's face.

The second man staggered backwards and Chess ushered Penner behind him. He lunged at them again, but this time Chess kicked him in the chest, and he collapsed. The third man jumped between them and pushed Penner back against the railing. Chess wasn't fast enough to react, and the man grabbed him and threw him against the rail. Chess collapsed on the ground, sliding to the edge of the ship. Penner went to save him, but the man gripped him, and for a moment eyed his shirt.

Looking down, Penner realised how obviously the Tome stood out. With his gloved hand, the man reached for it, and Penner retreated. Just as he was sure the man would grab it from him, Fred swung in on a rope. She grabbed Penner by the chest and pulled him towards Chess. As she did, another man in black fell from the mast above them and slammed into the man pursuing him. Using her swing as momentum, Penner launched himself to Chess and pulled him back from the edge as two more men climbed over the edge. Penner cursed.

One of them sprung up behind Fred and wrapped his arms around her. She struggled for a minute, but with a shove of her elbow into his groin, he doubled over in pain. Freeing herself, she kicked him to the side like she was disposing of garbage. The man tried to grab onto something, but Fred grabbed a cup and threw it at his face. It shattered, and the man slid over the side.

"Damn. I liked that cup."

Before the final man could even get on deck, Chess gripped him by the throat. He yelled, and the man went limp as Chess lifted him over his head and threw him onto the deck. The man skittered backwards like a spider trying to hide.

"What do you want?" Chess bellowed. The man hesitated before trying to launch a small dart at them. Chess caught it in the air and turned it around, plunging it into the man's chest. He went limp.

Suddenly, the ship lurched to starboard. Everyone staggered, and Penner's knees smashed into the floor. All three of them turned to the wheel to see one of the robed men attempting to destroy the wheel with a hatchet.

Fred yelled, so loudly Cassandra shook, "Don't you dare touch my ship!"

She slammed down on a loose plank. It launched a small sword into the air. Grabbing it from mid-air, she launched it directly at the man's face. The man dodged it, but stepped into a lasso of rope at his feet. She took a small knife from her belt and cut a rope above her, causing the rope around his foot to constrict like a snake. His foot flew over his head as his head collided with the wheel with a strong thud. The rope dragged the man over to her, and he dangled in front of her. She made a fist and pummeled the man in the face. He went limp, dropping several weapons to the ground. Fred rubbed her knuckles.

"No one touches Cassandra without my permission. Why don't we make him our new anchor?" She grabbed the rope and hogtied his limp body. Despite the fact that he was larger and heavier than her, she moved him without effort. Penner had never seen how strong Fred was. In seconds she'd secured the hands and legs, and then tied the rope to the mast. For a moment, Penner wondered why he felt a mild tinge of jealousy for the man.

As she was tying the man up, Chess walked over to Penner and helped him stand. Once standing, they embraced, and Chess rubbed his back.

"You okay?" Fred asked as they pulled apart.

"I'm fine. Is he—" Penner pointed to the man. Fred shrugged.

"I'm sure he'll survive. I was thinking of pushing him overboard and letting him dangle for a while."

"Are you torturing him for information or—" Penner began.

"Honestly, that's just for him touching the ship." She crossed her arms. "What's up with your shirt?"

"I got the book, Penner said as he reached into his shirt to retrieve it. However, in all the excitement the shirt he'd used to wrap it had fallen away. He reached in to grab the book and pulled it out, only to discover that there was nothing preventing him from touching the cover.

"Open me," it called to him.

For a moment every light intensified. The world blurred as everything began to glow, and the sky was on fire. The place where his hand gripped the book began to burn like a righteous flame. He breathed, feeling the air pour into him like water.

He watched as Chess reached for the book, but he looked very different. His body was glowing. His skin bounced light and colours at wild angles His eyes glowed, and the book was on fire. It filled Penner's ears with a screaming voice that boomed around his brain. "Open me!"

Then it was over. With a swift motion, Chess grabbed the book and pulled it away. Shocked by what had just happened, Penner stumbled backwards. He turned to Chess and then looked back at the book. "What was that?"

"I told you not to touch it."

"That is what you've been reading?" Penner bit his lip.

"You weren't supposed to touch it."

"What the hell is going on, Chess? The book was speaking to me! What the—"

His thought was cut short when a flash of green appeared, and Penner felt a deep pain in his chest. There was a cracking sound, and he felt like he'd been flattened. A strong force knocked him onto his back, and he looked down to see a large arrow sticking out of his chest. He felt a sticky warm liquid fill his chest, but couldn't do anything. His body was frozen and still. The world grew cold and dark, and Chess gripped him behind his neck. There was a sound like a cannon, and Fred gripped her sword and rushed out of sight. The noises were getting quieter as everything began to turn grey.

"Don't pass out, Penner! Don't pass out." The voice sounded far away, and soon he couldn't hear anything. He kept his eyes focused on Chess as long as he could. He knew something was wrong, but he couldn't figure out what. Everything was so distant and strange. Soon there was nothing except echoes. Then silence. The world went black.

And then there was nothing.

And then there was something else.

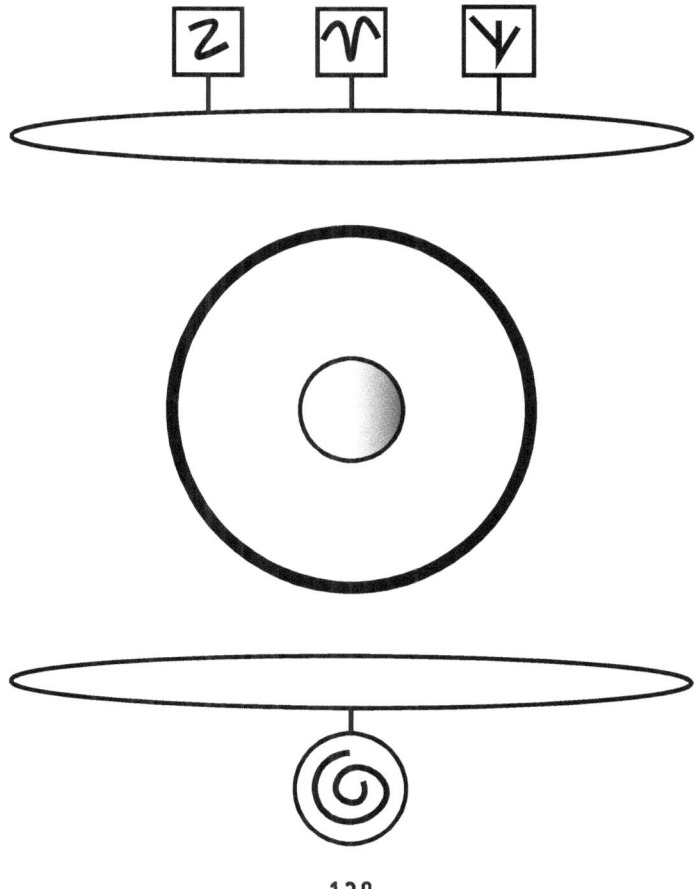

It was faint at first. A gentle hum in his ear getting louder. Penner felt nothing, but the sound was becoming clearer. It was music.

The sound of an orchestra filled his ears. Dozens of instruments playing in perfect unison. He could feel the music filling his soul with warmth. A feeling of comfort surrounded him, and he could feel his body slowly becoming warmer. Soon, he became aware of his body and realised he was sitting in a plush, beautiful chair that smelled like vanilla.

He opened his eyes and saw he was in Raina's study.

He was sitting in the beautiful red chair, which felt better than he'd imagined. He scanned the room, which was just as luxurious and beautiful as he'd remembered. His eyes danced around the room before settling on the massive fireplace that roared beside him. He felt drawn to it and walked over to get a better look. Shapes appeared in the flames before fading away and dying back into shadows. Shapes of people, animals, and cities, and then an arrow which formed above the flames. It hovered for a moment, before blasting from the fireplace and disappearing as it collided with his chest. His hands reacted as if he was putting out a fire as he patted his chest. To his surprise, there was no heat, no arrow. No pain. Then he realised there was no feeling at all. He breathed a sigh of relief as a puff of smoke slid from his mouth.

"You're fine, Penner," a warm voice cooed. For the first time, he turned to see Raina sitting in the other chair, but her hair was blocking her face.

"Is this a dream? Where am I?" he asked as he returned to his chair.

"Somewhere. You're with me."

Penner scanned the room.

"Chess?"

"Is not." Raina held out her hand and offered Penner a glass. He didn't recognise the beverage in it, but it smelled expensive. "It's just you and me, for a moment."

He accepted the drink. "Wh-what am I doing here?"

"You're fighting for your life." She smiled at him. "Best get comfortable."

"What?"

"Don't worry. You have every hope of surviving. You just need to relax, because we have some things to discuss."

"Like what?"

"Why not start at the beginning?" she purred. "Are you a man who fears death?"

"Doesn't everyone?"

"We only fear what we don't understand. What do you know about death?"

"I have seen enough of it to know I don't like it." Penner took a sip.

Wherever he was, at least he still had taste. The drink was rich and fruity and luxurious. It tasted like silk felt. "I know that I will see more of it in time."

"In time, yes." She leaned forwards, the shadows on her face resembling a skull. "Death is hard on all of us. The final goodbye. Being robbed of everything you could have had. The final chapter that closes the book on our lives."

"A tad dramatic, aren't we?" Penner asked.

"I'm an actress. It comes with the territory." She brushed her hair behind her ear and looked like herself again. "Death is cruel and unfeeling, but fair. It comes to everyone despite how you lived. It is, in essence, the great equaliser, but what do you think happens to the soul when we die?"

Penner paused. "Well, the Temples say we live on. That our soul passes through time and space to become another, until eventually we have lived every life. One Soul that binds the universe in a loop of past, present, and future lives. Everyone is everything at different times and points."

"That doesn't answer my question. What do you think happens?"

"I suppose we die," Penner said. "I don't care what happens after that."

"Do you ever think about it?"

"I try not to. My knowledge on the subject is limited by my lifespan."

"So, right now, as you lay dying, I ask you one simple question: what do you live for?" Her face was illuminated for the first time. The light from the fireplace danced across her face. Despite this, all he could see was her eyes. Two beautiful eyes full of energy, and he could feel the answer burning inside of him.

"Chess." He blinked and could see Chess reflected in her eyes. As if he was staring back at him. "I love him."

"We know that." She smirked as her face began to fall back into shadow. "The universe chose him for a good reason. But this time there is something wrong with the picture."

"The universe chose him?" Penner asked. On some level, this made sense. Everything had changed that night, and the only explanation was that he could not explain it. Something had been driving their destiny, and now it had led them here. She didn't seem to acknowledge his question. They both knew she didn't have to. The answer was too big to deny it any longer. "I am not a man of the faith. These beliefs are—" He paused. "The stories can't be true. The world can't be the way the temples make it out to be."

"There is some truth in every story. But right now, there is too much to tell you and not enough time. The journey that Chess is on is a one-way trip. You know what the end is supposed to be."

Penner frowned. "I suspected, but—"

"Every year, a sacrifice is demanded so that the Gods may be satisfied. This time, however, something is wrong. They're telling you things. They're revealing secrets to you that you should not be privy to. Because of this, people are coming after you two. Actively working against you both to make it harder. They're sending false prophets, and they do not want any of you to survive. You must be careful, Penner. Take care of him, because I think the rules of the sacrifice have changed, and you both must be wary of what's to come."

Penner wanted to ask more questions, but his throat felt like it was full of water. He could feel himself slipping back into the darkness.

"Your love will protect you. And if you two are wise, maybe it will save you both."

The smell of fresh-baked bread was the first thing he noticed when opened his eyes. The second thing to hit him was the intense pain that radiated from his shoulder. Penner was aware of every painful heartbeat that thumped through his chest and had to bite his lip.

Despite the pain, his chest itched like crazy. He tried to scratch at it, but his hands were restrained. Several ropes tied him to a wooden slab. He pulled against the restraints, but the effort just sent waves of pain coursing through him. At least he was still in the ship, and even better, it wasn't moving. Around him were broken windows and claw marks where he assumed those brutes had forced their way on board. The battle looked like it had been epic. Shame he had missed it.

He tried to yell, but no sound came out. His throat was raw and scratchy and when he coughed, he could taste coppery blood in his throat.

He blinked and noticed a small, familiar shape fluttering into view. A flash of green as the emerald spider sat in a web in the middle of a broken window. At least it was okay.

"You're awake." Penner felt a hand slide into his. He hadn't even noticed Chess sitting beside him and squeezed his hand. Though his body felt numb, he could feel heat radiating off him. It felt like it was filling his body with new life. Penner took the moment and felt Chess's warm lips lock onto his. "You beautiful idiot."

"What happened?"

"You got shot," Chess said. "The raiders tried to get on board for a while, but we managed to outrun them. We were lucky. You're very lucky."

"Because I got shot?" Penner coughed.

"Because you had this in your vest pocket," Chess said with a smile. He pulled out the small wooden block that Penner had received from the nameless monk, or at least what was left of it. The piece had splintered in half, with a large gash in the center where it had been struck from the arrow. Penner stared at it before trying to reach out.

"That's—wow." He tried to scratch at his chest, then looked up at Chess. "Can you untie me?"

"I don't know. I might have more fun with you tied up," Chess said with a twinkle, before relenting. With a shrug, he untied his hand and Penner gripped the block. It felt so brittle now. "The arrow missed your heart thanks to this thing. Not enough. Still going to leave a scar," Chess said as he put his hand over the bandage on Penner's chest. Penner smiled at him.

"Well, at least I'm not the only one." Penner ran his free hand over one of the scars on Chess's arm. It had healed but was still bright red, and Chess flinched when it was touched. Despite this, Penner gripped onto his arm, and Chess leant over and embraced him. "Damn, this thing is itchy."

He attempted to scratch his chest, but Chess stopped him with a kiss. He felt a hot tear on his shoulder.

"I thought I lost you," Chess whispered.

"So, we're even, then. How long have I been out?"

"Three days. We haven't seen the raiders in a while, but we suspect they're following us. Probably not happy about us heading towards holy ground."

"How far away are we?" Penner asked.

"We're closer. Likely there by tomorrow. If we don't have another episode." Chess smiled.

"Good. Do you know what's waiting for us there?"

"I think so. I know bits. Flashes." Penner looked over and saw the book laying on the shelf. He blinked and felt a shiver crawl over him.

"And that?"

"What about it?" Chess responded.

Penner frowned at Chess.

"What is that book, Chess?"

"It's necessary."

"Can you tell me anything about it?" Penner asked.

"Not really. It's hard to explain." Penner squeezed his hand. They looked into each other's eyes and smiled. For a brief moment, everything was peaceful. As Chess leaned in to kiss him again, Penner tried to untie his other arm, but Chess pinned it down with his leg. Chess climbed on top of him with a grin.

"What are you doing?"

Chess winked at him.

"Whatever I want. And I don't think you're in any position to stop me."

I have tasted death and I do not care for it. This is the first time I have been in peril. There are people out there hunting us down. Like animals. The idea is baffling.

I haven't told Chess about the dream, but I suspect he knows. I can't shake her words. This talk of gods. I don't like it. I hate that even a part of that book could be true. But if it is true, what does that mean? How can someone agree with some of the myths, but deny that my attraction to Chess is a problem? In the Temples, it is all or nothing, but the rest of the world doesn't seem to care what the book says.

Fred has proven a strong ally, perhaps even a friend. I believe that I can trust her beyond even what I initially expected.

Where is the truth when there is no clear path?

And this talk of sacrifice. I don't want to think about it, but it makes sense. He's marked for death. Chess is going to die, and I don't understand how to stop it. Raina thinks there is a way.

Maybe Chess does too.

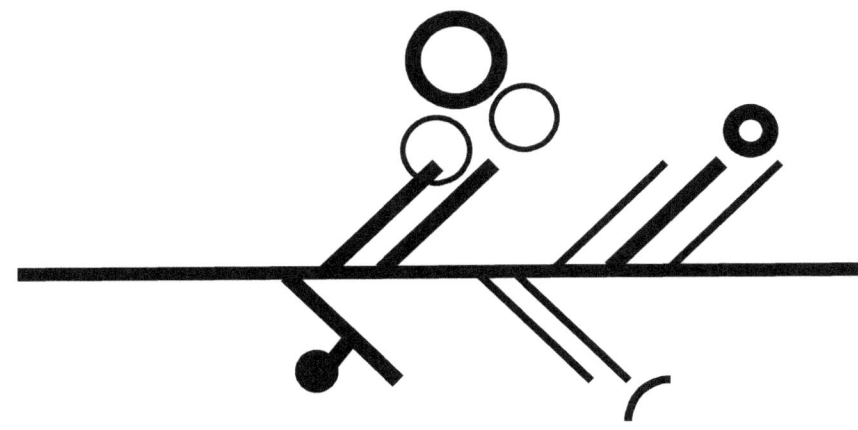

The wound stung like a persistent bug bite. Penner knew he would be fine. The pain was minor, but irritating, and it never seemed to subside.

When he breathed, he could feel it pulsing on his skin. When he closed his eyes, the pain intensified. When he looked at it the pain dulled, but only for as long as he could see it. They constructed a sling from Chess's shirt to prevent him from pulling it, and while it helped, the pain still crept through whenever his arm bounced. Fred insisted that they FIND a place to get it checked and stock up on supplies. Penner protested until Fred bribed him with a stay at an inn. Sleeping in an actual bed would do wonders for the healing process, she claimed. He couldn't refute that logic. And he craved a pillow.

Landing in a field a few hundred feet from the gates of a small township, they began their trek. They walked along a path through the edges of a lush farmland. The smell of crops and dirt filled the air. Turning a corner, he could see the outlines of buildings. A couple dozen houses around a large cathedral that was nestled in the hills. The sound of the cathedral bells echoed through the fields and he felt his stomach drop. Just once, he'd hoped to encounter a city that wasn't centered around the One Soul, but being this close to the mountain, it was unavoidable. It was close enough to loom intimidatingly over the horizon. Maybe this would be their final stop before arriving there.

They were greeted at the gate by an older woman in white. Her hair was blonde and held out of her face by a ribbon. Though she was advanced in years, she appeared healthy and strong from years of working in the field.

"Greetings, travellers, I'm Jadde. Blessing of the One Soul on you," she said, her voice sweet and song-like.

"And on you," Fred said. "We come from the Capital. My companion is injured. We were hoping to seek medicine."

"What happened?" Jadde asked, eyeing Chess up and down. Chess read-justed his vest as Penner stepped forwards, pointing to his shoulder.

Jadde looked shocked, before stuttering, and laughed when she saw him. "Oh. I just assumed from his—"

"I'm fine." Chess smiled through his words. "These two rescued me from certain death many nights ago. I'm almost fully healed, but my friend was hit with an arrow from a pack of Raiders."

"Is he poisoned?" she asked.

"We don't believe so. At least not anymore," Fred said as she peeled open Penner's shirt to reveal the wound. She came close and peered under the bandage. Penner blushed. The woman stooped closer and grimaced.

"It looks bad."

"It's not that bad."

"See those blue veins stemming from the wound? Slow venom. Raiders around here rarely use it, but it can pack a punch. Get him to the Temple. They'll be able to help him there." She smiled. "Can't imagine what you folks did to anger the lot of them. They only go after folks who've done something."

"Just unlucky, I guess. This voyage has been a cursed one," Fred said.

"Thank you for your kindness," Chess said as Jadde gripped his arm and peered into his eyes. Chess didn't flinch.

"If you don't mind," she said in a way that gave Chess no choice. She lifted and turned his arm around, studying the wounds.

"Such precise marks," she said. She looked Chess in the eyes and squinted at him. "Done by an animal."

"A very sick animal." They held their gazes for a moment before she smiled at him.

"Best get you folks to the Temple, then. They've got everything you need there. Just around the bend. It's the big building that looks like a Temple. Can't miss it." She laughed. Penner imagined she told that joke to everyone.

"Thank you." Fred nodded to her as they passed by. She gently grabbed Chess by the hand, and the two walked close. Penner bit his lip as he fought a wave of jealousy.

"Just be careful. There's danger in the shadows," she spoke directly to Chess, who nodded. Fred pulled them away and the woman called out, "Be quick. Your friend needs help sooner rather than later."

The path was easy and quick. In minutes, they were at the city entrance. Along the way, set up in the windows of the houses, were a variety of small shops. Some selling small woven items, others selling baked goods and freshly cured meats. For such a small city, they appeared to have enough business to provide for the town. Penner imagined they must get a lot of travelers seeking enlightenment from the mountain. He stared up at it and felt very small. He knew what this mountain represented to the chosen and the holy. A holy space where the veil between their world and the gods' home would be thinnest. A place where people could seek divine inspiration. He hoped he could avoid those people for as long as he could.

To distract him, he tried to admire the wares in the windows, but noticed that Chess was glaring at them. His attention was so captivated by the windows that he didn't notice a pothole and tripped as they were walking.

151

"You okay?" Penner asked as Fred helped him up.

"Fine. All good," Chess said, still looking at the windows.

"What is it?" Penner asked.

"There's something in the windows. It's following us," Chess whispered.

"Like a person? Someone following us? There's no one else on the road."

"So it would seem." He frowned. Penner looked at their reflections, and for a moment saw a shadow suspended above them. It was there for a moment, and as soon as Penner noticed it, it was gone.

"What is that?"

Penner stumbled.

"You okay?" Fred asked. She frowned at Penner. "You don't look good."

Penner turned to the window. He was pale. He felt something twist in his chest. The wound was burning hot as the smell of sizzling flesh filled his nostrils. He cried out as a burst of pain stabbed him. He clutched at the wound and collapsed to his knees. He coughed, and a trickle of blood splattered on the cobblestones.

"Quick, there's the inn. Let's get him inside," Fred said as she scooped his limp body onto her shoulders. Penner tried to keep his balance, but the pain was too sudden. His entire body was on fire, and his stomach felt like it was trying to escape through his throat. His vision went blurry and his breathing became quick. He could feel his heart pounding in his ears as sweat poured out of him.

Entering the inn was a blur.

"We need a room. And a doctor. An apothecary. Anything."
Voices echoed around him, but he couldn't understand them.

Penner caught brief flashes of the space.

The dark, wooden walls and the smell of lavender.

The rough feeling of an old blanket.

The terrible smell erupting from his wound.

The metallic taste in his mouth.

But his clearest memory was being laid on a bed that smelled like vinegar and spit.

It might've been seconds later or hours, but he could hear voices.

"He knew what he was getting himself into," Fred's voice said.

"He didn't," Chess said.

"He's not stupid, Chess."

"Isn't he? Why else would he—he has no idea what we're moving towards. You know where this path should end, but something is wrong. I don't know how to explain it, but—"

"Cross that bridge when it comes. Right now, we should let him rest."

And then, once again, there was darkness. But this time, there was no music. Only the echoes of Chess's voice as the pain in his chest began to dull.

Then, through the darkness he could see the mountain rising in front of him. A blue flame surrounded it as it stretched higher, as a stormy sky began to churn around him. He felt the rain, thick and fat, pelt his skin, drenching him, suffocating him. The wind ripped through him, and in the distance, he could see the outline of two beings wrapped in lightning. On one side, a Raven the size of a planet. On the other, a Snake that looked like it could wrap around the world. Then, rising between them, the shadow of a massive creature with pointed ears. Its teeth were lined with stars and it looked like it was screaming. Or maybe laughing. The noise echoed in his ears.

Penner looked down to see the Tome resting in his hands. He gripped it tight, feeling an energy like fire shoot through his body. His breathing was shallow and heavy. His chest spewed sickly ichor from its wound.

The Tome screamed at him, "Open."

A burning metal smell filled his nose. He held the book, and was about to open it when he looked up.

The massive beast looked crazed and hungry. Though he could only see shadows of its narrow features, it wanted something. Penner could feel its desire. It needed him to succumb. But why?

He looked at the sky, and for a moment the universe opened itself. A galaxy of stars ripped through the darkness and swirled into a familiar shape. He was looking into the eyes of the sky, and they looked like Chess's.

His grip on the book loosened, and he could feel it slide from his fingers. As it passed, the visions ceased, and once again, he was enshrouded in black. he window. He was pale. He felt something twist in his chest. The wound was burning hot as the smell of sizzling flesh filled his nostrils. He cried out as a burst of pain stabbed him. He clutched at the wound and collapsed to his knees. He coughed, and a trickle of blood splattered on the cobblestones.

"Quick, there's the inn. Let's get him inside," Fred said as she scooped his limp body onto her shoulders. Penner tried to keep his balance, but the pain was too sudden. His entire body was on fire, and his stomach felt like it was trying to escape through his throat. His vision went blurry and his breathing became quick. He could feel his heart pounding in his ears as sweat poured out of him.

Entering the inn was a blur.

"We need a room. And a doctor. An apothecary. Anything."

Voices echoed around him, but he couldn't understand them.

Penner caught brief flashes of the space.

The dark, wooden walls and the smell of lavender.

The rough feeling of an old blanket.

The terrible smell erupting from his wound.

The metallic taste in his mouth.

But his clearest memory was being laid on a bed that smelled like vinegar and spit.

It might've been seconds later or hours, but he could hear voices.

"He knew what he was getting himself into," Fred's voice said.

"He didn't," Chess said.

"He's not stupid, Chess."

"Isn't he? Why else would he—he has no idea what we're moving towards. You know where this path should end, but something is wrong. I don't know how to explain it, but—"

"Cross that bridge when it comes. Right now, we should let him rest."

And then, once again, there was darkness. But this time, there was no music. Only the echoes of Chess's voice as the pain in his chest began to dull.

Then, through the darkness he could see the mountain rising in front of him. A blue flame surrounded it as it stretched higher, as a stormy sky began to churn around him. He felt the rain, thick and fat, pelt his skin, drenching him, suffocating him. The wind ripped through him, and in the distance, he could see the outline of two beings wrapped in lightning. On one side, a Raven the size of a planet. On the other, a Snake that looked like it could wrap around the world. Then, rising between them, the shadow of a massive creature with pointed ears. Its teeth were lined with stars and it looked like it was screaming. Or maybe laughing. The noise echoed in his ears.

Penner looked down to see the Tome resting in his hands. He gripped it tight, feeling an energy like fire shoot through his body. His breathing was shallow and heavy. His chest spewed sickly ichor from its wound.

The Tome screamed at him, "Open."

A burning metal smell filled his nose. He held the book, and was about to open it when he looked up.

The massive beast looked crazed and hungry. Though he could only see shadows of its narrow features, it wanted something. Penner could feel its desire. It needed him to succumb. But why?

He looked at the sky, and for a moment the universe opened itself. A galaxy of stars ripped through the darkness and swirled into a familiar shape. He was looking into the eyes of the sky, and they looked like Chess's.

His grip on the book loosened, and he could feel it slide from his fingers. As it passed, the visions ceased, and once again, he was enshrouded in black.

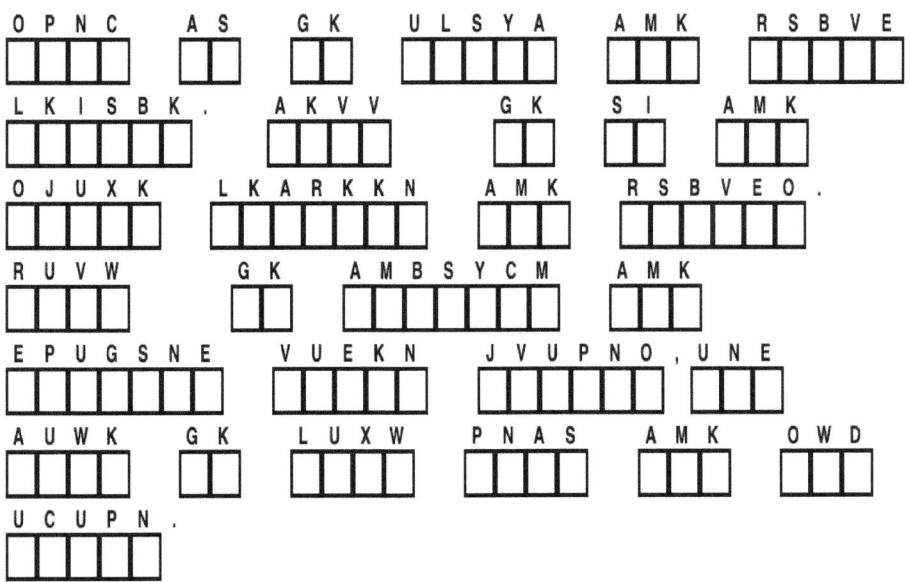

The smell of beef hit his nose and his stomach growled. Penner felt a softness below him as he slowly opened his eyes to see Fred and Chess sitting in the centre of a small room. The big windows were adorned with blue curtains that were tied at either end. The candles provided the room with a warm, lush glow and made it look like a dream. Penner didn't recognise the room, but approved of it.

"Hey," Penner said.

"Oh, thank goodness. He's alive," Fred said. "Neither of you had passed out in a few hours. I was starting to think something was wrong."

"Ow. My feelings," Penner snarked. She offered him a half-smile.

"Hey." Chess grabbed his hand. The contact felt good, but when he squeezed, Penner flinched. "Sorry." Despite a small twinge of pain in his shoulder, Penner felt energised.

"What happened? We were walking and then... here."

"Something about the air here must've triggered the poison in the wound. Could be the air. Might be the sulphur. Might've been that woman at the farm."

"It was the Mountain. Or some kind of thing in the Mountain," Penner said. "I think it's trying to kill me." Chess and Fred looked at each other with a confused look. Penner suddenly felt foolish. "Sorry, I just had a weird dream."

"Hey, it happens. When you reacted, we brought you up here and took care of you. We think the poison is out of you now." Fred gestured to the room.

"It's not bad," Penner said as he suddenly felt a chill down his spine.

"I could get used to having a bed again."

"You okay?" Chess asked as he grabbed his hand.

Penner shrugged. "Just a chill."

"No, it's not. There's something here," Chess said as he left Penner's side to walk to the curtains. Penner sat up and was surprised by how mobile he felt.

"We figure the poison was what was making your wound so unpleasant. But being here probably—"

"I can see the mountain." Chess looked out the window.

"It's hard to miss," Penner said.

"No. I can see the mountain." Chess bit his lip. Penner flung his legs over the side.

"You sure you should be getting up right now?" Fred asked.

"I feel fine," Penner said as he moved his body. Examining the area that felt tender, he poked at his shoulder. It was sore but seemed to have healed well enough. They had done a great job on his stitches. "I'm fine, right?"

"Yes, you're fine. I fed you some cud to detoxify your system as you slept. Should've worked the poison out by now."

"What the hell is cud?" Penner asked.

"Best not to ask," Fred said.

"Can you see it?" Chess asked as he turned back to them.

"The wound?"

"No. It. The thing that's been following us."

Penner and Fred both looked at each other.

"Well, I've been unconscious, so no?" Fred grabbed a piece of fabric and helped Penner wrap his arm in a sling. Chess continued to glare out the window. "You feeling okay, Chess?"

"Stop. It's right here. I think—I think I can—" His voice trailed off.

"What do you think? What are you—" Penner began to ask, but was interrupted.

"I see it!"

He jumped up so fast Fred and Penner were both startled. Then, in a flurry, he leapt out the window. Glass shattered over the street below them as Chess disappeared. A blast of cold air ripped through the room. So much for keeping a low profile.

"Chess!" Penner yelled as he leapt towards the window. He ignored the pain in his shoulder as he raced to it.

Moving slow was fine, but when he ran the pain throbbed. He suppressed it. He had to make sure Chess was okay. For all he knew, Chess could've jumped out of a ten-story building. He wasn't sure how high up they were, but when he approached the window and realised they were at least thirty feet up, he feared the worst. He peered out of the remnants of the window, but Chess wasn't on the ground. He was racing along a drainage pipe that hung around the rooftop. As soon as he saw Chess, he disappeared around the corner. He was running on a skinny beam, and Penner was amazed he didn't slip off. Penner turned to Fred, who appeared just as shocked as him.

"What the hell is he doing?" she asked.

"Why are you asking me?" Penner snapped. "Ow." He winced. The yelling made his wound pulse.

"Where is he going?" they asked in unison.

Penner whipped back to her,

"How the hell should I know? He's your—" Fred shook her head and took a breath. Penner attempted a burst towards the door, but Fred grabbed him.

"Stop. Penner."

"What?" he snapped.

"Pants," she said calmly.

Penner paused and looked down. His cheeks flushed.

He looked down and tried to find his pants, but couldn't. "Where are they?"

Fred offered him a pair. Penner cursed and threw them on. He wondered who the pants belonged to, but didn't question it further. With Fred close behind him, they raced down the stairs and were soon in the street.

Something was wrong. The hairs on the back of his neck rose. The road was quiet, especially considering how loud Chess had been when he burst out of the room. Glass crunched under his shoes, which he realised were on the wrong feet, and he scanned the buildings. They seemed taller from here. Perhaps this city wasn't as small as he'd thought it was. As he scanned, he could feel a strange sensation gathering around him. He felt nervous, and he couldn't shake the thought that something was watching them. His shoulder thumped, sending a shock of pain through his body. It felt like he'd been stabbed with a needle. He gripped his shoulder, trying to steady it, biting his lip to suppress the pain so he could move.

"I don't see him."

"Well, we know he went this way. Keep your eyes open," Fred said as she began to rush down the street. Penner dashed ahead, but Fred grabbed him by the collar and slowed him down. "But be careful."

"It's too late for caution," Penner spat. "We need to find Chess and get him back here."

"Don't forget that if they catch us, we could be detained. I don't feel like being questioned tonight."

"All the more reason to be quick about it." Then he saw it. "Think he went to the Temple?"

"Seems a safe bet. We keep getting drawn to these places."

"Let's just hope they're asleep."

They moved quickly, the lamp posts guiding the way. They cast an eerie glow like running through a haze. Penner felt the pain pounding through his body, and yelped when a shadow crossed their path. They tried to stop, but it was too late and they were seen. A man in a long black coat and large hat held his hand up for them to stop. Fred cursed.

"Where are you going?" Penner expected the man to be angry, but his voice was quiet and calm. He sounded concerned. "You folks are out after the curfew. Is everything alright?"

"Our friend, he's lost. We're searching for him. Trying to get him back to safety," Fred said. "Have you seen a man? About this tall? Strong stature? A couple scars on him?"

"You two are the only folks who I've seen out in hours. I'm just extinguishing the lights down the path here and—"

"If you're extinguishing the lights, why are they all on?" Fred asked.

"And why are they blue?" Penner nodded to the path.

The man looked at him, confused, and turned. He scratched his head. The entire row was glowing a brilliant blue as the lanterns flickered to life one by one.

"I didn't do that," the man said, looking at his lantern snuffer with a confused look.

"He must be down there," Fred whispered. Penner nodded.

"Witchcraft." The colour in the man's face drained and he looked at Fred and Penner with wide eyes. "I always read about this, but I've never seen anything like this!"

Penner could feel something knot in his stomach. Something was wrong. Chess was in danger.

"We need to help him."

"You can't go in there! It's not safe! I'll call the priests." The man tried to stop them. "Y'all best get back to where you were."

"We have to help our friend," Penner said.

"I can't in good conscience let you go. The One Soul will never forgive me if I let strangers get hurt."

"Come on, Penner. I don't like this," Fred said as she brushed past the man and began to jog down the road. Penner nodded towards the gentleman, who stood with his mouth agape in horror. He tried to keep pace with Fred but couldn't. The jogging rustled him too much, but he could still hear and see Fred in front of him. As he moved, the air became thick with mist. The lanterns burned from blue to red the closer they got.

"What is going on?" Penner asked.

"I don't know, but I don't like it," Fred said.

"It looks like blood," Penner said.

The flames went from blue to red. They intensified with each step. Somewhere behind them, the man called out to them. Or was he beside them? The fog made it hard to tell. Penner wasn't sure if he was calling for them to get away, or if he was threatening them, his voice was drowned out by the roar of the flames. All around them Penner could hear confusion as doors opened and people shuffled into the streets. He wasn't sure what they'd find, but he had to find Chess. He didn't care if he was in pain, he just had to be there.

The mist thinned out as they arrived at a plaza. Behind him the town, in front of him the cathedral that dwarfed the sky. Penner gasped when he saw it. Opulent and beautiful in its design, it was welcoming and threatening. It looked so much bigger up close. He stepped onto the plaza and felt a thousand eyes on him. He could feel his blood pounding in his skull. His eyes darted around, desperate to find some sign of Chess. He had to make sure he was okay. He scanned the Temple but found nothing. The flames around them intensified, and he felt a pull on his shoulder. He froze and turned to see Fred behind him. Her grip was tough and felt like she was pressing a hook into his tender flesh and twisting it. She pointed across the plaza and he held his breath.

There was Chess, standing like a statue in the middle of a strange steam that billowed around him. Small sparks of red-hot flame burst into life, as if he was standing on embers. He looked strong and powerful, but also terrible. Penner had never seen him so intense. The look on his face was contorted in pain. He wanted to help—but there was nothing he could do. Fred's grip on his shoulder kept him paralysed.

There was a thunderclap as the Temple doors closed, and a man in white strode out to face Chess. He took a few steps out onto the plaza and raised his chin. His cheek was red, as if he'd been hit. Chess had a dribble of blood falling from his lip. It looked like the two had been sparring, but Chess looked worse for wear. The man in white robes looked like a ghost, and Chess looked determined to eliminate him.

Without saying anything, Chess held his hands out to his sides. The burning fires that surrounded them began to grow bigger and brighter, intensifying as his fingers stretched. A wind swept over them, and Penner bent to keep his balance. The flames blazed until the entire plaza was blinding light. Penner had no idea whether Chess was doing this, or whether the man in white was responsible. Either way, it was terrifying.

Suddenly the earth shuddered. The ground felt like it was tilting. His balance was thrown off, forcing him and Fred to use each other for balance.

"What the hell is going on?"

"I have no idea," Fred said. "Just stay back until we can make a move."

The world was warping. Penner felt weak as he watched Chess and the man circling around each other, as the world distorted and stretched. The cathedral swayed like it was alive. The ground rippled, sending waves across the plaza. Penner tried to focus, but everything was spinning. He had no idea what was real right now and what wasn't.

The man stood at the base of the cathedral as it began to bloat and sway like branches in the wind. The spire elongated and twisted, becoming tall and thin. Penner stood there, stunned, and watched the building grow to look like a scorpion tail. The imposing spire held above the building as the man stood at its base, his arm held high above him.

"What is happening?" Penner asked under his breath. He clenched hard onto Fred's arm, trying to focus.

Fires swirled and danced around Chess. The lamps stretched out their flames and surrounded Chess in a wall of fire. They formed a shell around him, which blazed so hot Penner felt like it was suffocating him. The world warped and melted around him.

Then Penner blinked, and the world returned to normality. Chess wasn't bathed in flames and the building hadn't turned into a giant scorpion. The man in white stood with his arm up as Chess yelled at him. Chess still looked battered, as if he'd tried to enter the building multiple times.

"Let me pass!" Chess exclaimed.

"None may enter but the blessed!" the man screamed.

"It's in there. If you don't let me in, I'll have to draw it out!"

"What you are asking is against everything we stand for. Leave this town or you shall pay with your life!" The man whipped out a dagger and held it above him.

"So much for our rest," Fred whispered. Penner gripped at his chest. He shook himself, and just as soon as everything seemed to calm down, the pulsing sensation in his chest intensified. With a guttural yell, Chess raced towards the building and the man in white bent his legs.

Another blink, and Chess was now a bird the size of the plaza, drenched in flames as the building reared back its tail, preparing to strike. His wings were so hot the ground began to melt like butter. Each step sent small explosions ricocheting around them. The world became warped and crazed as the doors of the cathedral elongated, forming massive teeth that opened to consume him.

"What do you see?" Fred asked.

"Something impossible." Penner rubbed his forehead, trying to make the images go away. In another blink, Penner watched everything return to normal again.

He couldn't be sure what he saw was real, but he watched the man grab Chess by the arm. Chess tried to sidestep him to enter the cathedral, but the man slashed at him with his knife. Dodging with less than millimeters between them, for a second it looked like Chess would get into the building. But then the man pulled back on Chess's arm and, with a quick thrust, the man flipped him over his shoulder. Chess flew through the air and collided with the doors of the cathedral. Before he could fall to his knees, the man grabbed Chess by the shirt and flung him down the stairs. Chess's limp body tumbled down before landing with a thud.

"You dare to defile this holy place, Abomination!" the man bellowed.

Penner wanted to rush to Chess's side, but Fred held his arm and gripped tight.

"Don't. There is nothing you can do to help right now."

"I have to try."

"No. You have to wait. When the time is right, we get him out. I doubt they'll want us to stick around after this. We need to make a break for Cassandra as soon as we can. I don't think they'll take kindly to us after this."

She motioned her chin to the street behind him. He hadn't noticed, but people were filing out of their houses. There were dozens of people in the streets behind them: men, women and children alike. More of them were emerging from the mist, and he could only wonder how many more there were. He bit his lip as the people surrounded them. Penner's fists began to shake. Everything was telling him to help. He wasn't sure how long he could resist.

"There is something—" Chess coughed up blood. How many attempts to get in had he made? He wiped his mouth as he stood up. "—in there that I need."

"There is nothing that you need! You think you can enter without being pure?"

"No one is pure." Chess raised his hands as if preparing to fight the man.

The priest shook his head. Chess looked weak and was barely standing on his feet. He didn't stand a chance.

"You talk nonsense. You must go." The priest descended the stairs until he was standing next to Chess. Sluggish, Chess launched a punch at him, but the man easily dodged it and Chess fell to his knees.

"I'm not leaving without it. This is your last chance to let me in."

The priest laughed. He circled around Chess and grabbed him by the hair. He pulled it back, exposing his throat. Chess tried to fight back, but his struggles were futile by this point. The man almost looked like he was enjoying it.

"Heresy must be punished. As an example to anyone who dares to defy the words of the One Soul! This defiler has attempted to reach beyond his place, and now we must send him back to the depths he has slithered from!"

The man raised his knife triumphantly. It hung in the air to slash Chess's throat, and for a moment, Penner wasn't there. He flashed back to when he watched a Templar execute the one he loved. It was happening again. He felt a tremendous heat erupting inside of him, and then everything stopped. He glared at the man in front of him, and there was a perfect silence as time stopped. Before Fred could stop him, Penner was moving. He wasn't sure what holy fire filled him, but he wasn't in control.

His body moved of its own accord and raced towards Chess.

Faster than he thought he could move, faster than what should have been possible, Penner was standing between the two men. He felt his fist propel out and hit the man in the face. The shock on their faces was tangible. As he staggered backwards, the man loosened his grip on the dagger, which fell from his hand. The blade nicked Penner, but the priest still managed to strike him with enough force to knock him into Chess. The two of them collapsed in a heap, and Penner yelled in pain. He looked down to see that his chest wound had reopened, and blood was slowly beginning to soak through. They locked eyes, and Penner watched as Chess flooded with rage. Chess bolted to his feet as the man continued to yell at them.

"Who are you to defy the sacred?" the man screamed over them. "This punishment is not for you. Do not inter—"

The man's voice cut out and Penner looked up at him. The man had stopped moving. He hung suspended in the air. His body froze as his hand began to claw at his throat in a desperate motion. He opened and closed his mouth like a fish out of water. His eyes bulged and he began to turn pale.

Penner pressed his hand to the wound to prevent it from getting worse as he sat up. Looking up, he saw Chess glaring at the man as the flames began to surround him.

"You hurt the man I love," Chess said. His voice was low and angry. His expression was cold and intense. "You speak of the Soul but you know nothing about it. You know nothing of the gods who live beyond our Realm. What you know are fables twisted to serve agendas. But I am different."

The priest began to float, hovering above the ground. His feet kicked at the air below him. Chess raised his hand, his fingers hooked like he was holding onto an invisible spear. Penner could feel a tremendous heat radiating off of him as the priest began to float higher.

"I have read the invisible language. I have spoken to the Old Ones. I am what you should fear."

Chess spread his fingers, and in a violent motion, the man's arms spread so quickly that Penner was surprised they didn't fly off his body. Chess slowly opened his fingers further, and the man's hands were stretched to their limits. His body began to shake as his fingers began to snap. They twisted and contorted as Penner heard every bone in the man's hands separate with deafening pops.

The man was screaming in agony, but no sounds escaped from his mouth. Penner felt sick and was staggering onto his feet when he felt hands on his shoulder. He turned and was thankful to see Fred behind him. She looked as scared as he was.

"Time to go," she whispered.

"You are unworthy!" Chess screamed. He was barely audible over the roars of the air. "You do not deserve this place or the worlds that inhabit it!"

The man looked like a puppet, limp and dangling on broken strings. His throat erupted in screams for mercy that echoed around the plaza. Then the screams stopped, only to be followed by the sickening crack of every bone in his hands shattering. He blinked, and the image of Chess and the man changed to a glaring inferno. Each of them being consumed in flames. It was like he was being pierced by a harpoon of light. Chess had an expression of rage that made it hard to recognise him.

"You will pay!" Chess bellowed as his entire body became a black flame.

Chess twitched his hand, and the man was slammed back into the Temple doors. His large hood fell off his head, revealing a pale, skinny man. His terrified expression amplified. He looked like a horrified child.

Penner couldn't take it and ran to Chess.

"Stop, Chess! Stop!" he screamed as he grabbed Chess by the shoulders. Instantly the heat dissipated. The flames evaporated as the man dropped to the ground. He writhed like a tortured insect. For a moment, Chess didn't move. He just stood there with his arm outstretched as his incredible rage was replaced with nothing. His eyes went wide. A pathetic whimper escaped from his throat. He began to shake, mouth agape as he watched the priest attempt to writhe away from him. His arm fell to his side, and he turned to face the crowd that had formed around them. They looked stunned, unsure whether to scream and run, or riot. Any second, they could attack the intruder who had tortured the monk in front of their eyes. The fear filled the trio as they looked through the crowd. The gravity of what had just happened filled him. Torturing a holy man in the shadow of the mountain. Abusing him in front of his congregation.

"What have I done?" Chess whispered. He shook as tears filled his eyes. Penner grabbed him by the elbow and tried to pull him through the crowd.

"Let's go," Penner whispered.

"Wait," Chess said as he looked back at the cathedral.

He reached out his hand, and the doors flew open so fast they broke off the hinges. Blasting inwards, they bounced around the inner sanctum, leaving gashes of destruction wherever they touched. There was a scream that carried out of the space. Penner felt a wind whip by him, but it passed before he could figure out what made it. Then Chess took a deep breath and turned to the others.

"To the ship," Fred said softly. Chess nodded.

Looking at the group was frightening. It was the first time Penner paid attention to them. Some looked angry, but most were terrified. Penner slipped his arm under Chess and took a step forward. A few people in the crowd moved to block their way. Others stepped back, looking fearful. Penner held up his hand to block projectiles, but the gesture was enough to spread fear. They tripped over themselves to clear a path. Penner grunted.

Chess felt heavier with each step, and his own wound was dribbling down his chest. Chess looked barely coherent. His breathing was erratic, and he was reduced to a quivering mess.

They moved through the crowd, never letting their eyes off the mob until they were at the edge of the plaza. As soon as they could, Fred shouldered Chess, and the three ran as fast as they could to the ship. At first, the crowd didn't follow, but soon they began to chase. A few of them followed. Then a few more, until a small gathering was stalking them from a safe distance. As Cassandra came into sight, the crowd became bolder. Voices yelled at them. A rock hurtled through the crowd and hit Penner in the back. Exhausted, they tried to run as fast as they could, but the crowd was closing in fast. They could reach Cassandra in time, but would they be able to get airborne?

Once on board, Chess separated from Fred and sat in the corner. Penner tried to make sure he was okay, but he was catatonic. As the sounds of the mob closed in, Fred finally pulled him away and took them both up to the deck.

"Are you okay?" Fred asked.

"Am I okay? Did you see what happened to him? What happened to -?"

"I know, but are you okay?" Fred asked.

Penner snorted before taking a breath and closing his eyes. He inhaled and mentally scanned his body. Everything was attached, at least.

"I'm fine. Shoulder wound still hurts. Feeling a bit nauseous and dizzy, but I'm probably still a bit poisoned, so that's to be expected, no?" he said, frustrated.

"Good. Start untying," she ordered. Penner nodded and began to untie the ropes that held them down. As he worked, he looked down at Chess and frowned. "Fred, what was that?"

"That was—" she began. "I've never seen anything like that before."

"Not even with Cassius?"

"No," Fred said. "That was different. That was unexplainable." The mumble of the mob was growing louder, and Fred cursed. "Another night launch. In the middle of the mountains, no less."

"What do you need?"

"A miracle, preferably. Just keep untying," she urged. "We don't have much time before they show up."

"How far can we get?"

"It's a cold night and the air in the mountains is thin. We're not going far. I'd give us three or four miles, tops. Let's just hope they don't catch up."

There was a massive lurch as the last of the anchors was hauled up and Cassandra began to float. The glowing light of torches illuminated the woods as it surged forwards. Penner grabbed hold of the side as the ship tried to balance itself without the aid of thermals to keep it afloat. Before the mob could converge on them, Fred steered them into the valley.

Barely clearing the trees, Penner wasn't sure how long they'd be able to keep afloat, but with Fred at the wheel he was surprised by how soft the take-off had been. Under the cover of night, they might be able to escape unscathed. The mood was tense. As the dull roar disappeared into the distance, Penner felt restless. He looked down to where he knew Chess was.

"D-do I go to him?" Penner asked.

"Up to you," Fred said. "I'll keep watch. You still need to get well before we go anywhere. We've had enough close calls on this trip. Don't want you dying now from blood loss."

Penner hesitated. "I think I'd like to stay up here with you for a bit. I just need—I just want to see the stars for a minute."

"Sure," Fred said as she sat on the railing, looking back at the town. If they were being followed, there was no sign of it.

This forest must have been more dense and dangerous than the other ones. The entire city was dark and empty. Penner lay back and looked at the stars. He took a deep breath before closing his eyes, and within seconds, he was asleep.

"The stars are beautiful tonight," Chess said. Penner opened his eyes to see Chess lying beside him. He was staring at the stars and was close enough to touch, but Penner didn't move. It felt like there was more than inches between them.

"Yeah." Penner tried to speak, but his throat was dry. "What—"

"You can ask it."

"Are you okay?" Penner asked.

"I don't know. It was something new," Chess replied.

"It was—" Penner paused. "It was scary."

"I know. It felt different. I could feel something overcome me. I mean—I feel it now. All the time. But it's always been good. Or at least controllable.

But that? That wasn't good. I don't know what made me—" A hot tear shot down his cheek. "I've never done that before. I've never had to or felt the need to—but when he hit you, I—"

"I'm sure it was nothing."

"The whole world went white, and I felt this rage," Chess exhaled.

"Maybe it was just a one-time thing."

"I don't think it was. I think the whole thing was planned," Chess said. "That thing that was following us. The thing in the windows? I think it's been following us since the arrow. I think it might even have been the arrow. What if it was the poison? What if it was the point of our whole ambush? What if it's following us now?"

"That doesn't make sense."

"We're up against something that doesn't make sense, Penner. What if I go too far next time? What if I go so far that there's no way back?"

"You're not going to get like that. Not again."

"You don't know that." Chess paused. "When it came over me, I felt it. Like, really felt it. Like, there's a part of me that knows it on a personal level. I think I know why we're going to the mountain."

"Why?"

"You're not going to like it."

"Try me." Penner slowly moved his hand over to Chess's and gripped tight. Their fingers intertwined, and Penner kissed them one by one, starting from the pinky. Chess returned the kiss, and for a moment everything was warm. The world around them melted, and it was just them lying beside each other.

"I think it was Mobo." Penner paused. He knew he should balk at the idea of an elder God looking down on them, but because of what he'd seen, he didn't argue. At least, not yet.

174

"Mobo. The Raccoon Elder God. One of the Divine Three?"

"Don't laugh."

"I'm not. I'm fine. It's—" He flickered back for a moment and was once again standing in front of the massive beast made of thunder and darkness. The idea didn't seem silly at all. It was starting to feel deadly serious. "I believe you." Chess clung to him as he sat up. He looked at the stars and suddenly felt like they were watching him. "Whatever it is, whatever is going on, I'm here."

"I was so afraid I'd lose you. Everything just went dark and I—" Chess paused. "If it happens again, I—"

"It won't." Penner glared up at the heavens. "We won't let it."

Throughout his life, Penner had developed a variety of skills that had served him well. Hunting was never one of them. He had tried many times when he was younger, but had come up short. Fred, however, was the best hunter he'd ever seen; gifted with bows, knives, and traps, he followed her through the fields, carrying two animal carcasses on his shoulder as she pulled back her bow and easily netted a third.

"Impressive."

She picked up a slain rabbit and frowned. "Smaller than I expected."

"Still a good shot," Penner replied. Fred smirked at him. She threw the body at his feet and Penner tied it up. She looked proud.

"Three should be enough for the week. Not much meat to be found in the mountains. Unless you catch a goat or two."

"Have you ever done that?"

"What do you think?" Her smile was his answer. Penner looked up to the mountain. Every time he looked at it, it looked bigger.

"So we're going to be getting there soon, then?" Penner asked.

"I'd say tonight," she said. "Are you ready?"

"I wish. I have no idea what I should be ready for. Do you?"

"No idea. Anything could happen. After these past few days, and with the volatility of the mountain—" She looked over to him and wiped off her blade.

"What do you mean?"

"This mountain is said to be the birthplace of the world. Some even called it Mobo's Mountain." She chuckled to herself, but just hearing the name Mobo made Penner nervous. Her wipe was deliberate and slow. Making sure to soak up every drop of blood. "Maybe it is."

"What did you and Cassius do when you got here?"

"We didn't come here. We went south. In the middle of the revolts and the slave rebellion. In the middle of the power vacuum when the royal family was overthrown. It was the last place on earth anyone would want to go, but we dove in head first."

"And what happened?" Fred didn't say anything. "To Cassius. What happened to Cassius?"

"With Cassius, it was different. He was unpredictable, but he never did anything like—" She motioned with her hand. "Well, he never lost himself in power. He kept doing things that didn't make sense, and there were moments when I didn't even recognise him, but he never did anything that big. He was ordinary the entire time, but that was a long way from here. He lost himself in his mind, not in bending the world to his will. Maybe the powers here are stronger—angrier? I don't know what to warn you about, or what you should be expecting, but it's good that you're here. Had I not been there for Cassius,

I'm not sure he would have made it as far as he did."

"What happened?" Penner asked. "Who was he? I don't really know anything about your journey."

Fred paused and flashed him a smile. "I think it's better that way."

"But there must be something," he said. She took her bow and lifted it as she looked into his eyes. He was worried she'd fire an arrow directly into his face. "Fred?"

With incredible reflexes, she lifted the bow up and let an arrow fly into the tree canopy. A few seconds later, a small brown bird fell from the branches, and she casually walked over to retrieve her arrow.

"I was the daughter of a Judge," she began. "He let my mother run a bakery that we worked out of, when we wanted to. One day I met Cassius, and from there the story was typical. We were arranged to be married, and he was—" Her face lit up as she spoke. "He was a beautiful man with a good heart. Halfway through our engagement, he came to my house in the middle of the night, raving like a lunatic. I couldn't understand what he was saying, but he begged me to come with him. So, I did. And then everything changed." She hacked off a branch with her knife. "I do mean everything. My life changed in a night, and I traded in a calm life in the village for a new one in the clouds." She snapped a branch off with an angry crack.

"Do you regret it?" Penner asked.

"There are parts I miss. The village in the mountains. Friends. Most of my family," she said with a smile. "But mostly, I just miss him." She pulled the arrow from the bird and slung it over her shoulder.

"So what happened to him?"

"The same thing that happens to all of them." She sighed. "Come. We need to leave before the villagers catch up with us."

"Do you think they're still following us?"

"I'd rather not find out."

The day hung heavy on Penner's shoulders.

If he squinted, he could still see the village in the Mountain's shadow. While no one had sought to attack them yet, their proximity was troubling. He wanted to leave, but the day looked to be against them. What had started as a beautiful morning had descended into a cold and miserable one. Flying was tricky and the clouds around them were thick and wet, causing Cassandra to float slowly, and without the heat to make the steam, their engines were puttering. Fred had assured them it wouldn't be an impossible route, but it wouldn't be an easy one. As the sky churned, Cassandra was battered by the winds. Thankfully Fred knew the sky well enough to avoid the more dangerous zones, but the turbulence was inevitable. The ship would float itself there without everything, but the going was slow and turbulent.

Below deck, Chess hadn't moved much. He was sitting beside the hammock, staring at the spider as it spun another web. By now Penner had expected the web to cover most of the wall, but it mostly contained itself to the makeshift window. He had grown to like that spider. He had named it Micah.

Clutching at his stomach, he made his way down the stairs. Chess didn't look well. His eyes had big dark circles under them, and his skin was unnaturally pale, even for him. He looked more like a goblin than a man.

"Did you eat?" Penner asked.

"As much as I could. I can't taste much right now. It all tastes like ash. Everything burns."

"Need water?"

"It's too wet for water." Chess looked up at Penner. His eyes were bloodshot and wide.

"I can feel it getting closer."

"Feel what?" Penner asked as Chess pointed towards the helm of the ship. "The Mountain?"

"Whatever lies within the Mountain." Chess hung his head and took a breath. "I can feel it, and I don't know what to expect."

"Neither of us does. That's the point of going there, no?"

"I don't know if it's safe."

"Judging by our stops so far, I'd say safe is out the window," Penner said as he gently rubbed Chess's back. "Just breathe. I'm here."

"I'm breathing," Chess said as he curled into Penner—which was hard to do in the hammock.

"Good. Keep it up." Chess nodded and sat up, peering back at the spider again. Penner kissed him gently on the forehead before standing up and stretching. Whenever they spent time in the ship, he could feel knots forming all over his body. The rigidity of the ship made him tense and uneasy. He let out a yawn and walked over to Chess's pack, which was splayed out over the floor in a heap.

He reached down and grabbed it as he shook his head. He couldn't figure out how Chess managed to make such a mess in a short amount of time. Had they been back in their house he probably would have said something, but right now he was at a loss for words.

As he was lifting up Chess's jacket, a book fell out and landed in front of him. Without thinking, he grabbed it, and suddenly felt the air around him turn to smoke. He blinked, and the world was on fire. The air around him was liquid flames that smothered the oxygen out of his body. He tried to inhale, but the sheer force of the heat felt like it was burning his lungs out from the inside. As he looked at the book, amidst the living fire he could see the cover staring at him. On it was a beast peering at him with dark red eyes on a black body. Its shadow, a creature with thousands of arms trailing from its underbelly.

It emerged from nothing and screamed into his head, "Open me!"

The creature opened its mouth with rows of sharpened lightning teeth and sunk its jaws into Penner's skin.

Just as the flames had appeared, in the blink of an eye, it all vanished. The book was just a book, and the world was as it should be. Chess was still sitting, looking out the window at the cold, wet air. But Penner was no longer cold. He could feel a heat burning inside him. He felt the book, which was once again just a collection of ink and paper bound by a soft, silky cover. He gripped it so tight he could feel the spine bending.

"Chess? What is this thing?" he asked. Chess turned around, and as soon as he saw what Penner was holding, he leapt to his feet and tried to snatch it out of his hands. Penner pulled it back, not wanting to let the book out of his hands. He had to grab it tighter.

"What are you doing? Don't hold it!" Chess said, unsuccessfully attempting to slap the book out of his hands again.

"Why not? What is it? What is this thing? What is it doing to you?" Penner felt it, soft and silky in his hands. It felt almost like liquid slowly seeping over his skin. Like gentle blood slowly dribbling down his hands.

An anger bubbled up inside of him. "What is it doing to us?"

"Penner!" Chess yelled. "Put the book down! Now! It's not for you!"

"No? That's because it's all for you! Everything is for you!"

"Put the book down," Chess tried to touch him, but Penner dodged it.

"Why? It's because of this that we're here! That we're flying to who knows where to do who knows what!? Because of this? You're going to die because of this!"

"Stop! Penner!" Chess yelled.

"I'm not losing you Chess! I won't let this—"

"Penner! You're on fire!"

The smell of smoke distracted him as he felt a hot sensation licking at his feet. He looked down to see small flames flickering up his pants. The distraction was enough to pull his attention away for a moment. Chess kicked Penner's hand, smashing his knuckles. With a yelp, Penner let go of the book, which Chess slammed into the wall. Gripping onto his shirt, Chess lunged into Penner. The momentum threw Penner onto his back before he could react. Chess grabbed a satchel at his feet and threw it over Penner's flaming pants.

Having had no time to react, Penner collided hard with the floor, knocking the wind out of him. His vision spun for a moment as the world returned to normal. The heat that was permeating off him began to dissipate, and once he had caught his breath, he massaged his head.

"Ow," Penner moaned as he turned his attention to the book, which had landed beside the door. It was a few inches from him, but the acrid smell was suffocating. It looked unscathed despite the smoke that poured out of the cover.

Carefully, Chess removed the bag from Penner's burnt feet. It looked like he had just walked over hot coals. He could feel the burns, but they weren't bad. Compared to the pain in his chest, they were nothing.

Had Chess not smothered the flames it would have been another story.

"Wh-what happened?"

"I told you not to touch the book."

"But what happened? I only touched it for a moment and—"

"It feeds on fear."

"The book?" Penner sat up. "The book is alive?"

"No. It's not a just book. It's a Tome. They're manuscripts that talk about the mystical things in the world. They're normally there for enlightenment, but this one is different. There's something... wrong with it. There's something connected to the book. It's whatever is connected to me. From what I've gathered, it's Mobo. He's the only one who makes sense. It wants to subvert what's come before, and it needs us to go to the mountain—but the closer we get, the stronger it gets."

"And the more it wants—" Penner said.

"I'm lost, Penner. I know the legends. I know what I'm supposed to do, but this is a lot. I don't want to do what I think I have to. I mean, if they demand sacrifice, then—" Penner frowned. He wished there was something he could do. And then he remembered what Raina had said.

"You won't die, Chess. I won't let you."

"I don't think you get much of a choice here."

"Like hell I don't," Penner said. "I'm here for a reason, just like you. If you think you're going to die, then my job is to ensure you don't. The gods want you to sacrifice yourself? Screw them. They'll have to get through me first. I'll keep you safe. I'll protect you." Penner stood up in a dramatic way to signify his seriousness, but immediately lost his balance and fell onto his back.

Chess laughed. "Oh yeah. You're doing a bang-up job."

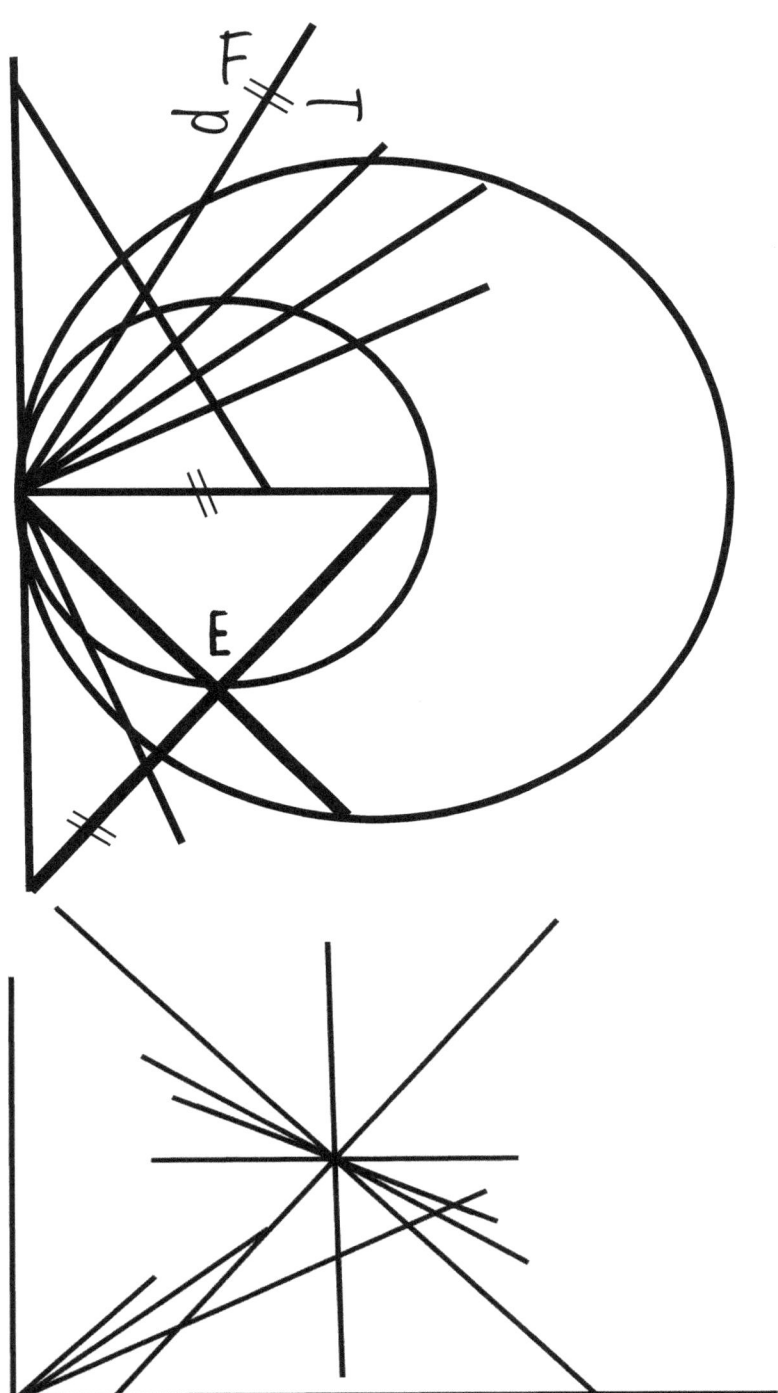

It is a unique form of intimacy and heartbreak when you realize you know the scent of your lovers blood
It is a unique form of love to know your lovers favourite star
It is the ultimate form of togetherness to see yourself through their eyes

There was a moment. A few hot seconds in the flames when everything came into focus. My hatred spewed out of me, and the really terrifying thing was that it was real. Some god or creature didn't put those feelings into me. They were mine. A part of me does, and likely always will, resent him for what he's done. To me. To us. I know now that we will never go back. But I wish I had some clue as to where we should be going next.

I want this journey to be over, but I know the end is coming faster than I want it to. Everywhere I look, I see that damn mountain and just ask myself, why? What is it about this place that keeps drawing us in? What is it that scares me so much?

So, what do I know? Well, I'm flying in a class four ship into enemy territory, and we're likely going to be facing off against an army of monks as they worship their Elder Gods, one of whom wants my Chess to die at a mountain where his power is its purest? I'm not a fan of this idea.

And for that thought, how much of the religion is true? If Mobo truly exists, what does that mean for the others? What the hell am I getting myself into? Do we even stand a chance?

Every part of my logical brain says no. But maybe we can stupid our way into something special. Maybe we have more of a shot than I think.

Or maybe this is it.

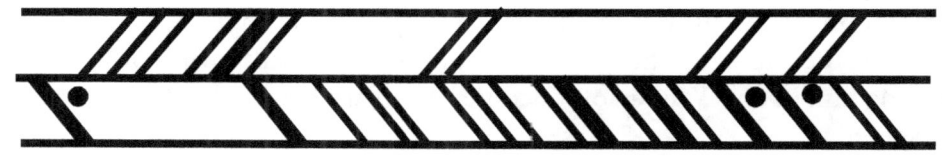

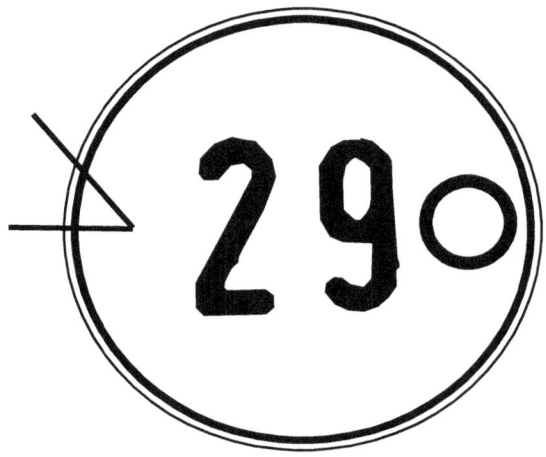

It was afternoon. The rain had cleared and the day had warmed.

While Chess and Fred were above deck, Penner was soaking in a small tub of water. He hadn't bathed in days, so he was thankful for the tranquility. There was a chill in the air, but the tub was warm enough to ease the tension from his muscles. Though his shoulder still stung and his feet ached from blisters, he lay back in the makeshift tub and tried not to think about what was to come next.

Then, as he looked at the ceiling, he saw a shadow pass over him. At first he thought it was Chess and started to sit up, but then felt a cold, sharp piece of metal pressed to his throat. He clenched against the edges of the tub as he felt the blade press into his skin. He could hardly breathe without the knife splitting him open. "You're not welcome here. Turn back or die," a raspy voice whispered.

"Who—" The blade pressed in. "Who are you?" Penner croaked as he tried to look at his captor. The man evaded his gaze, but pressed his blade again, sinking most of his face beneath the tub. Water splashed out along the floor as the knife pressed into him. He held his breath.

"You desecrated a sacred place and stole from us. You spat on our generosity and forced us to interfere in your sordid affair. You will pay the price."

"What do—" Penner tried to speak but choked on the water that rushed into his mouth.

"You stole from us. You lied to us. You desecrated holy places with your presence. We have every right to kill you. It is time to atone."

"I don't know you!" Penner exclaimed, but the man pressed him down so that the knife was holding him under the water.

"Quiet, or you drown in your own blood," the man said. Penner could do nothing but nod as the knife was slowly lifted off his throat. He emerged from under the water and coughed as the man gripped his mouth. With great force, he slithered his arm around Penner's neck and strangled him against the end of the tub. Penner's hands shot to the man's arms, clawing at them as he tried to get enough leverage to breathe.

"Your companion stole a match."

"A match? A-are you kidding me? I can get you another match—"

"The object is inconsequential. You took what was not yours from a holy place. Actors must be accountable for the fruit of their actions. The item is nothing. The mandate is everything. The match you stole may have been used to light a candle or a bomb. Either way, you have taken something without permission and have put us in peril. You brought this on yourself."

"I didn't steal!" he croaked.

"You are responsible for the company you keep. We are all one soul. We are all responsible." The man tightened his grip. "We will have our retribution and be made right in the eyes of those who are watching. We know who you two are and what you do in the dark. Who you are is enough to justify your execution, and we will not be merciful. We will wait for you at the Mountain.

187

This is your warning. This is the only chance to turn back."

Penner felt the arm loosen around his throat and half swam, half threw himself to the other end of the tub. Coughing, he rubbed his eyes and turned to see a flicker of soot dancing in the wind. The knife hung in the air for a moment before falling into the water. It looked as if it would pierce his leg, but as soon as it hit the water, the entire dagger dissolved into nothing and disappeared.

Penner, still coughing, stood up. Panicked, he whipped around in an attempt to see where the man had disappeared to when Fred appeared behind him. She didn't appear to mind his naked appearance.

"Someone was here," he sputtered. His voice was hoarse.

"What are you talking about?" she asked as Penner coughed. He threw his arm down to grab his tunic and did his best to cover himself as he staggered out of the tub.

"A man. Someone was just here."

"That's impossible."

"Is it? I almost drowned! A man was here with a knife against my throat, and whoever it was, he threatened us because we stole a match."

"Did you?"

"Chess did."

Fred looked at Penner suspiciously. He walked over to the space where the man had stood and pinned him against the bath. There was nothing there except for small traces of black powder. She knelt beside it and dragged her fingers across it. Lifting it, she sniffed a small sample and her eyes narrowed.

"I don't know what happened, but he was here. He grabbed me and forced me against the edge of this, and I couldn't breathe, Fred. I couldn't move. I just lay there with a knife against my throat like an idiot."

"If what you're saying is true, then there was nothing you could-."

"I could have tried."

"And you could have been killed. And this?" She lifted the powder up for him to examine.

"He turned into ash and floated away." She smirked at him. "Which sounds crazy, I know, but—"

"It doesn't prove he was here, but it doesn't prove that he wasn't."

"Do you believe me?"

"As much as I believe anything else," she said.

"There's more."

"Of course there is."

"He said this was our last chance to turn back. Said he's going to kill us when we get to the Mountain."

"Better get dressed, then. We should be there by nightfall."

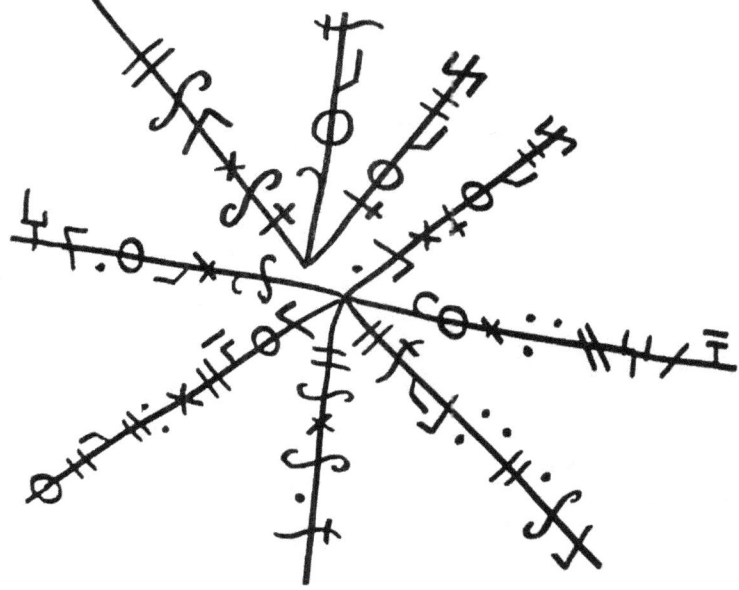

The sheer size of it is unlike anything I'd ever seen. The Mountain has always appeared big, but now, it dwarfs everything around it. I can't even see the top of it from where I stand.

Even more surprising is that I expected people. I don't know why, but I always imagined monks and pilgrims wandering all over this place, but it's empty.

That being said, I can still feel that strange knife against my throat. I don't know who that man was, but I feel like just being here is an act of defiance. Maybe an act of defiance against the temples? Maybe just against the world itself?

I wish I could say for sure.

I wish I knew what to expect from this place, but now that we're here, I have no idea. Will the Gods burst forth from the book and consume Chess? Will the Mountain come alive, or maybe just send an avalanche to swallow us whole?

I think I know why our ancestors worshipped this rock. I think I could believe that this rock was the birthplace of the world.

They arrived in time to make camp for the night. It wasn't fancy, but it was comfortable. Penner hardly slept. His mind raced. Who was that man with the knife? Had he actually been there? He rubbed at the scabs on his feet and dabbed another one of Fred's strange salves on them. Chess nuzzled into his chest and was laying still for once, but Penner suspected that he'd got just as little sleep as him. When Penner had awoken, he wasn't even sure what time it was, but he could feel Chess pressing against him in the hammock.

You should at least try to sleep," Chess urged him, but Penner's body felt like he had ants crawling through it. He wanted to get up and run, but his body couldn't move. He was too tired to rest and too alert to sleep. He squirmed, trying to find a comfortable spot.

"I can't. You know I can't."

"I know it's hard, but you have to try."

"I don't want to try," Penner said as he felt Chess interlock his fingers with his.

"But you must. You have to."

"I don't have to do anything."

"But you should. It's the right thing to do." Penner squeezed Chess's hand. He smelled good.

"Since when have we ever cared about the right thing to do?" Chess sat up and slowly got out of the hammock. The shift almost threw Penner off, but he gripped the edges and shuffled into a seated position. Chess walked to the window and stared up.

"It's bigger in person," Chess said.

"I know."

"I'm scared."

"I know," Penner said as he tried to stretch.

"It's a mountain. You've seen mountains before."

"None like this. I'm amazed you can still see the stars. It blocks out so much of the sky."

"Yeah," Chess said, his voice sounding cold and distant. "I think I need to be alone."

"Is that safe?"

"I think we moved out of safe a long time ago," Chess said.

"Okay. Do you want me to—"

"No. You sleep. I'm going to go for a walk." Chess walked back to Penner and kissed him on the forehead. Throwing on a pair of pants, he walked towards the deck. "I won't be gone long." It was dark, but Penner could still see

Chess's hand grip something in his bag.

"Are you going to read it?" Penner asked.

"Go to sleep," Chess said, and disappeared onto the deck.

Penner tried to turn over and go to sleep, but just seeing the cover of the book gnawed at his mind. He shivered, but didn't know if it was because of the night air or the book. Just thinking about it, he could feel the hairs on the back of his neck stand on end. His hand still pulsed from where that shadow had bitten it. He closed his eyes and could feel the book staring at him, calling out to him. He could feel it piercing his mind and his thoughts.

After what felt like hours, he felt sick. The thought of Chess reading that book kept bouncing around his brain. He felt like something was pulling him towards Chess, and he couldn't ignore it anymore. He stepped off the hammock and made his way onto the deck. Once on top, he saw Fred sitting on the bow, staring out over the horizon.

"Where's Chess?"

"He's gone for a walk. I think he wants to be with his thoughts," Fred said without moving.

"Do you ever sleep?"

"Only when I need it," she said. "You should, though."

"I'm not tired," Penner said.

"Then join me," Fred replied. She looked back at him and smiled. With a sigh, he shrugged and made his way to the edge of the ship. He brushed the railing, as if clearing it of dust, and settled himself on the edge of it, facing away from the mountain.

"You're missing the view," Fred said.

"I've seen enough," Penner replied. "I should go find him."

"Let him be."

"But he's reading that book."

"He needs to."

"No. He needs—" Penner paused. "Me."

"Do you understand what is going on?" Fred asked.

"Do you?"

"I know enough to let the man do what he needs to do," she began. "Let him read it."

"But it's dangerous."

"He's a grown man. Let him assess the danger for himself," Fred said.

Despite himself, Penner let out a yawn, and could feel his eyes getting heavy. Though he was fighting hard to stay awake, his body was betraying him.

"I'll be back. It won't be long," Penner said. He gripped onto the ropes that Fred used to bounce down to the ground. He launched himself into the air, and stumbled as he landed on the dirt. He wasn't sure how Fred managed to make it look so easy.

He wandered the path, following the thick smell of burning air that guided him. He couldn't be sure how he knew where to go, but before long he found himself off the path and wandering through the forest. He knew that monks, thieves, or beasts could be following him, but he had to get to Chess.

He found him in a clearing. He sat by a small fire that blazed so hot, Penner was surprised that the clearing hadn't set itself on fire. Chess looked like he was talking to the fire, but the roar of the flames drowned out any sounds that Penner would've been able to hear.

At first Penner wanted to pull him away from the fire, but when he looked at it more closely, he realised it was just the book. It was open, laid on the ground, as thick hot flames burst from it and danced through the air.

"Join us," a voice whispered in his head.

Penner looked around to see what had called out to him and paused. The thought that maybe he'd been brought out here, not to save Chess but to join him, made him comfortable. Slowly, he made his way over to the flames and sat opposite Chess, with the fiery book in between them.

He wasn't sure what he'd been expecting, but he could still hear nothing over the roar of the flames. Instead, he sat and watched as Chess conversed with the book. After a while, he began to see images fluttering in the fire. He wasn't sure if he was just growing tired or searching for meaning, but the flames began to be a comfort, and he could see what looked like a bird, a snake, and a beast all playing with a pearl. Symbols began to appear in the flames, some of which mirrored the scars on Chess's body. He began to feel his body fill with energy as he sat. As if he was waking up.

He wasn't sure how long they sat there, but by the time the flames had died down and retreated back into the book, the sound of birds filled the air. The pages were charred and burnt. The world was slowly waking up, and he felt refreshed and ready for the day. Chess, however, looked terrible. Large dark circles under his eyes and ruffled hair made it look like he'd been awake for weeks. His clothes were torn, and some of his wounds had reopened.

"We should get ready," Chess said.

"Are you—are you okay?" Penner asked.

"I'm fine," Chess said. "Come on, we've got work to do."

"Can we just stay here? For one more moment?" Penner asked as he reached out and grabbed Chess's hand.

"Sure. Just one more."

Excerpt from "Essence of the One Soul"

Do not cry for me
        for I have known
from the beginning
            what I must do,

and I willingly came along
                    and did it.

Do not fear
        for what comes after this
            for it is not for us to know -

but rest assured that I am ready to face it
        with my head held   high
and my arms   o u t s t r e t c h e d.

We have been deeply blessed
        to have found each other,
            too have been together
                    too have known and felt our love
    is to have known that the universe is good,
            and just,
                    and patient.

To have known you has made this life worth living,
        and so I shall go to the unknown
            with no fear of d e a t h -

because I have had a life
                    And a one
        that I loved.

"It's just a simple expedition." Fred smirked. "I don't know why you decided to dress up for it."

"Putting a vest on doesn't constitute dressing up," Penner defended. "It's likely to get cold up there. You can see how high it is."

"How high do you think we're going?" Fred asked.

"I have no idea." Penner turned to Chess. "How high are we going?"

"We'll find out. I'll know it when I see it," he said. "We follow the path and go from there." Chess exhaled and began to walk, following a brown dirt path that ran alongside the mountain.

He wasn't moving as confidently as he normally did. His lack of sleep made him look drunk as he plodded his way up the mountain. Any attempt that Penner had made to talk to Chess had been brushed off, and he refused

197

to talk about last night. After several attempts Penner had stopped trying, and was now just making sure Chess didn't hurt himself.

"At least we're not climbing straight up," Penner said, attempting to lighten the mood.

"I still brought my hook. Just in case," Fred said, patting at her belt.

"You have a hook?" Penner wasn't sure why that surprised him.

Despite the rocky terrain around them, the path was surprisingly flat. There was a thick underbrush of trees on both sides that filled the forest with animal and bird noises that echoed off the massive bluffs. He wasn't sure how long they'd been walking when the ground changed, but at least the view had been pleasant. The dirt path had transformed into a smooth, grey rocky surface, and the trees had thinned out until there were only a few that grew along the side of the rocky mountainside. Greenery became sparser with every step, until it was just barren path winding through dead rock.

After walking for what felt like hours, the path became much steeper. It carved into the mountain. Arches made of stone began to line the path as the trail became unpredictable. Though they were climbing, Penner didn't realise how high they'd got until they came to a threadbare wooden bridge. While the bridge was sturdy, it swung back and forth above a realm of nothing. He tried not to think of plummeting to his death, but with each step, it was getting harder. He didn't want to look down, but couldn't stop himself. He could barely see the jagged stones that lined the bottom of the gulch.

"Just keep moving," Chess said, encouraging Penner as he held out his hand. "Take your time. You're doing fine."

"Is there another way around?"

"It's the path. Trust the bridge," Chess said.

Penner looked into his beautiful grey eyes and, for a moment, thought back to when they'd met. He looked into his eyes and felt his resolve begin to build. For a moment, Chess looked like the man he'd fallen in love with. So he took the next step.

Though Penner had never been afraid of heights, he'd never been this high before. The experience was dizzying, and with one uneasy step, he felt his feet hit the bridge. It wobbled, and he had to clench onto the rope sides just to keep himself steady. He put his other foot in front and focused his attention on Chess. He walked until he finally made contact with the stone pathway once again. Shaking, he collapsed into Chess's arms. He exhaled and laughed as he looked up at Chess, who laughed with him.

"Still in one piece." Chess gave him a congratulatory pat and for a moment looked like his old self again.

"I need to stop. Just for a minute. I need to stop." Penner felt the adrenaline pumping through him.

"Okay. Sure," Chess said as he grabbed Penner by the shoulder and sat him down by the rocky wall.

"You two make it look so easy," Penner said.

"It is so easy. The danger is just in your head. You did good for your first time," Chess said.

"Here. Have something to eat," Fred said, producing a handful of seeds which Penner accepted. They were flavourless, but comforting. Chess sat beside him. His arm draped around his shoulders, Chess pulled him into his side, and Penner exhaled.

"We've been higher than this in the ship, you know," Fred said. "You'll be fine."

"Yeah. But that was—the ship doesn't feel real. That was different. Very different."

"You did fine. One down," Chess said.

"There's more, isn't there?"

"No. Yes. Lots. But they'll probably get easier."

"Grand," Penner said as he felt the wind whip through him. He shuddered, and Chess held him tight for a minute. "Wait, are there actually more?"

"Only one way to find out." Chess gave him an affectionate squeeze.

Neither wanted to say anything, but they both thought the same thing.

This could be the last intimate moment they'd get. Despite the thought being in the back of their heads, neither acknowledged it. Penner closed his eyes and imagined them back home, sitting on the edge of their bed. He imagined how they'd sat for hours, and wished he could be back there. He wanted to go back to before, and for a moment, it was everything he wanted it to be. But when his eyes reopened, Chess was getting up to walk away. Penner reached out and grabbed his hand, which made him pause.

"Stop. Wait." Chess froze, before slowly settling back down and sitting beside him again.

"Yeah?"

"You—I love you, Chess."

"I know," Chess said, with a smile appearing on his tired face. "I love you too."

"And whatever it is that is waiting for us, as long as I have you, it's worth it. This will all be worth it. I just want you. I just need you."

He hadn't realised he was crying, but he felt a tear on his cheek. Chess reached over and brushed it off with his thumb before they locked eyes and kissed.

"I know," Chess said, a tear staining his own cheek as he pulled away and made his way back to the path. "We need to keep going. When you feel well enough—"

"I'm good. Let's go," Penner said as he shook himself off.

"You've got something in your eye," Fred said as they followed Chess. Penner nodded, and brushed his eyes with the sleeve of his shirt. Everything would be okay, he told himself. He tried really hard to believe it.

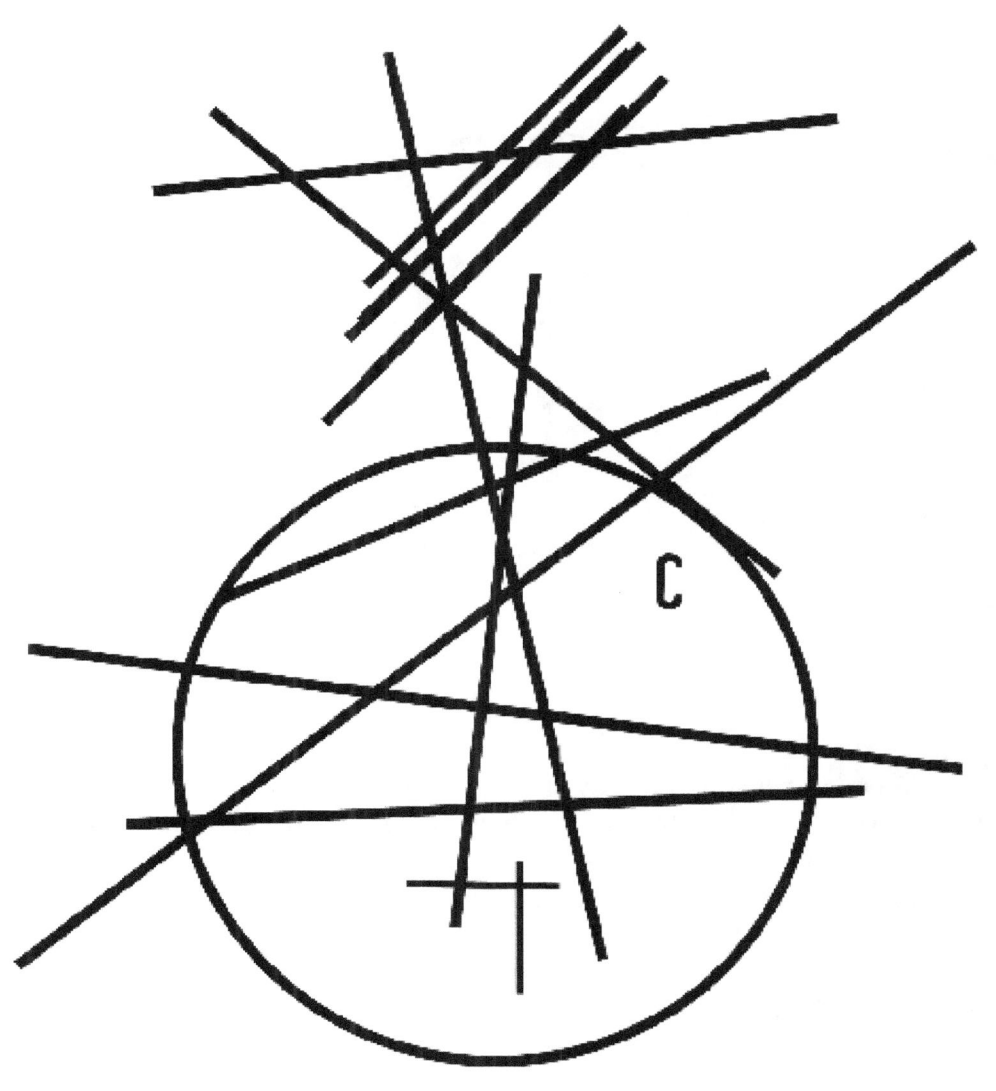

nkedbfxɔɘvirlwɿqḭḭƨƨɘlmƌou

lɣɿl ɒʇɒƨxiʜ ɣɈ lɔlɒx ʜlɒx mʜu Ɉlmɒ xɣɈḭɈiʇ lɈm Ɉiʜ ɒlɒʜ ɣlwɈxlwiɣ xʇo Ɉlmɒ ix mlllʜ Ɉiʜ ʜɈupu ʜɔio lo ix ɣlwɈxlwiɣ

After another short eternity of climbing, they arrived at a massive pile of rocks. Swords, staffs, and flags were stuck in the pile like pins in a pillow. Despite the rocky terrain, there was a variety of grasses and flowers that sprouted from it, and groups of fireflies that blinked as they danced around it.

At this point, the wind around them had picked up, and despite his vest, Penner still felt chilly. He wasn't sure how Chess and Fred had managed to stay so warm all the way up, but he wished he'd brought along a scarf and gloves as well.

"What is this place?" Penner asked as Chess approached the shrine.

"Looks like a space for the travelers who have come before," Fred said.

"But there's so many. There must be dozens—"

"A moment of silence," Fred cut him off, and Penner shut his mouth.

Chess knelt by the shrine and touched it. Penner watched as he bowed his head and took a breath. After a moment, Chess got up and shook his head.

"Voices," Chess said as he tried to clear his ear. "So many voices."

"You okay?" Penner began.

"One moment. I'm listening." He nodded as if listening to instructions.

He reached down and grabbed a sword and threw it at the rocky wall. The shrine fell apart as boulders, swords, and flags toppled over the cliff, slamming into the ground below. Penner was shocked, and looked to Fred, who looked dumbfounded. He took a moment to look at the sword and saw that Chess had thrown it hard enough to stick it into the wall.

"What are you—" Fred began, but Chess held up a finger to silence her. He walked over to the sword and pulled it out of the wall, sending several other, smaller rocks with it. As he pulled it out, the rocks fell away, revealing a cavern that bore deep into the mountain.

"You should show some respect for the dead," Fred sneered.

"It's not a shrine, it's a test. If the dead want my respect, they could have earned it in life. Now they won't shut up about it. The voices are so strong here," Chess said as he threw the sword over the side of the mountain.

Penner listened as it clattered on the way down. Despite not seeing anyone on the mountain so far, he couldn't be sure no one would hear it. Chess turned back to the hole in the wall and walked through. Penner began to follow him, but Chess held out his hand and gently pushed him back. "You can't."

"What?" Penner frowned. "Why not? Chess, I've come this far—"

"This far but no further," Chess said, looking down the tunnel that led into the mountain. "I need to do this myself."

"You can't do this yourself. That's the reason we came along. That's the reason I'm here."

"Exactly. This far and no further," he said. Penner tried to push his way inside, but again Chess resisted him. He tried again, but Chess grabbed his face and looked into his eyes. Penner could see him trying to look strong and determined, but all Penner could see was his fear. It filled him with dread.

"I can't let you go in there alone," Penner said.

"You don't get a choice this time," Chess said as he gave Penner a soft kiss on the cheek. "I'll be back out in no time. Trust me."

"Fine. I'll give you ten minutes," Penner said as he clenched his fists. Chess smiled at him, and then turned his back and entered the cavern.

The darkness was thick, and he disappeared in a few steps. Penner stood there until he couldn't even hear the sounds of his footsteps echo around the chamber. It took every fibre of his being to resist running in after him. If Fred hadn't been standing over him, there was a good chance he would have followed despite Chess's protests. But he stood and waited for what felt like eternity. Soon even the sound of the steps stopped, and he was left with nothing but the darkness.

"He's crazy if he thinks I'm not going to follow him."

"You're crazy if you think I'll let you interfere," Fred replied.

"How long has it been?"

"Three minutes."

"Feels longer." She gripped him by the shoulders and steered him away from the cave entrance.

"Have a seat. Let him do what he needs to do." With a grunt, he left the blackness of the cavern path and walked over to a pair of makeshift chairs Fred had created for them out of the fake shrine. Penner grabbed a small rock and began to fidget with it. He had hoped it would clear his head, but all it was doing was making his mind race.

"Stop that," Fred said, causing Penner to take the rock and chuck it over the cliffside. He listened as it echoed down the side.

"I'm nervous, okay?" In a burst of energy, he exploded onto his feet. "Why can't I follow him? What do I do now? How can we—"

"Shut up and breathe," Fred said. "Just trust him."

Penner gazed into the cave one more time. He could feel hot air rising out of it. Like the cave was alive and exhaling salty, sticky air all over him.

"I just want to make sure he's okay," Penner said as he started to make his way to the cave, but in a flash Fred was on her feet, blocking his way.

"Give him time."

"But—" Penner paused. "What if there's something in there waiting for him?"

"There probably is," Fred said. "But we have to let him do this himself." Penner looked at the cave and then back to her. With a frown, he hung his head.

"I'm just worried that those men are in there. The ones who—the ones who showed up when I was bathing and—"

"That was probably a dream. If not, we left them behind days ago."

"But they said that was a warning."

"Probably just to scare you," she said. "Just let him do what he needs to. Come on. I'll put on some tea."

"Do you always have tea?" he asked.

"Of course I always have tea. I'm civilised." She smirked. "Now come. Have a seat and let him do what he needs to." Reluctantly, he followed her to the rocks as she produced a small metal circle and a small jar of water that she placed on top of it. "You remind me of myself. Back with Cassius. So protective and loyal. It's cute in its own way. "

"I just wish I knew what was going on," he said. "I just want to know he's okay. There could be anything in there. Thieves. Bandits. Dragons. Those men might've been zealot enforcers here to cleanse the world of the heretics. Us and our scandalous forbidden love."

"That's a bit of a stretch."

"After everything we've seen, I wouldn't be surprised," he sighed as the smell of freshly brewed tea began to fill his nose. For a moment he closed his eyes and thought back to his home. The world they left behind. He could see it so clearly: the teapot by the window, the curtains, the smell of bread baking from the bakery down the street. For a moment, he felt a tremendous home-sickness, and gripped the sides of his pants.

"What are you thinking about?"

"The simple things. The simple times. The times before this."

"Things are rarely simple, and the Good Old Days are an illusion. Things were just as complicated back then. Just in a different way."

"In a very different way," Penner said as he watched the smoke pour from the kettle. "I still miss it though."

"Tell me about it, then," Fred said. "Tell me everything."

"Where do I begin?" Penner chuckled.

"Just start with whatever comes first," Fred said.

"Well, it wasn't special."

"Then start with you," Fred prodded. "Who was Penner?"

"No one, really. I grew up in the law. Top of my class, with a good family. They died when I was about fifteen or so, and I poured myself into books. Mom was a gardener, Father was a doctor. Spent my draft years in medical training. They used our house as an office, and I remember apprenticing with him when I was young, so it was a natural fit. After they died, for a while the village took care of me, but I didn't understand it at the time. I wanted to be alone, so I pushed everyone away. After a while it worked, but I was forgotten, and the world moved on without me. I was forgotten everywhere but at the tavern, and then I met her."

"Her?" It was the first time Penner had heard her sound genuinely shocked.

"Her name was Sam. She was amazing and short-tempered." Fred smiled. "It didn't take me long to love her. She coaxed me out of the tavern and back into the world. But the world saw her differently."

"Why?"

"Well, Sam was a woman, but her body, her body was that of a man. One day she was attacked in an alley, and then—" He froze and stared into his cup. "They discovered her and brought her in front of the Temple. They killed her as an abomination. Thankfully, I was never discovered, but—"

Fred reached out and rubbed his shoulder.

"I'm sorry."

"It's a long time ago now."

"Wounds like that can take a lifetime to heal," she said.

"Well, I haven't been a huge fan of the One Soul since then." He sniffled. He hadn't even realised he'd been crying, but wiped his eyes and turned his attention to the opening. "I can't let something like that happen to him. To us."

"It won't," Fred began, but was interrupted by the earth shaking. There was a boom, and Penner could feel everything rumble under his feet. It felt like the earth had shifted. His eyes immediately shot to Fred.

"What the-?" he asked.

"I don't know." She turned back to him. Suddenly there was a flash in the entrance of the cave, as a bolt of light shot from the entrance and disappeared into the sky.

"Well, what the hell was that? Did you see that?"

"What was what?" Fred asked.

"A light. Just for a moment, I saw—"

"I didn't see anything," Fred tried to reassure him.

"What if we sent Chess into a trap?" he asked.

"We didn't—we couldn't have," Fred tried, but it was no use.

Penner's mind was out of control and his body was already in action. He raced towards the opening as fast as he could. He blinked, and for a moment he saw the outline of something in the doorway—like a shadow was watching them. In a blink, it was gone, and Penner shook his head.

In a matter of moments, Fred was by his side. As she entered the space, the ground where they had been sitting moments before split, and the rocks fell into the chasm. Fred and Penner raced inside as the last of the firmament below them evaporated into nothing.

As they entered, the entrance was buried as an onslaught of rocks covered the path. If they hadn't moved, they would both have been dead. He couldn't see anything in the darkness. She gripped onto his shoulders and he tried to calm his breathing. Penner's hands were trembling. Hers were strong and cold as steel. She reached into her belt and pulled out a small glowing ball that gave them just enough light to see each other's faces.

"We almost died," Penner said.

"You'd figure we'd be used to that by now," Fred said. "Damn. I just lost my favourite teapot." She struck a match and used it to light a miniature lantern that hung from her hook. Penner peered down the stairs into the darkness.

"I don't think we have a choice anymore."

"Well, we can't go back," she said. "We go in. But be quiet and be careful."

"Stay close," he whispered.

He wasn't sure what they were walking into, but could feel himself growing anxious as they stepped into the darkness. He held his hands in front of his face, keeping one hand resting against the wall as he moved forwards. Despite the glow from Fred's lantern, he couldn't see his fingers.

The darkness was absolute and ate the world around him. He could feel the walls closing in on him. The dark was so complete, it was suffocating. The only sound he heard was Fred's footsteps behind him. Though he could reach out and touch her, he had no concept how far away she was. The sounds were growing more distant. His paranoia was getting the better of him. Every now and then, he had to stop and reach out to her just to make sure they were both still there.

"How far do you think we've gone?" he finally asked.

"Just keep going," she whispered.

With each step, they drew closer to whatever it was they were chasing. He couldn't be sure, but the ground felt like it was sloping down. It felt like they were descending into the centre of the mountain.

A soft glow appeared in the distance, casting the slightest bit of light in the rocky cavern. Everything got brighter, but not enough to illuminate the whole tunnel. It was enough to see that the tunnel was cylindrical in shape, with just enough space for them to both walk without hitting their heads.

They turned a corner and saw the light source—a single candle attached to the wall. At first it looked perfectly ordinary, but as they approached it felt strange. The flame danced like it was being battered by winds. Penner held his hand up to it, but the air around it was still.

"There's no wind. Why is it dancing like that?" Penner asked.

"That's not what I was looking at," Fred said as she pointed to the wall behind the candle. Penner looked at them and saw hundreds of symbols covering the wall. He had seen them before, covering Chess's notebooks and papers and skin, but there was something different about these.

They didn't look exact, almost like whoever had made them had been in a hurry. Curious, Penner reached out to them and felt a warm, sticky liquid coat his hand as he felt the writing for himself.

"Blood," Fred muttered.

"Of course it is," Penner said. "Because why would he walk in here without writing bloody symbols on everything?" He bit his lip.

"We don't know it was him," she said.

"It was," Penner said. "I recognise the scent." Penner shook his head as he found himself flashing back to Cassandra. Holding Chess in his arms as he ran to the village as he bled out. He was blinking to try to clear his eyes when he turned to the ground. A twinkle caught his eye, and he noticed small drops of blood along the ground.

"He'll be okay. Just breathe."

"Just breathe." Penner repeated the phrase in his head a few times as he blinked a few tears away.

"Come on. We follow the trail." Fred smacked him on the back. Penner nodded as he followed. She tracked the blood drops into the darkness of the tunnel.

Though it was dark, soon they came across another candle, which helped to illuminate things further. Still more symbols covered the walls, ceilings, and sometimes even the floor. But with each candle they crossed, the symbols became looser and more distorted. It was as if Chess was making the symbols more quickly as he went deeper. As if he was running out of time. Maybe he was being chased? Penner wasn't sure if it was his mind playing tricks on him, but in the darkness, the blood scent was thicker. It was so pungent. He began to gag as they marched deeper. He tried to block out the images of Chess bleeding, but with each candle, he was becoming more and more concerned. He wasn't sure if they'd passed twenty or a hundred.

"He's going to be okay. Things are going to be okay," Fred repeated.

It helped. But he didn't believe her.

After a hundred more steps into darkness, he could feel the ground change. The path below them began to slope down more steeply. The stone ground became more regular and took more concrete forms. Soon they were racing across stone slabs. Why anyone would decide to tile a mountain trail path was beyond him, but Penner didn't think about it. He just had to get to Chess.

After what felt like hours, they arrived at a door. It was solid wood, with more scribbles scrawled across it in red. Underneath Chess's brutal, bloody symbols were a series of golden lines. Each of them was elaborate and ingrained into the wood—but he recognized them.

"It's the same symbols," he said as he pushed the door. Then he pressed harder, but the door wouldn't budge. Fred joined him, and together they grunted as they tried to force it open.

"It won't budge," Fred grunted.

"It will. It has to."

"We can try to find another way in—"

"No. This is the way in." He took his hands off the door, feeling Chess's blood thick on his palms.

It was still warm, but he could feel it getting colder. He grunted as he thumped his shoulder against the door. The impact sent a stabbing pain straight to his shoulder and he gritted his teeth. He pressed himself into the door. He had to find a way to open it. Whatever had opened the door for Chess, had now sealed it shut behind him. After pushing, pulling, and even trying to slam the door open, Penner collapsed in a frustrated mess. He rested his head against the doorway and felt a hot tear slide down his cheek.

"Please—" he whispered. Frustrated, he rested on his heels and looked at the door again, and saw something strange. The symbols that had just appeared to be random shapes and patterns seemed to shift and change into what appeared to be a single word. Penner read it over and over until he was sure of what it was saying, and then stood up to look at it.

He turned to Fred. "Do you see this?"

"What do you see?" Fred asked.

"Sacrifice. It says sacrifice. Why did it not say that before?" He turned to Fred, who gazed at the wall and frowned.

"Where?" she asked as she scoured the wall.

Penner reached out to show her, but noticed something strange. His hands where the shadow had bitten him were bleeding through the bandages. He unwrapped his hand and watched as blood freely poured down his hand. He could feel his hand being drawn to the door like a magnet. The droplets of blood even curved towards the door as they plummeted to the ground.

He didn't feel any pain. He reached out and pressed his hand into the doorway and felt a shock run through him. He pushed. With a click, they opened, and Penner ran through the doorway into a room unlike any he had ever seen before.

The interior of the room was a large dome. The center of the space was a pool of glowing white liquid that was a combination of fire and water. Through the air, small balls of light floated like glowing ash. It was surreal and beautiful, but also terrifying and unnatural.

Then Penner saw him. In the middle of the pool was Chess, suspended above the water like a bird. He was still, and had he not been floating in the air, Penner would think he was sleeping. His eyes were closed, and blood flowed down his hand and dripped into the strange water feet below him. He took a step towards Chess, but Fred held him back as he seemed to notice the pool below him for the first time.

"What is this place?"

"I'd rather not find out," Fred said as Penner knelt down at the edge of the path. "What do you think you're doing?" Penner leaned over the edge and reached down to the strange liquid. Before Fred could protest, he touched it, before recoiling in pain.

"Hot?"

"No. Cold. You know how some things can be so cold that they burn?" he said, shaking his hand as he tried to regain feeling in it.

"That was a stupid thing to do."

"I had to try," he said looking at his hands. To his surprise, the bite seemed to have disappeared as his hand glowed for a moment. The blood trails remained, but the wound itself was sealed.

"Look!" he exclaimed.

"What happened there?"

"The bite."

Fred smirked. "The one you got from the book?"

"Whatever it was. That's not the point. Look."

"How convenient." Fred looked at the water. Penner once again returned to the edge of the water. He knelt beside it and undid his shirt. Pulling off the bandage, he looked deep into the water.

"Don't do it," Fred said.

"I have to try," Penner said, and before she could stop him, he threw his other hand in and gathered a small amount of the fiery liquid in his hand. It burned and froze him, but he took a small splash of the flame water and placed it against his chest.

He inhaled. The pain was so intense he thought he was dying. He could feel the pain not only shoot down his skin, but also inside of him, like daggers piercing his entire body from the inside. He wasn't sure if he screamed, but the next thing he remembered was lying flat on his back and looking up at a very unamused Fred.

She frowned. "What did you expect?" Though the pain had been searing, it had already passed. He examined his chest and smiled. He pressed his arm up and down as he touched the area. It felt like there wasn't even a scar. "I had no idea places like this actually existed."

Penner got to his knees as he rubbed his chest. He looked out to Chess and frowned.

"Why the hell did he bring us here?"

"I'm more concerned about how he got out there," Fred said. "How do we get to him?"

"Swimming is out of the question," Penner said. "We'd sink in seconds. I don't want to know what happens if you spend too long in there."

"I could tie a rope to you and see how far I could throw you."

"I don't like that idea."

"I was joking," Fred said.

He wasn't sure that she had been.

"Is there anything we could attach the hook to? Something we could use to swing across?"

"Not likely," she said.

"Well, he didn't just fly out there!" Penner exclaimed. Then he paused. He was floating in the air. It was possible he'd done just that, but it didn't help them right now. "Maybe there's a path?"

"Do you see one?" Fred asked. Penner frowned as he looked around the circumference of the dome. No path. No trail. Barely a ledge running along the outside.

"Nothing." Penner gritted his teeth.

"There has to be something. He couldn't have just floated out there," Fred said.

"Why not? He's floating now!" Penner turned to Chess. "Chess! Chess, how do we get out to you?"

"He's not responding."

"This is absurd! He's floating, and we can't even get out there to grab him." He looked around the ground they were on and shuffled his feet. His eyes scanned the pathway, looking for some sort of rock or small item he could grab. "Maybe I can throw something at him? Do you still have your hook?"

There was a strange echo coming from the water, and Penner turned to it. A small set of ripples emanated out from it, and Penner leaned in closer. It wasn't far away, but Penner could see something moving under the surface. It was hard to tell with just how bright the water was, but he could see them. "Fish."

"What?" Fred asked.

"Look, there are fish in the water. Can you see them?"

"I think so," Fred responded as she peered into water. "They're huge."

"They look strange."

"They look more like they'd belong in an ocean or something. How did I not see them before?" Penner watched them moving under the surface, swimming slowly but deliberately.

"They're swimming in a circle," Fred said.

"No. I think they're swimming around Chess. Look!" he said as he pointed to the waters that swelled underneath Chess. It seemed that the closer they got to Chess, the more the fish tried to pile on top of themselves. Almost like they were stacking on top of each other to get to him.

The more he watched the large black blobs, the more he became convinced that he could find a way across them. "I'm going to try something."

"You're not seriously considering this, are you?" she asked as Penner removed his vest.

"I have to try."

"It's a magic pool filled with giant shadow fish. What part of this sounds like a good idea to you?" Fred took Penner's vest.

"There's enough of them. If I can walk across them—"

"It's still a terrible idea." Fred frowned at him, but Penner felt his courage building.

He couldn't explain what was compelling him to do something so stupid, but he knew this would work. At least, he hoped this would work. He stood on the edge of the lake and felt the energy lapping at his toes. He took a deep breath and looked over to Chess, still floating peacefully above the waters. He took the rope from Fred's waist and tied it around his own. Giving her the other end, he hoped the rope was long enough for him to get to Chess without having to let go.

"Just in case," he said. Fred nodded and grabbed his hand. It was shaking as he put his foot above the waters. Before he could step out though, Fred pulled him back.

"You sure about this?"

"My feet can't get worse. I have to get to him somehow."

"Okay. Just let me brace myself. I don't want to be pulled in there with you." She kicked out her feet and lowered herself so she was braced, before nodding to him. Holding the rope in her hands, she nodded, and he turned to the edge of the fire lake.

Holding his breath, he lifted his foot and stepped out onto the water. He was aiming for the fish, but as he was about to feel its slippery skin under his foot, a white hand shot up out of the water and gripped his heel in its hand with incredible strength.

Shocked by the sudden feeling clasped against his ankle, Penner's other

217

foot followed, so that a second hand reached up and grabbed onto it. He looked through the water to see the massive fish looking at him. The white hand jutting from its forehead like a mutated unicorn. Penner's mouth hung open at how silly the creature looked that he didn't notice the other fish that held his other foot.

Now steady, Penner lifted his back foot up and the fish relinquished its grip. He stepped forwards, where another fish was waiting to grip his foot in its hand-horn. He stepped forwards again as the next hand shot up to grip it, and soon he didn't even notice the fish anymore. Step after step, hand after hand appeared to grab him and keep him moving. When he was comfortable, he began to move at a faster pace. Racing to close the gap between him and Chess. He began to jog, and each hand shot up to catch him.

"What the hell are those things?" Fred yelled. Penner staggered and motioned for Fred to shut up. She didn't. "What will you do when you get there?"

"I don't know yet!" Penner yelled. "I'll figure it out."

Each step made him more nervous. Inching closer, but feeling more unsure. What would reaching Chess accomplish? He had no idea what was keeping Chess aloft, and wasn't sure what bringing him down would do. But he knew he had to get closer. In addition, the fish that grabbed his ankles were gripping tighter. His momentum slowed to a crawl as he fought them to release his feet. Were they trying to pull him under? He was becoming unsteady, and if he wasn't careful, he would fall into the strange electric force that lapped closer with each step.

Then, there he was. One leap away, floating just inches from him. But when he tried to free his foot, another hand reached up, freezing him in place. He wanted to wrench free, but the grip was too strong. His leg wouldn't budge and he began to tip forwards. The water inching closer, Penner tried to leap again, and managed to wriggle one of his feet free.

However, with much of his momentum lost in the struggle, he was forced to reach out as far as he could in an attempt to catch Chess's legs.

The contact was brief, and barely there, but it was enough. As soon as Penner physically touched him, whatever energy was keeping him afloat vanished. Gravity kicked back in and time slowed. What he did know was that they were falling, and he was close enough to Chess now to grab onto his legs. Somewhere in the distance Fred yelled out to them, but he didn't hear her. Instead, he felt his body collide with the flames that rushed up his body. It stung with incredible precision, like he had a thousand needles piercing into him. He tried to grab hold of Chess, but there wasn't enough time.

Penner looked up to see Chess blink a few times, as the water rushed around them.

"I'm sorry, but—" Penner began.

"You're late," Chess said with a smile.

Before anything else could be said, the world around them sunk, as the strange liquid consumed everything around them.

Whatever he had been expecting, this wasn't it. He had expected pain unlike anything he'd experienced before. He had expected to be drowned under deadly waters. He had expected fire to smoulder all over his body and burn him and Chess to a crisp.

Instead, what they found was nothing. A blank void on all sides that shimmered with a blinding light. The world around him swirled and imploded on itself like a thousand burning suns. Every colour was reflected on the walls as the sound of music and drums swelled in his ears.

He opened his mouth to scream, but before he could say anything, the taste of wine and nickel filled his mouth. Every part of his body felt like it was being saturated with every taste and smell imaginable. His entire body vibrated with the feeling of being alive. He felt powerful and complete.

And then he saw Chess naked in front of him too. He was glowing. His skin was luminescent. Each line he had cut into himself was now a brilliant light that seemed to shine through his body. With no sense of gravity, he pulled himself close to Chess and felt his body. Every touch felt like lightning bolts rifling through them both with the force of a hurricane.

He reached his hand up to Chess's picturesque face and pulled himself closer, so that they were both looking into each other's eyes. When he did, he could see every moment they had ever spent together. All the good times, all the bad, circling within his eyes like a small galaxy that only they knew.

With a passion unlike any he had felt before, they kissed. Their naked bodies pressed into each other with a fury. It felt perfect.

It felt right.

The moment was perfect, but Chess pulled away, and when Penner followed suit, he turned his attention to what Chess was looking at. In the distance, but somehow as close as Chess, were two ghostly images that danced through the strange world, yet remained still as they watched. Two figures were looking at them: one with wings and one with a long tail. Though he couldn't prove it, he knew they were watching them, and for a moment, he felt Chess tighten his grip on him.

They looked into each other's eyes and spoke without making a sound.

Chess looked at him with a reassuring look that said, we could stay here forever, and Penner felt sad knowing that they couldn't. He looked to Chess with a smile that said that they should, but he knew it wasn't going to happen that way.

Then Chess smiled and pulled his hand down so it was level with him and Penner. In it was the rope that Penner had wrapped around him. Penner looked deep into Chess's eyes as he pulled back and saw something he had never seen before.

Penner watched as he slowly dissolved into nothing. Before Penner could react, the eyes of a beast appeared before him, and he felt himself dragged through space until he was somewhere very familiar.

The world around him was moving slowly as he looked around to examine their old bedroom. Everything was where he'd left it. He looked in front of him and saw Chess.

"Chess?" he called out, and looked over to see them both sleeping in bed.

Chess had his mouth open with a string of drool dangling from his lip. He had kicked half the covers off and had conquered much of the bed. Penner wasn't sure how he could be in two places at once, but when he looked down, he could see flashes of silver dancing around his hands. When he looked around the room, he quickly realised when and where he was. This was the night the adventure had started. He was now standing there, and symbols swirled around him.

He felt something on his shoulder and when he looked, the Raven was perched there. He could feel its voice in his head.

"The world is circular," it whispered. Everything else melted away and it was only him and the bird standing in front of Chess in their old apartment. Chess yawned and sat up. His eyes were drawn towards Penner, but he wasn't sure exactly what he was seeing. "You have a choice."

"I don't want a choice."

"You can give him the knowledge. Or you can walk away now," the voice chirped.

"I can refuse?"

"And you wake up in the bed as if nothing has happened. You will remember nothing, and life will continue."

"And if I do?"

"You will have set the entire journey in motion. You can give him the knowledge, or not. You now know what it is that we need—" Penner looked at the bird and frowned.

"If I do this to him—" Penner asked. The bird didn't respond. "Why would I do this?"

"There is always sacrifice," the bird fluttered to his other shoulder. "We choose the ones who are able to do Our work in a world that has gone deaf. We choose the ones who can do what needs to be done. Since the beginning of time, we have required this. Since the first. Since the next. Up to today."

"But why this? Why does this need to be done? What are we doing?"

"You are together in a place. Bringing life back to a space that has been drained. There must be a sacrifice to keep us connected to this world. Even if we made this world, we are but forgotten shadows. We are present but unseen as the world follows dead words and the echoes of the miracles of our past. If we are to survive, we need you." Penner looked at Chess, who now seemed to be curiously prodding at him. He wondered what he was seeing.

"Why does it need to be us?"

"Because you were the ones who could do it," The bird said. "We are sorry, but no one before has succeeded. You two are our best chance. But the choice is yours."

"The choice is mine." He looked down at Chess and paused.

"We just want to help. Our Brother seeks to destroy—what was once a trickster has become so much more."

"Mobo," Penner said. "So you need us to—"

"You need to know our truth. What began as a sacrifice has become a fight for our survival. Please help us."

When he looked at himself in bed, he looked so peaceful. He looked so ignorant of everything that was to come. He knew that he loved Chess, that had never been a question. But when he looked at Chess, he knew that he didn't have a choice. He reached his hands out to either side of Chess's face and kissed him.

A torrent of energy burst through both of them. He watched as the Chess that was evaporated and blended with the Chess that was there now. The past, present, and future became one as the Raven passed through his body and flooded into Chess. As they kissed, the world that was disappeared, and the two of them were floating in the ethereal space.

They pulled away from each other and looked at the figures in the distance. The Raven and Snake were there, but a third one appeared between them. While the Snake and Raven seemed gentle, this other spirit felt more chaotic. Penner could feel a heat bubbling off of the being as it began to slowly crawl towards them. Its various hands swayed as it moved.

The other two looked like they were trying to stop it, but the being made of hands began to claw around them. Its long spider-like limbs stretching out and drawing closer to them. Almost like it was trying to keep them there. There was something behind that final beast that filled him with fear.

He gripped tight to Chess, and then a force ripped them from the world.

Penner felt a sharp tug as the rope that was still tied to him propelled them through the blank world. He watched as Chess was pulled through the glassy surface of the water and soon felt the sensation washing over his skin as well. Being dragged out of whatever it was they had been in was much more painful than going in. If going in had felt like cold flames, this was like scraping every cell in his body through broken glass. The incredible light that had filled his eyes disappeared, and he felt like black oil had been poured into them.

The taste in his nose and mouth turned sour as vomit as the air became thick and rancid, making it hard to breathe. He collapsed. It felt like he'd been trampled by a horse. He saw strange shadows standing over him. He coughed, feeling like his insides were about to burst out of his chest. Choking, he pushed himself to a sitting position and blinked to clear his vision. He shook his head, feeling as if his brain was sloshing back and forth as he tried to make sense of the world.

"We need to get him out of here," a female voice said. He blinked a few more times to see the face of Fred looking down on him. Or at least a fuzzy blur which he hoped was Fred.

"We need to go back the way we came."

Chess. He was alright. Penner breathed a sigh of relief and looked over to the shadow that he assumed was him. Chess still appeared to be glowing, and was definitely naked. Before long, he realised he was too.

"Cold," Penner said, his voice sounding hoarse and unused. He shook as he tried to pull himself up as he felt a piece of fabric fall on him.

"Good thing you left me your vest," Fred said. Penner grabbed it, feeling the fabric on his skin. Was this the same vest he'd left with her? It felt so rough and coarse in his hands. He threw it on and fished out his handkerchief from his pocket. He secured it into a makeshift loincloth to afford him a moderate sense of decency. Chess didn't appear to bother.

Getting to his feet was difficult. His balance was shaky, and every step felt like he was walking on broken glass. Fred put one hand on his back and attempted to stabilise him, which helped.

"It's a little drafty, no?" Penner squeaked, his voice still strange and un-familiar.

"It'll keep you humble," Chess said, wearing nothing but a smile.

"I look ridiculous," Penner mumbled.

"You've never looked better," Chess said with a smile. Penner looked at him. He was glowing. "Come on, we need to get moving."

"Wait. Do you hear that?" Fred asked.

"Gurgling," Chess said.

"What could—" Penner began, but Chess had already grabbed his arm and begun to move them around the pool.

"Let's not find out. Quickly, out the exit on the other side." For a moment Penner wondered how Chess knew that, but for some reason, he realised that he felt like he'd known it as well. For whatever reason, he had a vague idea of the layout of the entire mountain structure now and was acutely aware of where he was in it. He wasn't sure how, but it just made sense.

Then there was a crash. An ash white hand shot out of the water and stretched out long, nimble fingers that looked deformed and skeletal. Then another burst forth. And another. The entire pool was churning as the burning water began to spark and spill over the sides of the pool.

"The exit," Chess said, pushing Penner in front of him. "Get him to the exit." Penner felt Chess let go of his arm as Fred collided into his back. He was almost knocked off his feet as she pushed him along with the force of a train.

"Keep moving," she hissed.

"But, Chess—"

"Keep moving!" she barked, once again pushing him towards the exit.

"I can't leave him."

"We don't have a choice right now! Let's go! This is no place for us!"

Penner turned over his shoulder to see Chess standing at the edge of the water as they rushed into the exit. He tried to fight back, but she kept him moving forwards.

"I have to get back to him," he said, more to himself than Fred.

"No, we have to go!" Fred said, giving him an insistent nudge. Penner stumbled, but managed to catch himself before wiping out. In fact, he caught himself easily. He looked up to see Fred, who looked different then he remembered, but he couldn't put his finger on why.

When she went to push him along, he became very aware of how she was moving. She always moved with grace and purpose, but it seemed slower now—like she was moving through water. As she approached, he evaded her hands and, with a quick sidestep, slid right past her. He was moving fast, almost as if the space between everything was shrinking. While Fred had great reflexes, before she could grab him, he was already running back to Chess.

It had been a matter of seconds, but already the dome itself had transformed. A hundred long arms thrusting up from the water, pressing into the ceiling. Each was as thick around as a person.

"What are you doing, Penner?"

"I'm not leaving here without you," he said, grabbing Chess by the arm.

"You have to—"

"No. I don't. Damn the Gods. Damn fate. Damn the sacrifice. We carry their knowledge now. We're the first to encounter them and survive. You won't be sacrificed here—it's a trap. Mobo wants to imprison you. He doesn't want us to share what we know—"

"And what's that?" Chess asked.

"That even two heretics can find the truth. I know it now—you must too. This whole thing has brought us here to be the messengers—not the sacrifice. We can still escape. You know we can. Come with me." Chess looked at him, and a single tear fell from his eye.

"Yes," he said. "Let's go."

This time, he would be the one dragging Chess along. He wasn't going to leave without him. Not this time. With a firm grip upon Chess's wrist, he dragged his lover back up to where Fred was waiting.

"I got him," Penner said.

"Why did you bring him along?" Fred asked.

"It's all part of the plan," Penner exclaimed. He could feel Chess's hand in his. He squeezed it just to make sure it was real. He was almost starting to feel excited at the prospect of them all surviving this.

"I hear it," Chess said.

"Is that—chanting?" Penner asked.

"It sounds like it," Chess said as they made their way up a set of stairs.

"Monks, most likely. They're likely here for the ritual."

"How did they get here?" Penner asked.

"No time for chats! Just run!" Fred exclaimed as she led them through the tunnels. "Move it, Boys!" Penner turned to Chess, who gave him a wink. Something very strange was going on that he couldn't figure out. He chased Fred through the tunnels, trying not to think about it. Hopefully there would be answers before long.

The world around them was getting darker, as there were fewer candles to light their way. Had they burnt out or just sunk back into the walls? Despite this, Penner could still see effectively, and for as minimal as his clothing was, he felt surprisingly warm. Behind him, Chess kept close, making sure they were moving. He could feel his excitement becoming momentum. We're getting out of here. We're going to make it.

The path changed, and for a minute, Penner dared to believe they'd done it. Then, as they were climbing stairs, Penner felt something brush against his arm. At first he thought it was nothing, but when he felt it happen again, he forced Chess to stop.

"Fred, wait!" he called out, but she had already vanished through the dark. They'd have to catch up to her on the path.

"We don't have time for—" Chess said as he almost barreled into him.

"Stop," Penner yelped. Chess froze in place. "I feel something." His eyes went wide as he eyed the wall and extended his hand to Penner.

"Move to me. Now." Penner watched as a long, ugly hand twisted its way out of the rock. He held his breath as he and Chess began to back away from it, easing their way up the path. Then, a large eye formed on the fingers and began to ooze the glowing metallic water. It wasn't bright, but it cast enough of a glow for the hand to focus on them. As soon as it saw them, the hand lunged at them. Penner staggered backwards and fell when he saw another hand slowly emerging from the ground, more rapidly this time. It reached out to him and would have grasped him, had Chess not gripped him by the vest and ran him out of the way.

"It's him—" Penner gasped.

"Just keep going. We've gotta get out of here," Chess said. Penner staggered to his feet and they ran. Soon, they would get out of here and catch up to Fred. Soon, they would be safe.

More hands emerged from the walls, each seeking to ensnare them as they passed. Dozens of them lunged as they passed by, a few getting dangerously close. At one point, one of the hands grabbed at the vest Penner was wearing and ripped off a chunk of it. As it pulled itself back into the stone, it left the fabric embedded in the rock. Penner wondered what would have happened if they'd grabbed him instead. He didn't want to find out.

"Duck. Left. Jump!" Chess instructed as they made their way through. They narrowly missed getting snared by the hands, but they couldn't keep this up forever. Luckily, they were getting closer. Penner could feel the afternoon air on his face. "You're doing good. Just keep your head low and keep moving. Keep going," Chess encouraged, and before long, Penner could see a glow coming from the end of the tunnel. They were almost out of the mountain.

"Where is Fred?" Penner asked at one point, but Chess ushered him along, refusing to let them stop.

"Just keep going. She's alright. Just keep moving."

"I can feel the air!" Penner exclaimed.

"Just keep going," Chess said. "No matter what happens."

"We're going to make it!" Penner exclaimed as he ran through the door. The cold air tickled his skin. He never thought he'd feel so happy to be cold. He began to laugh as a few tears threatened to burst from his face. "We did it!" he exclaimed, then suddenly realised that Chess was no longer holding his hand.

"Goodbye, Penner." Penner turned around to see Chess at the door, but he wasn't alone. He was ensnared with dozens of hands. Hands on his neck, legs, waist, and chest. Each of them long with skinny, narrow fingers that seemed to stretch out unnaturally and dig into his skin.

"Chess!" Penner yelled.

"Catch," Chess said as he threw Penner the small red book.

As soon as the book left his fingers, Penner watched as all of the hands tugged, and the ground beneath Chess opened and sucked him in. As soon as the chasm had opened, it closed, leaving Penner alone at the mountain entrance. In a millisecond, Chess was gone, buried underneath a stony path. Penner flung himself to his knees as he attempted to dig and scratch at the ground. The ground was solid, but he scratched and clawed at it until his fingers bled. After what felt like eons, he had to give up. It was no use. It was solid stone once again, and Chess had been swallowed by it like it was quicksand.

"No. No, no, no, no, no..." His breathing became shallow as he pressed his hands against the ground. Forming fists, he battered at the rock, trying to get it to budge, or open, or split. He screamed as tears began to pour down his face like an avalanche. This couldn't be it. He had to be okay. Then, he felt something. He closed his eyes and felt a soft, gentle tapping on his brain. A soft, subtle heartbeat sound that he would recognise anywhere.

Chess was still alive.

He couldn't figure out how he knew, but he did. Taking a deep breath, he closed his eyes and felt it again. This time it was closer. He opened his eyes, and saw the book. The red book which seemed to emanate with a strange energy, uncovered and exposed. For a moment, he contemplated taking it and throwing it over the edge to never see it again. But then, when he reached his hand out to it, he could feel something on the tips of his fingers. A subtle heartbeat pulsing from the book.

He'd been told never to touch the book, but he had no choice right now. If this Tome was going to help him get Chess back, there would be nothing that could stop him. He grabbed the book, opened it, and the world went white.

ZPV LOPX IPX TPNFUJNFT
ZPV GFFM MJLF TPNFPOF JT
XBUDIJOH ZPV?
UIFZ BSF.
UIBU JT UIF FZF PG NPCP.
IF CSJOHT DIBPT.
IF CSJOHT GFBS.
IF CSJOHT UIF DPME PG
XJOUFS BOE UIF
TUPSNT JO TUNNFS.
CF IBQQZ XIFO IF JT OPU
UIFSF GPS JG IF JT DMPTF,
UIFSF XJMM CF OP QFBDF
GPS UIF MBOE.
UIF EFDJNBUJPO. UIF UFSSPS.
UIF CSJOHFS PG UPSNFOU BOE
XJDLFEOFTT.
IF JT NPCP.

It felt like he was being submerged into ice water. Every inch of his skin stung with a wicked chill. Needles felt like they were being raked all over his body. Every inch of his skin felt like it was burning, and then he felt nothing at all.

The air was thicker than water, and when he breathed in, it felt like he was drawing tar into his lungs. He wasn't sure if he was choking, drowning, or just dying, but he could feel the atmosphere pressing down on him from all sides. It was strange, but at the same time familiar. It was the same as when he'd plunged into the spring. He wondered if it was the feeling of passing between realities.

Penner opened his eyes, allowing the feeling to gouge them. The light was blinding, but expected. There was no atmosphere around him, only white energy that seemed to beam at him from all angles. It was bright. Silver streams of liquid energy floated around him, circling him like snakes. Then Penner felt something strange. His hands felt like they were burning with energy, and he knew something was close.

He could see the book in his hands, but instead of being a simple red book, it was alive. It twisted and squirmed in his grasp like a slimy creature. Silver liquid pooled in the middle of the burnt pages, and he could feel it dripping out and spilling over the ground.

Then he felt a shadow on him, which was a strange sensation. He could feel the light being blocked out by a figure, but when he looked, he could only see a strange shadow shimmering at the edge of his vision. As more and more of the silver liquid pooled in the centre of the book, the figure became more and more visible until he could see it clearly.

A large beast that seemed to be made of blood and gold that dripped off of its skeletal frame. The lumpy creature was as large as a Temple and Penner knew that he'd seen it before. What had felt so small on his shoulder was now a terrible beast that looked more dead than alive. Maybe it was. In this realm, the two seemed to coexist simultaneously.

"Mobo."

"You cannot save him. I have him." The creature spoke, but its mouth didn't move. Its skull was partially visible behind the golden ooze that seeped off of him. Its fur was matted from centuries of neglect as a thousand hands extended from its belly, each twisted and deformed. Its eyes were a sunken ocean of blackness that bore into his soul and didn't reflect back.

"He belongs to me!" Penner exclaimed. The beast laughed with a roar that shook the ground. He could feel the earth underneath him rebelling.

"From the beginning, I have been overlooked. I have been passed by. I have been the one abandoned and left behind. While the others received praise and adoration, I got nothing. So now nothing will come from nothing. They demand death to stay connected to this world, and I will take it for myself." Penner felt a holy fury building inside of him.

"You will not keep him. He is mine. Damn your sacrifice."

"He is already mine. You can't stop me. I know how it feels to be left behind. Now you shall be bound to me in that feeling. You shall know what it feels like to be alone. You shall know how it feels to die," Mobo whispered, and the world shook. Penner recoiled and flung himself to the ground to protect his ears. He squeezed his hands over his face to block the assault of sound that pounded into him.

"You can't stop me."

"And you can't win. I am a god. You are nothing. Your sacrifice means nothing, and you shall die."

And then it ended.

Penner opened his eyes. He was laying on the ground of the tunnel entrance. A few inches in front of him, the red book lay open, its papers smouldering as it consumed itself in its flames. Whatever was left of it from last night was now disintegrated. He picked it up and it felt dead, as if whatever had possessed it before had passed on. He took what little of it was left, rolled it up, and put it in his vest pocket.

Then he scanned the mountain. There was no sign of anything, but he could feel that something pulsing in it. He got up, scrambling onto his hands and knees and wiping off the dirt. His entire body burned and felt like his skin was ripping itself apart. He got onto his feet, coughing at how thin the air was. He knew what he had to do and raced back into the tunnel. If this was where Chess had been pulled, this was where he'd go to find him.

For some reason, this time the tunnel didn't make him scared. It was like he could sense the twists and turns before he could see them. His senses felt more elevated now, and the journey was easier. In no time he had descended deep into the heart of the mountain—but then something made him pause.

He smelled something. It was a scent that was strange but familiar that drifted through the tunnels. He was at a fork in the road, with a light on one side and a small dark hole on the other. He knew the path with the light would lead him to the basin of fiery water, but this other one seemed more important. He turned to the tunnel and plunged into the darkness and saw her. Fred stood a few feet in front of him, pinned to the side of the wall by dozens of stone hands. They covered her head to toe. No less than fifty hands pinned her to the wall, each twisted and clutching at her body.

When she looked up to see Penner, her eyes went wide. She mouthed for him to get away, but he wouldn't.

Penner gripped one of the hands around her neck and attempted to pull it away, expecting some kind of struggle from it. Instead it disintegrated into dust. He had pulled another one off just as easily when Fred extended her hand and Penner pulled her out. The hands fell lifeless and pathetic at her feet. Some shattered, others just rolled away, but they couldn't hold her. Fred clutched at her throat and coughed before reaching out and balancing herself with Penner's help.

"Are you okay?" he asked. She nodded.

"We need to go," she spoke softly. Her voice sounded hoarse, like she'd been screaming. "Thanks for coming back for me."

"Not just for you, but I'm glad you're safe," Penner said.

"Where is he?" she asked. Penner pointed to the main chamber and Fred nodded.

"You're going after him, aren't you?" Fred asked.

"I have to," Penner said. "You should go back to the ship."

"I can't stop you, can I?"

"Do you really want to?" Penner asked.

"You need to do what you need to do," Fred replied. "I'll be at the entrance."

"I'll see you soon then."

Fred looked at him and paused. She grabbed his shoulder and tried to smile.

"I wish I could go with you. But I can't. If that thing sees me—I don't know if you'll be able to stop this. But if you have to try, just come back to the ship. Try to survive."

Penner looked into her eyes and noticed that for the first time they didn't sparkle. He shook her hand, and then pulled her into a hug. For a moment they stood there, silent. Then, without a word, she stood back with a half-smile and left. Penner walked back towards where he knew he had to go and focused on his scent. He was going to get Chess back.

He ran. He ran as fast as he could. Despite the fact that the air felt like acid. Despite the fact that he felt like he was getting heavier with each step. Despite the blackness that he felt pressing in all around him. He ran to get to Chess.

He wasn't going to leave without him.

The mountain trail seemed easy to navigate now, but the hands had made many routes through it impassable. After trying many tunnels downwards, he finally found a small path that led up to a ledge that overlooked the main chamber. Perched twenty feet above the crackling waters, he could still feel the electricity buzzing through the air. He was too high to be able to climb down without plunging himself into the water, but he could at least see what was happening. But as he looked down, what he saw was unexpected.

Chess was floating in the pool. His naked body unconscious as he lay exposed to the world. Everything in the room was churning. The small lights that had danced around the room were now blood red, and they bobbed up and down so fast they looked like they were vibrating. In the water, or more precisely, standing on the water, were hundreds of figures.

Each was dressed in a dark robe, like the monks that had swarmed the ship. He wondered if that's who they were, but how hundreds of humans could get in here was beyond him. Maybe they were the ones who had found him in the bathtub. Maybe they just lived here and emerged from the lake to take part in the rituals. He wondered for a moment if perhaps these were the fish who had helped him step across them before.

The idea seemed ludicrous, until he realized that it was very possible that was exactly what they were. As they stood, a thick black smoke seemed to penetrate through the room.

There was chanting that was echoing through the room. He wanted to believe it was the hooded figures, but couldn't see any of their mouths moving. He couldn't even make out their faces from this angle.

Then, as if from a dream, hands emerged from the water's edge and began to slither out from around the edges. The monks didn't appear to notice. The hands stretched out longer and more imposing as the monks continued to chant, while they seemed to invest all their focus into Chess.

No one seemed to care that the water seemed to be gaining sentience as more and more of the long, broken arms filled the space. It didn't take long for one of the arms to act out, and Penner watched as one of them gripped the throat of one of the monks and forced them under the water. There was little more than a yelp as the hand quickly re-emerged to strike again.

Soon the monks began to notice. Maybe they could sense something was wrong; they began to swarm the hands. Some hands lunged at the monks and tore them in half. Some monks tried to claw at the hands that began to plunge them into the water they had been standing on. They looked to be fighting the hands back. Panic filled the space as the chanting gave way to brutal screams and chaos.

Then there was a flash. The monks were standing there, but there were no hands. Just a sacrifice. A victim sent there to die to appease the gods. This was how it should have been. A quiet dignity and an act of sacrifice. Not the chaos that surrounded them currently.

The world returned to focus, and he watched as the first long bony hand reached Chess. It gripped him by the wrist as another grabbed his shoulder and pulled. They looked to be attempting to rip him apart. Penner wanted to yell, but he couldn't. He watched more hands grab onto Chess as they suspended him over the water. The monks that hadn't tried to flee moved out of the way as the hands slowly lowered into the water. With only seconds left before Chess would be submerged, Penner couldn't help himself.

"Chess!" he screamed. He knew he was running out of time. He had to get down to them.

Chess's eyes shot open, and he looked up to see Penner standing on the ridge just seconds before his face was plunged below the waters. As soon as he broke the surface, the water began to churn and change. Any monks who had been fighting on the surface were pulled under the water like it was nothing. The chants were silenced, and the room itself became deathly still.

More hands started to funnel into the water, as the strange silver water churned before turning into a solid grey mass. It was becoming stone. Penner watched as the remnants of the water began to solidify around Chess. For a moment they made eye contact, and Chess mouthed something to him. Penner didn't need to hear it to know what he had said. Penner couldn't take it anymore and launched himself over the ledge. What had been liquid only moments ago was now solid rock, with the occasional hand poking through it. Penner ran as Chess reached out to him. Penner had run fast before, maybe he could still reach him.

All Penner could see of Chess now was his face. A few more hands emerged and pulled him under. Chess tried to reach his arm out to Penner, but it was too late. As the last of him was pulled under, Penner arrived. He put his hands against the ground and slammed his fists down, attempting to break through the stone, but there was no use. Chess had once again been devoured by the hungry earth, and Penner didn't know how to get him back this time.

He lay there. He wasn't sure for how long, but he waited. He waited for the room to shatter, or for the monks to reappear, or for Chess to emerge from the depths, but none of those things happened. The ground below him was now just rock and he was alone. But he didn't cry.

As he lay there, he stretched his hand over the rock and pressed down. For a moment, when he closed his eyes, he could feel another hand pressing against it. He felt a heartbeat, however faint. It was subtle, but it was enough.

Rolling onto his knees after what felt like an eternity, Penner pressed his lips to the space where Chess had been. Taking his time, he slowly peeled himself off of the ground and stood up. With one long exhale, he made his way back through the tunnels and up the mountain.

Within minutes he was out of the wretched caves. Fred had been true to her word and had waited for him, which he appreciated. As they walked down, she pointed something out to him about the mountain. It had ruptured. Maybe it was his eyes playing tricks on him, but the entire mountain looked to have cracked in the center. It didn't look stable—the mountain looked dangerous and precarious, as if a gust of wind could topple it over. He hoped he'd never have to go back in there.

The trip back to Cassandra was a silent one, but seemed to take no time at all. Penner had no idea what to say. His brain was swimming. His thoughts were a mess.

He lay down in the hammock that had fit them both and suddenly felt how large it was when he was alone. It felt cold, and when he wrapped himself in a blanket, it offered little comfort.

He closed his eyes and took a breath. He wrapped himself and for a moment felt like someone was lying with him. He imagined the feeling of an arm around him and inhaled, for a moment smelling a vague note of cinnamon. The feeling was so real, and then he felt a soft voice echo in his head.

"Go to her."

The voice was so clear. Penner's eyes whipped open and he shot up in the hammock.

"Chess?" he exclaimed.

But when he looked around, there was nothing there. Feeling the force of his loneliness as palpably as the air, he shook his head and got up and walked over to the sink to splash water on his face. He took a breath and looked at himself in the mirror. His eyes were red and puffy. The bags under his eyes were dark. He looked terrible.

But then, something strange. The mirror began to flicker like it was a picture show. It was only for a moment, but the glass shimmered like water.

He stared at it dubiously and then caught an impossible reflection of a fire-place within it. A rich smell filled his nostrils, and he raced back up to the deck.

"Fred, I know where we need to go."

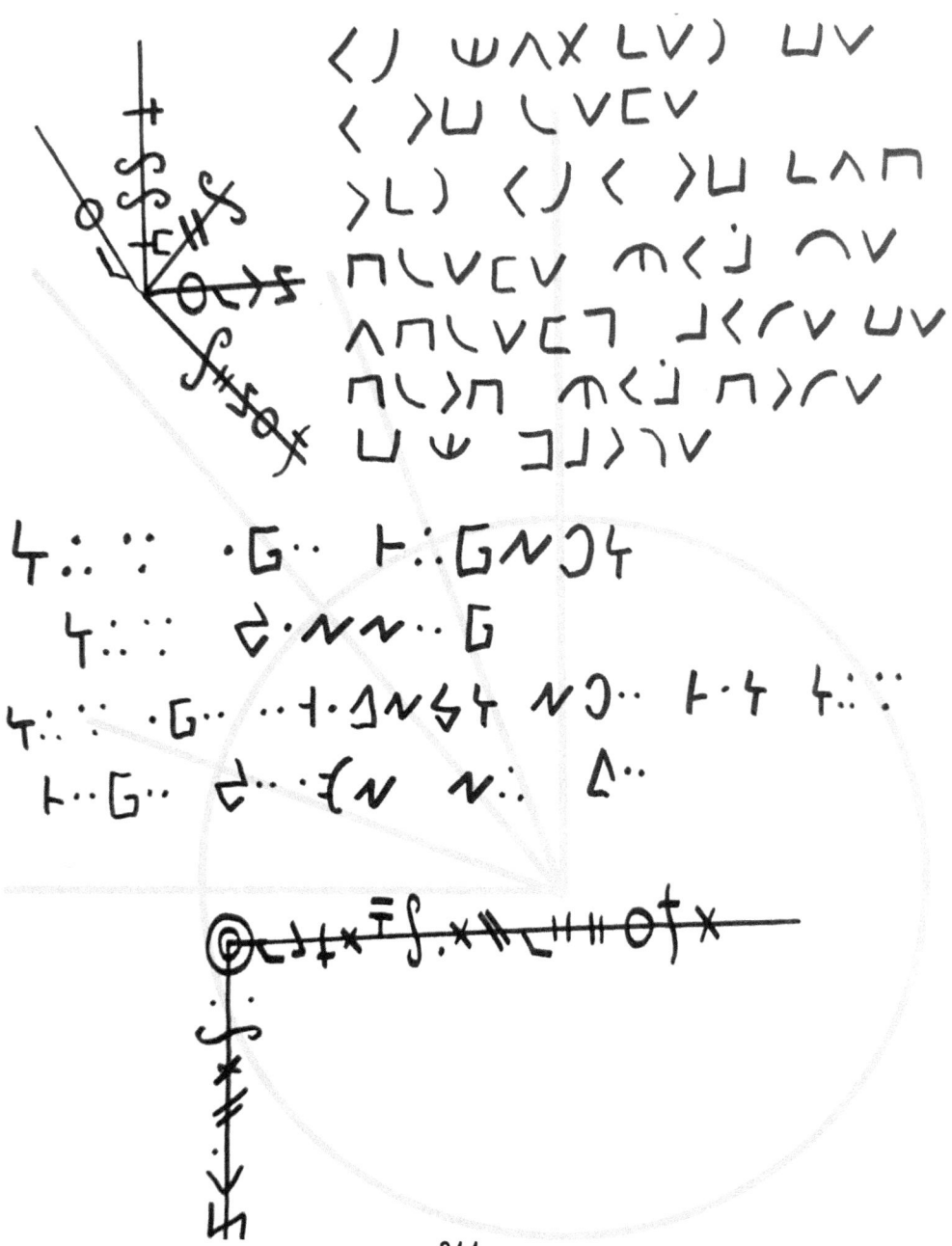

"I hope I didn't keep you waiting." Her calming voice announced her presence before he had even laid eyes on her. The gentle scent wafted in, and he turned to see her beaming at him.

"For you, I'd wait as long as necessary," Penner replied, taking her hand in his and kissing it.

"Such a gentleman. I never had any doubt you would be." She gripped his hands with both of hers and looked deep into his eyes. "I am so sorry to hear what happened."

"That is actually what I wanted to talk to you about," he said.

"Well, considering you got back here alright, I would assume we have much to discuss. Where is Fred?"

"She didn't want to come. I am sorry to arrive unannounced."

"Well, considering you are waiting in my bedchamber, I doubt they would have let you in."

Raina smiled as she walked behind a changing screen and threw her dress on top of it.

Much like the rest of Raina's estate, her bedchamber was everything Penner had imagined it would be. Large, luxurious and red. Plush velvet seemed to be her fabric of choice on everything.

"I hope you don't mind my intrusion."

"Penner, I have had men far less beautiful than you in here. The real question is whether or not I'll let you leave." She swept out from behind the screen wearing a silk gown that barely covered her ivory chest. She smiled at him. "How are you?"

"I am—" Penner paused. "I have much to discuss with you."

"Well, ask away. I'm an open book."

"Speaking of—" Penner said, pulling out the remnants of the Tome. It was little more than cover and ash now.

"I trust it was useful then?" she said, taking a pin from her hair and stabbing the book before walking it over to her vanity.

"It was. There was a lot in there." Penner walked to the window that he'd snuck in through and looked out over the city. "He was supposed to die, wasn't he?"

Raina nodded. "Those who are chosen are marked to die, yes. They are to be sacrificed to honour the Gods and the Creator and keep the gates between the worlds open. If they die on the way, then their body is carried to the pool of creation and laid to rest so that they may be with the Gods there."

"But not all the gods," Penner said, pointing to the Tome. Raina smiled at him.

"No. Not all the gods."

"How long has this been going on?"

Raina shrugged. "As long as there has been. I don't know how it began, but I do know that what happened now has never happened before."

"He's not dead, is he?" Penner asked.

"You sense it too then. No, he is not," Raina said, but her face became serious. "But there is something wrong. The Beast has stolen him for himself."

"So, do we need to steal him back?" Raina laughed.

"You're talking about taking on a god."

"I suppose I am. Can it be done?" Penner replied.

"You'd be best to forget him. You'd be best to leave him behind and move on."

"Like Fred? Like you?" Raina frowned.

"I did great things with my life. And Fred is a woman of the skies now."

"But if you could get them back, wouldn't you?" Penner smirked. Raina had a twinkle in her eye.

"You're talking about heresy. You're talking about taking on not just a religion, but the gods behind it."

"It's just one God. And when you think about it, I'm just talking about getting the man I love back," Penner said. "If I can make it so that no one else in the world has to go through what I'm going through, I'll move hell and high water. I want him to live, and if I have to kill myself to make that happen, I'll do it. So, are you with me or not?"

Raina smiled at him.

"Let's get started."

EPILOGUE

The chains that bound his hands were heavy. He hadn't expected them to be light, but after countless hours with them rubbing his wrists raw, he was ready for the death that awaited him on the other end of this venture.

The airship maneuvered through the countryside with all the speed of molasses. The cramped quarters, the thick smell of burning copper - he could think of few things less enticing to die in. But when found guilty of a crime - even if the charges were fallacious - it was only a matter of time before the cold kiss of death would accept them into the beyond.

He looked out the window, or what passed as a pathetic excuse for a window on this poor excuse for a ship. The mountains sprawled below them, opening on a grand forest that looked dense with life and darkness. He knew these forests well - he had studied them time and time again when looking at maps of the rebellion's plans. They had always considered this area of Avaria particularly important if they were ever to build a successful rebellion. The untapped resources were incredible.

He pressed his back against the wall and attempted to brush his hair away from his face, but the chains made the motion futile. Instead, frustrated, he attempted to blow the strands away from his eyes. It didn't work and he looked out the sliver of window that he was privy to.

Then he saw it. A familiar darkness in the distance. A dark storm cloud that spiralled unnaturally in the afternoon sky. He held his breath when he realized that it was heading right to them and braced for the chaos that he knew would follow.

The bolt of noise and fire blasted from the cloud to the ship and rocked it so hard that it tore the hull of the ship in half. The air was ripped from the vessel as wind whipped around him. If he had been fully coherent in the moment he would have realized that the ship had lost a significant part of its structure. The only thing he was absolutely sure of was that he was falling. As he looked up at the ship as it listed away from him, another bolt from the cloud smashed into the ship sending debris and metal showering down over the countryside.

Had this beast been sent for him? To destroy any and all remaining seeds of the rebellion. The sentence of death in a work camp had seemed uncharacteristically merciful for the governance. Death by assassination by demented sky dragon seemed much more appropriate.

But as he fell, the beast didn't seem to pay him any mind. It wouldn't matter- the beast would ultimately destroy the ship and the fall from this height would surely kill him. He thought back to his family - the people who he had fought so hard to protect and closed his eyes.

If he was to die, then he would die peacefully. He had fought a great fight and their side had come up short. If they had done all they could, and it had all been in vain, what else could be done.

Then the voice filled his mind.

"Brave Coward- Your time is not done yet."

The air was knocked out of him as the ship exploded and the winged beast rocketed past him. If his time was not up, he would surely find some hint of destiny in the forest. If this was the end, then at least he would die knowing he had done his part.

If this was the end then it would be the end. But if it was to be something else - then he would have to see what happened next.

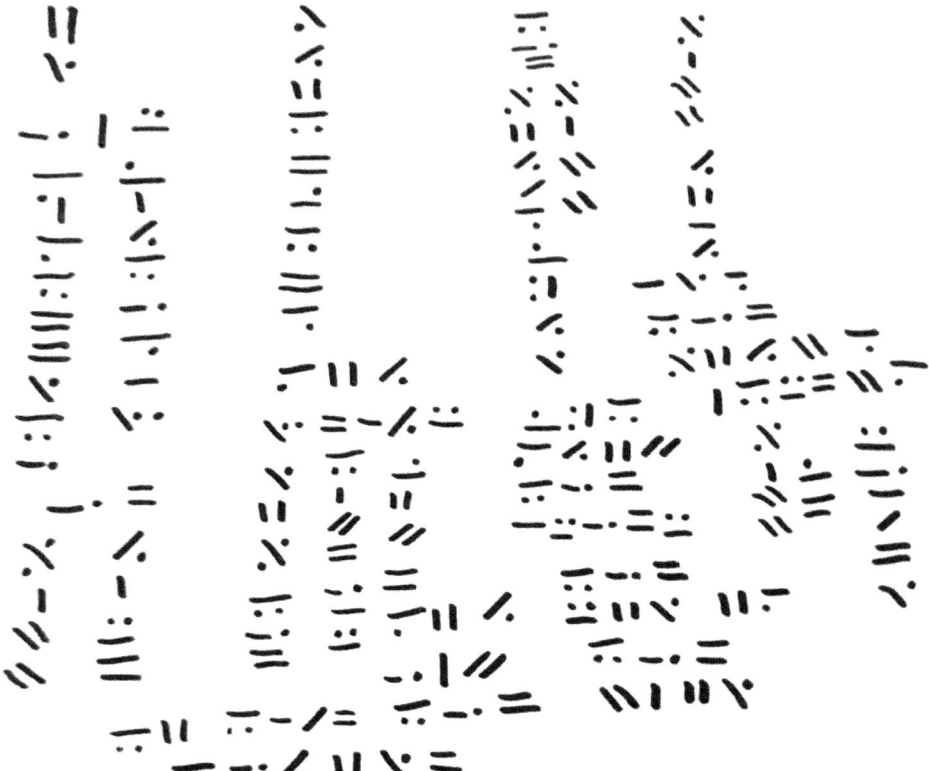

ABOUT THE AUTHOR

Matti McLean is a creative artist and writer from Northern Ontario. He is continually pursuing new creative endeavours from body painting to game design and always seeks to keep his projects challenging and his pursuits eclectic. He loves challenging accepted social norms and has the radical belief that people are human and we should all be nicer to each other.

Renaissance.
Diverse Canadian Voices

Renaissance was founded in May 2013 by a group of friends who wanted to publish and market those stories which don't always fit neatly in a genre, or a niche, or a demographic. We weren't sure what we wanted to publish exactly, so like the happy panbibliophiles that we are, we opened our submissions, with no other personal guideline than finding a Canadian book we would fall in love with enough that we would want to publish and sell. Five years later, this is still very true; however, we've also noticed an interesting trend in what we tended to publish. It turns out that we are naturally drawn to the voices of those who are members of a marginalized group (especially people with disabilities and LGBTQIAPP2+ people), and these are the voices we want to continue to uplift. To us, Renaissance isn't just a business; it's a family. Being authors and artists ourselves, we are always careful to center the experience of the author above all else.

pressesrenaissancepress.ca
pressesrenaissancepress@gmail.com

If you enjoyed this book,
please consider
leaving a review
where you purchased it!

MURDER AT THE WORLD'S FAIR
MJ LYONS

The year is 1893, and airships cloud the skies over the bustling metropolis of Toronto. The city is set to host the world's fair thanks in no small part to the work of two fantastical inventors. The New World Exhibition is to be a celebration of cultural and technological marvels; roving automatons, clockwork contraptions, the world's biggest steam-powered paddle boat, all to be fully lit by the wonder of electricity! On the day of the grand opening, young Norwood Quigley, aspiring journalist, photographer and scion of a world-famous airship magnate, stumbles onto the scene of a murder; the victim: a Prussian Ambassador; the perpetrator: a Chinese assassin, or so the powers-that-be say. In truth, the suspect is Jing, a roguish but amiable youthful delinquent. Concerned by Jing's claim of innocence and his assumed guilt by higher powers, including the British Empire's military, Norwood is thrown into a grand intrigue that hinges on Toronto's world fair. As chaos consumes the celebrations, he fears that his influential family is being manipulated in a plot to create an international incident that will lead to a war that spans the world.

pressesrenaissancepress.ca

BLOOD STATE
RALUCA BALASA

Three generations ago, the Modernist Mission arrived on the ice planet Tählti to find it already inhabited by the Firsts, humanoids who have evolved an antifreeze glycoprotein in their blood. With the next ice age nipping at everyone's heels, the Modernist government will do anything to get the protein – even experimenting on the Firsts in secret. Despite Modernist general Lucian Devereaux's best efforts, what began as a medical research facility to ensure his people's survival becomes a concentration camp. When an exiled vigilante learns this secret, he threatens to tell the world and spark a war between Modernist and First – a war neither can afford before the ice age. Surrounded by enemies, Lucian must figure out whom to trust, or neither subspecies will survive much longer.

Raluca Balasa has penned a dark, gripping tale of colonialist and indigene as the world around them begins to freeze. Blood State is a slick, twisty, chess game of a novel that sucked me in and held me until the last page.
– Stephen Graham King, author of *A Congress of Ships*

pressesrenaissancepress.ca

www.ingramcontent.com/pod-product-compliance
Lightning Source LLC
Chambersburg PA
CBHW051338020726
47501CB00007B/2145